INTO THE ETHER

INTO THE ETHER

DAVID SHERER

For further information, contact:

Thousand Acres Press
825 Wildlife
Estes Park, CO 80517

ISBN: 978-1-7362988-4-8

For Jeffrey Chappell—my teacher, friend and creative inspiration.

AUTHOR'S NOTE

Though the names of the characters are fictitious, some of the places and institutions referenced in the book are real. The technical descriptions of medical procedures and practices are the author's sole creation, and do not necessarily reflect current practice.

PROLOGUE

Billy Ray Devereaux was fixing to meet his maker. Staring up at me from his dull, dead-fish eyes, Billy was strapped and shackled to the gurney within the drab, hospital-green tiled walls of the Execution Chamber housed in the Louisiana State Penitentiary. Having exhausted all his appeals for clemency, Devereaux had made peace with the fact that before enough time had passed for him to digest his last meal of a double bacon cheeseburger, French fries and a Dr. Pepper float, he'd be dead.

The condemned, a man who made his money selling the fish he caught in the Mississippi River, had been convicted of triple murders in the first degree. The evidence against him, including DNA analysis and eyewitness accounts of him fleeing the scene after he had murdered his son-in-law, daughter and 10 month- old granddaughter, was overwhelming. The facts were indisputable: on the night of July 29, 2021, while visiting his daughter Lula in Baton Rouge, Billy had "lost his temper" and knifed his daughter's husband, Nicholas Dees, to death. He then turned on his own daughter, attempted to sexually assault her, and after hearing and ignoring her pleas, killed his granddaughter Brianna and then her. Witnesses recalled a clearly deranged and dangerous Devereaux leave the apartment in a blood-soaked shirt and notified Baton Rouge police, who were able to pick him up a mere two hours later outside of a strip club.

After a trial that lasted a little more than three days, Judge Wilbur Watkins returned, with uncharacteristic gusto, a sentence of death by lethal injection. It had taken the jury of seven women and five men a mere 33 minutes to find him guilty on all charges.

"Anything you want to say?"

He looked up and said, "Just tell my momma I'm sorry."

Four minutes later, with no agonal screams, movements or any sign of struggle, Billy Ray was dead.

CHAPTER 1
OCTOBER, 2023

Most people know me as Alex Crisfield, but my real name is Adrian Wren. I grew up in the suburbs of Washington, DC, in Glen Echo, Maryland. Glen Echo is one of the stranger little towns in America. It started out as an old Indian village, then in the late 1800s hosted a type of compound seen only rarely in our nation, a Chautauqua. This was as close as one could get in those times to a commune, and it was based on liberal principles and improving education, especially for women and minorities. Theatres, cottages, lecture halls and an amphitheater were built there to enhance the life and intellectual growth of the people who settled there. After some Great Depression-related financial setbacks however, Glen Echo, and the neighboring town of Cabin John (rumored to be a bastardization of "Captain John") became a center for housing of military personnel and weapon-research scientists and engineers between the Great Wars, and even had a section where descendants of Black Civil War slaves had lived for generations. But over the decades following World War II, DC and its environs had become virtually recession-proof and housing prices steadily grew. My parents' house, which they purchased in the 1970s for about $95,000 on Yale Avenue, sold for $1.7 million just a few years ago.

My dad, Augustus Wren and native of Chicago, was a general surgeon and my mom, Alice was a violinist for the Capital Symphony. In the 1970s and 80s they had three kids in succession: Charlie came in '79, then me '81 and finally, our late sister Gail in '83. Charlie was a stand-out athlete and scholar. If ever there was a golden boy, it was Charlie. He was an all-county receiver for the high school football team, straight A student and funny as hell.

Charlie, with his dirty blond hair, hazel eyes and angular face was destined for success. After high school he got a partial football scholarship to Yale (the only football player in our county to go there), majored in Political Science and then got into Harvard Law. After breezing through a legal post-doc at Oxford, he came back to DC and jumped on the partner track in contract law at Bainbridge, Weston and Howell.

Gail, the baby and only girl, was everyone's joy. It was impossible not to love her. Gail grew up a tom-boy, lanky and sinewy, with long, thick brown hair and blue eyes, the color of the Aegean. She began her piano studies at age five and by the time she was ten her talents were so great, so developed and refined that mom got her an audition with her orchestra. The conductor, Zoltan Rebroff, was so blown away, that he hooked her up with the best teacher at the elite Berman School of Music. At age twelve, she made her debut with mom's orchestra playing the Haydn D major concerto, complete with a four- minute cadenza Gail had composed herself for the first movement. It caused a sensation. The papers went nuts.

By the time she turned fourteen, she played the Mozart d minor in Philadelphia and then, at age sixteen, got a New Year premiere at Carnegie Hall playing the Liszt E flat. She seemed headed for stardom when tragedy struck: a growth on her shin turned out to be bone cancer—Ewing's sarcoma—and, after all the right treatments with all the right docs, she succumbed to her disease just before her nineteenth birthday. It killed all of us. My father has barely smiled since.

I got so messed up in college after Gail died that I had to take time off. After spending two months in near catatonia, I pulled myself together, returned to Stanford, and studied and swam like hell.

After just missing the Olympic qualifying times for the butterfly and freestyle, I did what was, in some Calvinist twist, destined for me: I applied to and attended medical school. I say "Calvinist" because for as long as I could remember it was just assumed I would follow in my dad's footsteps. After four tough years in medical school in Boston, I chose anesthesiology as a specialty because I did not want what my father had: an office with patients to see, staff and equipment to invest in, and all the overhead and regulatory hassles that running a large practice entailed.

By the summer of 2013, I had joined the anesthesia staff at Hamilton Memorial, in Northwest DC. By the fall of 2023, after years of working my ass off, a failed marriage and some garden variety ennui and burnout, a simple luck-of-the-draw occurrence in the day's OR schedule changed my life. It was the third case on a routine Tuesday in my favorite operating room with my favorite surgeon, that I crossed paths with a man who set all of this in motion: Chairman of the Federal Reserve Bank of the United States of America, "Long" John Silverstone.

After the 8 am gallbladder with Dr. Temple, the 9:45 breast

biopsy with the same, it was time for Silverstone's hernia repair (under local with sedation anesthesia) with Dr. Helen Footer at 11:15. I had scanned the schedule while I was checking out my narc box at the drug window (the Narxis computerized drug delivery system was down again for the umpteenth time) and saw the name, "Silverstone." The date of birth fit as did the whispers and presence of too many administrators and other worthless suits hanging around the OR. After the breast biopsy, I peeked into the pre-op area. Sure enough, there he was, all 6'6" of him. Rail thin, tanned, a mane of silver hair, in a stretcher and under a blanket, with his black wingtip size 15 shoes jutting out from under the covers and hanging over the edge of the gurney. He was absorbed in both *The Wall Street Journal* and his smart phone, while the two bodyguards, both obviously ex-military, one black and one white, sat on each side.

After setting up my room for his case, I grabbed a quick coffee and headed for the pre op area at 11:05. Rumor was that Footer was late again, tied up in the ER with some gunshot wound that had rolled in ten minutes before. Evidently, she was on trauma call that day. Only God knew when we'd start her case.

"Chairman Silverstone, I'm doctor Wren. Nice to meet you. I'll be your anesthesiologist."

"Pleasure's mine."

The two goons gave me the once over. The white guy lowered his glasses and squinted at my ID badge.

"Before we get started let me review your chart." I opened the EMR and reviewed his history: White male, aged 58, 6 feet 6 inches tall, 200 pounds. No known drug allergies. Past medical history noteworthy for mild asthma, tonsils and adenoids out at age 7, all labs, EKG and chest X ray normal. Only meds albuterol inhaler as needed and vitamin D.

"Chairman Silversto—"

"You can call me John."

"Sorry, John. When was the last time you ate or drank anything?"

"Last night at about ten."

"Breathing good today? No wheezing?"

"Nope, feel fine."

"When was your last asthma attack?"

"Oh, about six months ago, when I did the Cherry Blossom Ten-Miler. Pollen that day was hell."

"Oh, good for you. I did that race too. Let me listen to your lungs."

I took out my scope and listened. All clear. Heart regular. BP 133/66, pulse 66, respirations 16, oxygen saturation 99 percent.

"Open your mouth as wide as you can please. Now tilt your chin up." It looked like Fort Knox with all that gold in there. "Airway looks good. Now, we usually do these hernia repairs under local anesthesia with sedation. Dr. Footer likes it that way too. We don't seem to need general or spinal, epidural or general anesthesia, for that matter. Plus, your recovery time is quicker."

"Sounds fine with me."

"I'll check to see how late Footer might be and let you know."

In my head I rubbed my hands together. I had done plenty of celebrities before—senators, football players, actors, even The Speaker of the House—but no one with this much power, I thought.

I checked with the charge nurse and asked if it was okay to get Silverstone in the OR room, to make him more comfortable. To my surprise, she bought it and told me to bring him back. She probably wanted the goons gone and The Chairman out of her hair anyway.

"Chairman, uh, John. Let me take those shoes off you; you won't be needing those. And try to get these booties over your socks. Looks like there's no way they're going to fit. Well, at least I tried."

The guards beat it and I paged the Filipina nurse Esmerelda to help me wheel the Chairman back to OR 5. She soon appeared, 5 feet and 100 pounds soaking wet, and took the foot of the gurney.

"Just a little cocktail to start you off John…" I injected 2 mg of midazolam into his IV. "Gonna feel like two martinis in a minute."

After 30 seconds: "Wow, you ain't kidding! We could use these at our Committee Meetings!"

Once in Room 5, John moved himself over to the OR table, and Sonia introduced herself as the scrub nurse.

Sonia said: "I understand Dr. Footer will be a few minutes. So, I'm going to run to the bathroom while I can. Be right back…"

I wasn't sure John heard her. He was too in love with his cocktail. I put the BP cuff, EKG leads and pulse oximeter on him, got a blanket from the warmer and let him chill. Esmerelda too had gone out for a quick break. It was just me, John, the quietly hissing oxygen I had set to 3 liters per minute in his nasal prongs and CNN on the OR anesthesia desk computer. Soon John was snoring and I was scanning headlines: "Putin Offers to Meet With Prez," Washington looks forward to facing the Cowboys in Dallas (that's a big L right there), Brad Pitt is in a new biopic and, what's this? "Fed to Convene Next Open Market Committee Meeting on Monday, October 22." I thought for a moment and my heart skipped. I looked at the sleeping giant and back at the screen. My armpits got sticky. My throat was suddenly dry. The words "Open Market Committee Meeting" echoed in my brain.

I got up and peeked through the glass door. No one there. I looked at the screen again and stared at the floor, my hands on my hips. I just stood there a moment, like some tall, masked, medical statue. Back on the screen, the tiny stock market symbols flickered in greens and reds, like on a Christmas tree. By the time I had sat back down into my swivel chair the devil sitting on my shoulder had me by the throat. My years of experience and clear talents in handling disinhibiting drugs with tens of thousands of patients—children, teens, adults and the elderly of every size, ethnic group and physical status—crystallized in my brain. Maybe Christmas could come early this year, I thought.

I had seen time after time what midazolam or propofol or fentanyl or even ketamine could do, when used alone in sub-anesthetic doses, to get people to say things they would not normally say. But when used in the right amounts in combination, they were almost like a key to a lock; they synergistically opened the minds and mouths of patients, many of whom would die from embarrassment had they known the secrets they spilled out. Truthfully, in overall anesthesia practice, I was by no means a king or wizard. There were people who could do better nerve blocks than I could. There were colleagues who had better skills intubating people with difficult airway anatomy. But when it came to sedating someone to the edge of consciousness, someone who could get a cheating spouse or an embezzling businessman to fess up and be happy they did, there was no one even close to me. I knew this was true. I had seen my colleagues at work. And so had the surgeons. That's why for sedation cases, I was often requested, whether in the plastic surgery room, the urology suite, the eye room or the GI suite for endoscopy and colonoscopy. There was no doubt around Hamilton; I had "the touch." If I had served in World War II, I would have been the guy with the sodium pentothal syringe in his hand, titrating in the "truth serum" so that the intelligence folks could get the dirt from the resistant prisoner.

Without hesitation, I took out my syringe of fentanyl and gave John a half cc, or 25 micrograms. Then, picking up my 20cc syringe of propofol, I slowly injected 5 ccs of the milky "Michael Jackson" drug into the IV. I then hit John with 15 mg of ketamine. That, I figured, would be the clincher. After two agonizing and seemingly eternal minutes, I bent close to John's ear and said: "John, How ya feelin'?"

"Jes great, jes grayyyy…"

"John, tell me something. Where are interest rates going?"

The Chairman opened his eyes, his gaze flicking rapidly back and forth in sharp saccades, like an old, spastic electric typewriter gone rogue.

"Oh, oh, that?? Well, well, they, they…are goin' up! Up, I tell ya! You see the president…the president and I…"

His voice trailed off. With growing urgency, I said in a hushed voice, "The president and you are what!?"

Just then, both nurses entered the OR. I pushed myself back from the edge of the OR table.

Silverstone snorted once, hiccupped and began snoring, sounding like a buzz saw.

It has been said that The Chairman of the Federal Reserve Bank is the second most powerful person in the world. Presidents may be commanders in chiefs, generals may move armies and admirals vast fleets, but few people can control the daily lives of so many people like Fed Chairs. The Fed Chair is the acting executive officer The Board of Governors of the Federal Reserve System and wields tremendous power. Together with other voting members of the Federal Open Market Committee, seven of whom are members of the Federal Reserve Board, The Fed Chair presides over periodic meetings in Washington, DC and has first say in dictating monetary policy through interest rate adjustments, money supply manipulation and tweaking of other economic parameters.

That late afternoon after work I turned on at low volume my late sister's live-concert recording of the often dark Mozart Piano concerto in d minor, reclined on my living room floor and took my best dead-man yoga position (on my back, feet splayed out and my palms up). Attempting to take in the enormity and import of what was becoming a plan, I let my mind wander, drifting back to the poker games my dad had held at our home years ago each Thursday night starting at 8 pm and lasting usually until 1 or 1:30 am. Between the ages of 13 and 18, before I went off to college, I was witness to these games. I would sit off to the side, sketchbook in hand, and draw what were considered by people with an eye for artistic talent, realistic and even nuanced portraits of the men at the poker table. There was Vin Cerrato, a burly dark Italian in his mid-forties, who owned a scrap metal yard. Two other surgeon friends of my dad, the sleek and refined Jossi Berlinsky and the outgoing and at times boisterous Edwin Armacost were frequently there, as was the slippery red-headed crime lawyer Brian Dorland. Rounding out the group was a mortgage broker, the aging Benny Segalman, whose parents and much of his extended family were wiped out in the Holocaust. Benny was left with his brother Samuel, at the age of ten and twelve respectively, to join a partisan unit in Ukraine fighting the Nazis. The last member of the poker seven was Li Wei Eng, a perpetually cheerful and smiling Taiwanese plastic surgeon with whom my dad frequently golfed.

Sitting there at poker-table ringside, I was privy to the usual bullshit talk that men disgorge at the gaming venues: sports, money, business, politics, women—the whole laundry list. I learned a lot from those games about poker, politics and even a little about women, but it was the financial aspects that intrigued me. In particular, banter among Segalman, Dorland and Armacost was consistently geared to the stock market, and the three frequently tried to outdo each other with their supposed masteries of the intricacies or trading equities: puts, calls, going long, going short, margin plays and the like.

One evening at a poker game during the mid-summer, when I was working days as a checker at the Giant Food over at Friendship Heights making five bucks an hour (with benefits and a much-resented deduction on my paycheck for union dues), the three finance mavens got into it. In particular, Dorland went on about his propensity for "shorting" the market, where one wagers that stocks will fall and thus bets against them. I was taken aback by this concept, for at my young age I naively thought that the only way to make money in stocks (or on any investment, for that matter) was to have their values rise. Dorland said he had confidentially heard from an anonymous but reliable source two days prior that Icelandic Glacier Energy would soon lose its long-standing president and CEO to a sex and financial malfeasance scandal. The guys at the table teased him about insider trading but he ignored their jabs. In fact, I remember Dorland bragging, "Yeah, so this Adriel Einnarrson asshole or whatever-the-fuck his name is was caught by another two execs after hours in the board room screwing the Danish secretary. That and some fishy financial doings led the board, just this morning, to vote him out. This I learned two days ago, before it became public. Well, I call my broker and sez 'I wanna short Icelandic Glacier, and few other players in their sector, and see what gives'. Well, today my ship came in: Icelandic fell 11 percent today, and the two other companies in the sector took nice hits as well. Made myself a quick 25,000 bucks!"

Back at the table-side, I was flabbergasted. Twenty-five grand in two days!? All from a rumor? I figured "Shit at five bucks an hour, less dues and stuff, it would take me all summer to make a fiftieth of that! And he did it in two days."

As the next hopeful, slow movement of the Mozart concerto swirled in my brain, I relaxed further into the yoga pose and considered all angles of what happened today in the OR with Silverstone.

By the conclusion of that movement, one thing had become apparent.

My big break had finally come.

The Mozart now moved into its final dramatic third movement, the Allegro. I got up from the pose, took a swig of iced tea, moved over to my desk and reflected further. My head down, my hand absently scratching the back of my neatly cut blonde hair, I suddenly thought of an old friend. My "conversation" with the Fed Chair and my poker memories led me to think of a friend, Clete Shea, AKA "Cleesh," as in "Cli-che," due to his propensity to overuse hackneyed words and phrases, once we started, in tenth grade, to call him the nickname he came to hate. Cleesh and I lost touch after high school; me out to Stanford and him to U. of Chicago, where he studied Economics undergrad, and stayed on for a masters and doctorate in Economics. Presently, Cleesh has some wonky position with the SEC in downtown DC. We had been in contact regularly since I moved back. Cleesh was a bit of an oddball, but no one doubted his brains.

Draining the last of my iced tea, I picked up my mobile and called Cleesh to feel him out: "Yo Cleesh, it's Adrian."

"The Man! How's it hangin'?"

"Can't complain. How's work?"

"Nose to the grindstone. You know how it is. Wassup?"

"Listen. I got some questions for you if you got time. I got into a little, shall we say, argument with Charlie over interest rates and their effect on markets and I want you to settle a score. A case of Hennepin rests on it."

"Hennepin! That's serious stuff! Do I get a kick-back? After all. They say it's the beer that God drinks! Nectar of the Gods!"

"Yeah, well, that may be. If I win, I'll throw you a couple."

"Fox guarding the hen-house."

"Cleesh—stop! Now listen. I said to Charlie I thought that in general, sharp and sudden moves in interest rates can affect equities. 'Generally speaking' I said, 'but not always, a surprise upward tick in rates can cause a rapid fall, and vice versa.' Knowing there were other factors involved, was I right in my thinking?"

I could see Cleesh, through the mobile, pinching his nostrils the way he does when he's concentrating. There was a pause and a sigh. "This is what the hell you guys wager on? Not whether we're gonna get pounded by the Cowboys or who has the better track record with the ladies?"

Another pause. He continued, "Look Adrian. It's like this: Some folks, in the short term, and only when interest rates take a quick hike north "s -o -m- e people, (not me, of course), think they can make some bank on that. Hold on a minute. I got a paper in a file on my computer that was written by a buddy of mine, Tim Muller, back in '12. Hang on….oh yeah, here it is. Listen to this. In his analysis presented at an investment conference we both were at in Vegas he said:

'Any moves in interest rates have economic effects. When they go up, money in circulation goes down. But if you want to borrow, despite a lower inflation effect, it's pricier to do that. This affects how people spend. Higher rates lead to higher expenses which leads to lower earnings for companies that owe money. A rise in rates also makes, in the short term, people feel that fixed income investments, like bonds, CDs and money markets more attractive than stocks.'

"Ya know: flight to safety, they call it. Bear in mind Adrian, predicting short movements in the stock market is a fool's game. Nobody can do it."

"Yeah, I know, I know…but, what do think the odds are if…"

"Odds? Well, I don't have a crystal ball to show me that. I can say that if I was a betting man, I'd wager that more times than not in the short term, a surprise and dramatic rise in rates will spook the markets. IN THE SHORT TERM! And that's the name of that tune!"

"That's all I needed to know, Cleesh. Thanks! Hey, meet me for pizza tonight? Da Marco's in Bethesda? 7:30?"

"'Meet you'? Is a frog's ass watertight?! You bet. I got nothing tonight. And by the way, you're not planning anything stupid based on this discussion, are you? I'm not gonna hafta call my bosses on your ass, am I?"

"No, no. Just a bet between me and Chuck."

"Whatever, Crazy Man. See you tonight."

I met Cleesh at Da Marco's at 7 pm. He was in a good mood, having told me about a girl he met at a party in Adams Morgan the night before. I ordered a Peroni and he a Moretti. We both had the special: Da Marco's signature authentic Neapolitan tricolore pizza, with 00 flour, San Marzano tomatoes, and authentic buffalo mozzarella and fresh basil. Alessandro, the owner, baked it in a brick oven at high temperature. It was the only real pizza one could get in Bethesda.

I started to size Cleesh up. "So Cleesh, tell me, how's work?"

"You know, SSDD. Looking to move up the food chain soon. Up for a promotion in two weeks if all the ducks line up. If they don't I may bolt for the private sector. I deserve more money, fuck-ing-University- of-Chicago-fucking-PhD and…"

"That's great! Listen up. Gotta ask you a few questions. Kinda related to the bet I had with Charlie. "

"That again? What are you guys, obsessed? Don't you have anything better to talk about?"

"Listen, it's Hennepin, after all. Anyway, I told Chuck that knowing how interest rates would affect the market is useless since any large and atypical transactions by two-bit players would trigger a, you know, red flag."

"Wait a minute, Adrian. I thought this was only about a case of fancy beer, even if 'god drinks it' or not."

He wiggled his fingers heaven-ward, as if making quotation marks in the sky.

"It is just about the beer, but..."

He cut me off.

"Then what's all this stuff about 'large transactions by two - bit players'? Listen Hadrian..."

(He called me Hadrian whenever he judged me to be too full of myself.)

"Listen, Hadrian. In the first place, I told you my feeling on likely market moves, in the short term, when rates hike up. Secondly, I don't know what you or you and Chuck are up to but, whatever it is, A, I don't want to know and, B, don't do it."

"We're not up to anything, it's just that, well, I know this guy who claims he's gonna make a play on a tip he got from an insider and I, you know, was just curious as to how hard it is to pull off a score before a..."

"Oh, an 'insider'?"

Fingers wiggled again. He went on: "Let me give it to you straight. The feds, the SEC, watch strange moves in market accounts all the time. They live for this shit. There's a boatload of ways to get into trouble: moves by individuals or corporations that trigger FINRA reports; then there's whistleblowers, news reports, routine periodic SEC audits, accounting deficiencies, misleading disclosures, unregistered offerings. The list of possible red flags is as long as a donkey's dick!"

"Okay, Okay! I'm not doing anything of the sort. It's just that this guy I know is..."

"'This guy you know'. Listen Hadrian, let me tell you about a whale I know. His name is not Orca but ORSA. That stands for

Options Regulatory Surveillance Authority, which is a fancy name for a watchdog agency, like FINRA, that refers cases to us when even a tidbit of suspicious trading occurs, or our own analytics concur with reports we receive from these agencies. Sometimes it takes days, sometimes weeks, but let me tell you, these reports get filed and investigated."

Our pizzas arrived. The beers were half gone and the first, celestial slice went in my mouth.

"Cleesh. No one's doing anything. It's all about the bet. I'll tell my friend he'd better not try any illegal stuff and that the feds watch this shit all the time."

Cleesh, sprinkling oregano on his pizza, narrowed his eyes at me. He wiped the Moretti-foam from his lips with the back of his forearm.

"That would be wise. Tell your 'friend' to walk the straight and narrow. Now shut up and let's enjoy this I-talian fuel and rinse. Pass me the parmesan, will ya?"

I took a quick look at my finances. My net worth, despite my divorce settlement from five years ago, was healthy but not "fuck-you" healthy. I was beer and pretzels rich, not champagne and caviar rich. I was making about 25 grand a month minus the 8 grand a month alimony I was having to pay for five more years. There was no child support since we never had kids, thank God. I took out a piece of paper and calculated my net worth:

Assets: $1,822,444 in brokerage account. $599,077 equity in my condo. $323,988 in my 401 K, $25,000 in a life insurance policy and about $175k in an old pension plan, against which I could borrow. A 2019 C class Mercedes, with 35,000 miles. Some gold coins, antique watches, rare stamps and jewelry, all valued at about $25k.

Liabilities: The balance on my condo. No credit card debt. I owned the car outright.

I did some searching on the web about how to buy stocks and ETFs on margin. I looked at the calendar. It was Tuesday the 9th[th] and the Fed meeting was a week from next Monday, the 22nd[nd] of October.

If I was going to act, it had to be soon.

To consider leaving the life I had made for myself was wrenching. But it had been a long time coming. "Typical doc burn-out," a phrase that Cleesh would likely use to describe how I felt, didn't quite capture it. It was much more nuanced than that. There was so much more to it. A pig of a department chairman who did no clinical work, sucked up to Admin, kissing their collectively three-piece-suited asses with large donations to hospital charities while inviting them to weekend forays on his yacht he kept in Alexandria, the Gas-Man. I was also growing tired of taking care of people who did not take care of themselves. Since over two-thirds of my patients, like most Americans, were overweight or obese, my patient population was growing sicker and riskier to take care. Ever mindful of the fiasco of a lawsuit that dragged on for five years for my dad in the 1970s (it was finally dismissed for no merit, but not before, as I learned as a child, dad had lost 60 pounds from the stress and depression), I knew the longer I practiced, the more likely it was I was going to get sued. Stats show that a doc can expect to get sued every seven years, and I had been untouched by the litigation fairy for too long to play games. Then there was the misery of call.

Ask any doctor who must take on-call duties and he or she will tell you it's one of the worst parts of the job. Our call days used to start at 7 am (now it is 4 pm) and not end until 7 the next morning, in house (we had it easy, the surgeons and gyn folks had 36-hour shifts). The nights were filled with C- sections on high risk mothers, traumas like gunshot wounds and stabbings from Northeast and Southeast Washington and car accidents from the Beltway, along with the usual middle of the night appendectomies or bowel obstructions. Literally, I was getting way too old for that shit. All while our chairman, that fat Leonard Askin MD, with his bitchy wife, snotty kids, and hairy moles in the folds of his fleshy neck, slept comfortably in his house on Arrowood Road nights and all weekends, schmoozing with his society friends and admin buddies. I also resented the alimony I was still paying, to a wife who never used her law degree. My lawyer told me never to bring that up in deposition and that made me extra angry.

Then there was what all of us were calling "the screw." "The screw" meant lower paychecks unless certain metrics, set by Medicare and the insurance companies, were met. It meant more demands on our time and attention due to our mandatory electronic medical record inputs instead of paper charting. It meant a dedicated spy, who sat in the preop area to see if we washed our hands for a full minute with disinfectant between patient encounters. It meant all of this and more, and I was tiring of it, fast.

Looking back, I still can't believe I pulled it all off in less than two weeks. There was the consolidation of finances; the refinance to the hilt of my condo, the contact with my broker at Titus/Dixon Investments on how much margin I could leverage, the pawning in Northwest DC at Parliament Pawn Shop on 14th and P Streets of all my jewelry, coins, stamps and watches. There was a shell corporation to set up, a dummy company so that if I did make what I thought I could on this deal, I could hide the money long enough to have access to it from abroad. And then there was where to bank overseas; I needed a country that kept their clients' banking matters secret.

The brokerage leveraging was straightforward: the Titus/Dixon website said that qualified account holders could borrow up to 50 percent of their accounts' valuation. Then there was the issue of refinancing my condo. Calling my mortgage people in Rockville. I sweet talked Marina (the Latvian woman to whom I often brought Belgian chocolates) into working the refi paperwork for Ms. Simms, her boss and loan officer. I asked her if she could move the application to the top of her pile. "Kinda urgent, because I had heard rates might be heading up," I told her. Pending an inspection that she said could be done the next Thursday afternoon, Marina said I could pick up the 80 percent loan to value check by the following Monday or Tuesday. I promised her a box of Lindt's.

Wednesday midday, I spent time looking up places to incorporate. Everyone thinks of Delaware, for generic corporations, but the First State was too slow and, frankly, too conspicuous. To my surprise, it turned out that the state with the most private, easy to process and user-friendly corporations was Wyoming. I stumbled across the website of a company, Incorporation Services of Wyoming, touting the benefits of incorporating there. It bragged:

'Wyoming has the best asset protection of any other jurisdiction. Your LLC can be linked to a Domestic Asset Protection Trust. Wyoming law provides for no room for interpretation. Wyoming LLCs are confidential and private. There is no state tax for an LLC in our state. And our rates are much lower than other states. Also, there is a new law that means Wyoming's law is better than other states. Wyoming does not require corporation members or managers to be listed in public record. Shareholders are not listed with the state. There is no need for a nominee officer. Wyoming draws little attention and again, there are no state income taxes.'

It sounded almost too good to be true. I went to the application portion of the website. It was ridiculously simple. The application said that for corporations that were LLCs, or Limited Liability Companies, the "filer" (the party making the application) could be a third party. This was particularly attractive to me since I did not have to use my own name. By 10:30 in the morning, I had put in an application for Gail Force Holdings, LLC. I clicked to PayPal button to process my 65-dollar fee and was directed to a screen that said:

"Congratulations! Your application has been received. Within 24 hours, you will receive a notice regarding the status of your application. Please check your email, including spam file, for the notice. Have a wonderful day! Yours, Warren Tetley, President, Incorporation Services of Wyoming, LLC."

I could not believe how easy it was. That would have never happened in Florida, Maryland, or Delaware, for that matter.

To pitch a "no hitter" on call meant to sleep the entire night through: no C-sections, no calls from the main OR, no calls from the surgical floor on pain patients. "No hitters" were rare but not unheard of. In the many years I had been on staff at Hamilton, I had had probably an even dozen no hitters. How much more work I could get on Thursday to finish my research on how to disappear, how to most effectively short the stock market, tie up loose ends on my Wyoming incorporation and figure out where to hide my money away from the feds, should I have the good fortune to bet correctly.

The anesthesia gods were indeed smiling that Wednesday night. Except for a bleeding tonsil at 10:30 and one C-section and 11:45 pm, I closed my eyes at 1:15 and awoke at 7 that morning. A two hitter was more than adequate to feel refreshed enough to hand off the call and trauma beepers to my colleague Dr. Singh at 7:15, be home by 8:30, take a nap till 11 and get to work.

By 11 am I had felt awake and sharp enough to round out my plan. I had already arranged the Wyoming LLC, the application for refinancing the condo, the pawning of my valuables and the margin account with my investment company. All that remained was to research how to disappear, how to establish a bank account that was as secret as possible and how to quickly profit from a tanking stock market.

Coffee in hand, I searched "most secret banking laws by country" and to my delight instantly found a website describing what is called the financial secrecy index. This index, through its research and expert opinions, rated countries on their banking privacy laws and scale of their functions. It purported to be a politically neutral ranking, and incredibly, estimated that between 20 to 35 trillion dollars of private accounts were housed in banking secrecy zones. The most recent rankings the website reported were, in descending order:

1. Switzerland
2. Hong Kong
3. Singapore
4. Luxembourg
5. Cayman Islands
6. Panama
7. Malaysia
8. Isle of Man
9. Jersey and
10. Bahrain

I had heard of all of them but was least familiar with Isle of Man and Jersey. The Isle of Man is a British Crown dependency in the Irish Sea, as is Jersey. After reviewing the privacy rules, ease of account opening, accessibility by boat or ferry and the fact that the coat of arms for the Isle of Man, the triskelion, was three running legs joined 60 degrees apart at the thigh in a spiral design (I figured if I was going to be on the run, this was a good omen), I picked it. I googled the smaller banks on the Isle and came across the contact information for the accounts officer at Isle of Manx Crown Bank, Ltd. A Mr. Simmonds Armstrong-Wicke was the contact person for new accounts. I noted his phone number and the phone numbers and emails of three other Isle of Man banks and slipped the paper in my wallet.

Next on my list was the best way to rapidly short the market. I had known enough from past discussions with Cleesh, my investment counselors at Titus/Dixon, Dad, Charlie and my own reading and research that my choices were limited to two options: straight up stocks or exchange traded funds, or ETFs. While stocks were more liquid in that they could be traded intraday, I did not have time to research the literally tens of thousands of options in the equity world to make any intelligent choices in time for the fed meeting a week from Monday. ETFs, though not as liquid as stocks due realization of assessed value at the close of each market day, rather than intraday, was a better choice, I thought, since they were essentially baskets of other equities piled into sectors like precious metals, industrials, energy, healthcare and the like. My plan was to buy as many strongly bearish ETFs as my research and margin account would allow, evenly split, on a week from Friday's market day, wake up Monday early and put all my sell orders in by the close of business at 4pm. I had a lot from which to choose: there were S and P Bear shares, Mid Cap, Large Cap, Small CAP Bears, China Bears, Brazil Bears, Japan Bears—I decided I'd spread the love anywhere and everywhere, maybe 20 positions, and let the chips fall. And then there were the Ultras, that let me multiply my bets, 2, 3 and even

4-fold. That's where the real money could be made, and that's where I planned to park as much money as my analysis would justify.

The doorman called up at 12:55 pm to tell me the assessment guy was here from Calvert and Crossland Mortgage Company. After ten minutes of inspection, I asked Andrew, the guy hired to do the estimate, how much I could mortgage and when I could expect the loan.

"Well, seeing that the market's improved considerably since you bought in, let's see, 2015. You're looking at about a million fifty, maybe a million seventy- five.

I coughed.

"You mean total or 80 percent?"

"Oh, 80 percent. At least that's what Marina told me, right? You want the max? 100% loan to value?"

"Oh, yes, yes. The max. If that's doable."

"I'll run it by them."

"Great. Uh, when do you think it'll be processed?"

"Well, Marina; she's sweet on you, so she told me to run this down to Ms. Simms after my next appointment in Chevy Chase. I can get this to the office by, say, 3:30 to 4? "

"Wonderful! That works. Hey, want some coffee?"

"No thanks. Gotta get going. Traffic you know."

Andrew took off and I sank to the couch. The refi money would be ready sometime early next week. That would allow three days for my check to clear. If my incorporation papers could be obtained as early as the middle of next week, I thought, I could take a sick day a week from tomorrow, Friday the 19th (that would really piss Askin off), go through my checklist and finalize my plans. I could sell the car that Friday morning to CarMax.

The clock read 2:10 pm and I decided to grab a quick pita downstairs and head out to sign the margin papers at Titus/Dixon.

My investment advisor, Tricia Porter, an early thirty-something single woman with flax hair, killer legs, elegant hands, and an unfortunate smoking habit, agreed to meet me at 3 pm to go over the paperwork. As I left the apartment and headed to the elevator, a chill came over me. "I'm not gonna hafta call the SEC on your ass, am I?" My recent online research had triggered my conversation with Cleesh from earlier in the week. I turned on my heel and went back to the condo. I dumped my keys on the dining table and took a seat. I stared down at my blue Pumas. SEC. Shit. And what about bank deposits? Even I knew that any deposits above ten grand could trigger a notice to the bank feds, LLC or no LLC. How was I going to launder my money? Fuck!

I took out my phone and called Tricia at her office.

"Trish? Hi it's Adrian."

"Hello, Dr. Spitz! How are you?"

"Funny, Trish. Fine. Listen, I need to take a raincheck today. Could we meet next week, say Wednesday afternoon, the 17th, like 3:30?"

"Sure. No problem. I'll pencil you in. Got a hot date?"

"No Trish. Just something last minute. And do me a favor: stop smoking!"

"I'm trying, doc. Really!

"'Dr. Spitz'," I thought.

I put my phone down and thought about Tricia Porter. Even after such a brief conversation there was something about her that my mind couldn't shake. She called me "Dr. Spitz," clearly for the multi-gold-medal winning Olympic swimmer named Mark Spitz of decades ago and asked me if I had "a hot date." I knew she liked me. Her hints confirmed that. She was clearly attractive, smart, and funny. She had great taste in clothes and was always impeccably groomed. She smelled good, except for the cigarettes. Through the glass door and windows of her office, while waiting for her on several past appointments, I had witnessed the obvious care and courteous attention she had paid to her clients: an elderly couple who looked to her for sound financial guidance, a disabled man brought in by a friend whom she helped wheel through the narrow doorway of her office, and a young mother with three unruly children whom she placated with juice boxes and a few balloons and toys she had kept in a drawer. There was even a photo on her office wall of her with a teenaged Black girl on the steps of the Smithsonian. Tricia once had told me she was a Big Sister to the girl on the weekends and some evenings, through the organization "Big Brothers and Sisters of the National Capital Area."

But then there was the Ms. Porter I could not, at that time, know anything about: the child who at aged four had lost her mother to breast cancer with a never-to-remarry and devoted dad, an engineer from Seattle who moved east to help design aircraft engines for a Northern Virginia-based company; the girl who would blossom into an elegant blond wisp of a dancer and a formidable fencer who would win collegiate titles and become a Phi Beta Kappa caliber student at The University of Maryland. This dog-loving, energetic and curious child was first an ungainly, colt-legged creature who skipped through grade school, despite the loss of her mother, and magically transformed in high school to a young woman; lean – boned, graceful in her movements and light on her feet. Aside from her excellence in academics and athletics, she was funny, outgoing, and headstrong. When she saw something she wanted, she went after it. But she played by the rules.

She made many friends easily, most of them for life. She had been engaged twice before, to Paul an attorney and Raul, a diplomat's son, she being the one to break off the engagements. She had felt both times like she was "settling." She wouldn't have it.

She tried to keep her friends close, both male and female, but as her cohorts married, she felt more and more alone. Her close friendship with her co-fencer sorority sister at The University of Maryland, Ann Desmond, she cherished most. Desmond, a jewelry designer, was her last remaining single girlfriend and Patricia's wing man when they went out for drinks or to meet people. They spoke by phone almost every day and saw each other at least once a week. Ann had, for years, tried to get her friend to quit smoking. She actually had her now down to two cigarettes a day.

I couldn't say why I had never asked her out.

I went back to the computer. All my google searches on depositing checks to accounts, whether individual or corporate, said the same thing: deposits exceeding 10,000 dollars, or repeated deposits of more than $10,000 would indicate suspicious activity and could trigger an audit under the 1970 Bank Security Act, formulated under President Nixon's administration. Rules on this were tightened even more after 9/11 and our country's involvement in conflicts with Iraq, Iran, Russia, and Afghanistan. China, Mexico, and other Latin American and African countries with which we had security concerns, either through military conflict or the transport and sale of narcotics, compounded the enhanced security laws.

I sat at the table and stared over at the calendar. I had about ten days to get all these plates spinning at the same time. I recall thinking from past encounters and discussions with Charlie, Cleesh and at seminars related to protecting assets by moving money around that even if I was discovered to have committed a crime or crimes (since insider trading and money laundering certainly fit that category), there would be a finite and brief time before the authorities at the SEC and the feds watching the banks found out. I estimated that that time frame would be days at worst and weeks or, if I were lucky, months. I had to find a way to buy as much time as possible.

I was startled by the chime of my cell phone. It showed a Wyoming area code, the one I recognized from my web search.

"Hello, this is Adrian."

"Hello Mr. Wren? This is Warren Tetley calling from Incorporation Services of Wyoming. Is this an okay time?"

The voice sounded like tires running over packed gravel. I immediately imagined a large girth, a big belt buckle, a large Stetson and a bolo tie.

"Yes Mr. Tetley. It's actually Dr. Wren, but you can call me Adrian. What can I do for you?"

"Oh sorry Doc, I mean, Adrian. Nice to speak with you. Jest a quick question about your LLC application. I see the company name requested is "Gail Force Holdings." Is that the correct spelling? Usually, Gale in that sense is spelled G-A-L-E."

I could not shake the Wilford Brimley vision in my head.

"Oh yes, Mr. Tetley. It is G-A-I-L. That was my late sister's name. The company is to be named for her."

"Oh, so sorry to hear. I understand completely. That's a fine testament a brother can make. Me, my brother Walter died when we were boys. Shot himself with our dad's Colt by accident. 'Bout ruined the family."

"Sorry for your loss, as well. Anyway, how are the papers coming?"

"All looks good on my end. I see you wanted my company, that is, me, to be your filer for the corporation in question?"

I told him that that was the case.

"Happy to oblige! Then you should expect, barring any hold-ups, to be incorporated in the Cowboy State in, I'd say, let me see.... next Wednesday. October 17th. That work for you?"

"More ways that you can know, sir."

"Fine! Soon as the state's approval hits my email, I'll forward the papers to you and the hard copy you'll get in the mail. Also, will you be adding any officers other than yourself to the LLC?"

I rubbed the back of my elbow against the chair, paused and said

"Actually Mr. Tetley, there may be additional officers down the line. Can they be added later?"

There was an awkward pause on the line.

"Dr Wren, I mean Adrian, Wyoming is a very protective state when it comes to privacy and freedom of commerce without the government's nose up its rear like a rooting sow. Because of that, you can add or omit any names you like. It's your choice as to whom is listed as managers, officers or members on or off the public record."

I exhaled a sigh of relief. The ease of this process was astounding.

"That's terrific, sir. You see, I may want to be…what do they call it?…a 'silent partner' in this enterprise."

" 'Silent', noisy, it don't matter to us! It's my pleasure son. By the way, any plans to come visit us up here? It's beautiful country!"

I told him I'd like that, thanked him again and told him I'd await the papers he had promised. I turned off my phone and took a sip of cold coffee that was left on the table. On the table were sheets of research I had printed out about LLCs in Wyoming and other states. Now that I had a jurisdiction that did not require my name in a public record, I considered what other roadblocks and dead ends I might create to cover my tracks and thereby purchase the needed space to get me and my money gone.

One way do get that done, according to what I read, was to get a "registered agent," usually an attorney, who would be the recipient of all legal documents and other important papers on behalf of the corporation. After wracking my brain, I put the finished coffee cup on the table and snapped my fingers. For this purpose, I had just the man.

CHAPTER 2
ARRANGEMENTS

When I was married, my dad steered me to his estate attorney, Abe Levin, who advised me that since I was in a high-risk medical specialty, my assets were always at risk. In Maryland, where we all resided, there is an available but easily overlooked law that states if you hold assets with your spouse in a legal construct called "tenants by the entirety," husband and wife are, for all purposes, judgement-proof. But since I had been divorced, I had no way to protect my money. Any judgement exceeding my malpractice coverage made me open season for plaintiff's lawyers. Levin had retired five years ago and move to Florida, not far from where mom and dad now live in Delray Beach.

Then it occurred to me: I could augment my plan, take care of my "registered agent" issue and settle an old score all at the same time. I'd call Francis Devlin, Esquire. With offices on K Street and Chevy Chase, Maryland at Friendship Heights, he was a member of both the DC and Maryland Bar. He helped get the Montgomery County Executive, Elijah Dyson, elected. He had the ear of DC Mayor Caroline Rogers, Maryland Governor Sam Tilden and was a frequent visitor to The State Senate in Annapolis. This guy had a reputation as a fixer; he was a guy who could get the guilty off, cut deals in the back rooms, woo the charity and gala sets of Potomac and Georgetown and all the while look like St. Augustine. He also had caused a lot of pain for someone who means much to me.

It was the summer of 1991, and I was at home with mom after day camp at Landon Summer Day. She had been doing some housekeeping and tidying-up: getting rid of dad's old medical journals, some old sheet music that had orphaned pages, some out of date store coupons. She had put a photo album out that contained family photos from the past few decades Sitting cross-legged on the cool hardwood floor, I got to flipping through the pages and came across a picture of a man I thought looked familiar. Pointing to a photo that had AUG 1976 along the margin I said to her, "Hey mom, who's that man?"

She came by my side and, turning her head much like Gail did when she was curious said, "Oh honey, that's your father."

My mouth fell open.

"But he's so *skinny!*"

She put her hand to her cheek and, giving me a look I had never seen on her face before, remarked

"Well dear, I suppose he is. Adrian, listen, that was a bad time in dad's life. Mine too. I guess you're old enough to understand what I'm about to tell you. Dad was very depressed then. Very worried."

"Over what?" I asked.

"Well, he was being sued. For malpractice. It was early in his career. He was quite concerned it would affect his career, his livelihood."

"Who was suing him? And why? What did he do?"

"He actually didn't do anything. Wrong, that is. It was all a mix- up, a clerical mistake. You see, he found out a lady patient had cancer. After a biopsy. That's when they take a piece of your body out and send it to the lab for testing. And when he and the office kept trying to reach her, by phone and mail, they never got to her. Turns out she had moved. To Florida."

"What happened then?"

"Well, they sent it registered mail and all that. But they never got a reply. She left no forwarding address. So months later, like six months later, your dad gets a letter from a lawyer saying that he's going to be sued. Turns out her cancer had spread and she blamed dad for never telling her she had it in the first place. Except he tried to, but, as I said, they couldn't find her. He had insurance and everything but, you know your dad, he's a worrier. He worried when this news got out it would make his professional life quite difficult. And it did, for a few years."

"Years!?" I exclaimed.

"Yes Adrian. It dragged on and on. These legal things can. Eventually, the judge threw the case out. She said dad and his staff did nothing wrong. You'll understand a little better when you get older. But it took a toll on us both."

Eventually, I understood. Years later I came across some papers in an old shoebox in the basement of the house related to the lawsuit. I can never forget the name "Devlin" on the letterhead. The letters, to my reading, were full of threats, veiled in oddly polite terms. I never forgot that name. It looked like Devil to me.

Devlin represented to me all that I hated about Washington: power for power's sake. He, like the future lawyers, businessmen, lobbyists and other folks with whom I went to college, went on to earn what I perceived to be relatively easy money with a quicker path to financial freedom than I ever knew. It took me four years of college, four more of medical school, a year of internship and three years of residency a total of twelve yearsto even start to get to a point that began to resemble where they were in life. Law school was three years. Business school? Usually two. And then there were the guys who went into their father's businesses, making big money from the get-go. And no doctor I ever knew received stock options in a company he or she worked for. And perhaps worst of all: none of them understood the misery and stress of working 24 to 36 hours straight two to three times per week, year after year, with people's lives in their hands. All for 16 thousand a year for an intern and all the bad hospital food you could eat.

On my first break Friday morning I called his office. His assistant told me that he had had a cancellation for Tuesday afternoon at 1:30 and asked if I'd like to take that appointment. That was on the early side but if I could trade on-call with one of my colleagues for Monday, that meant I'd be off all day Tuesday. I told her I'd take it. A quick query to my buddies at work yielded the desired result: Danny Constance told me he'd let me take his Monday call for mine on the following Monday, no sweat. Danny always had my back. I felt like a shit that I'd certainly be gone by then.

Monday's on-call day started at 4 pm. That gave me most of Monday to research ETF picks and prepare for my Tuesday meeting with Devlin on K Street. I had decided earlier that day that I would try to talk Devlin into representing my LLC, perhaps even become an officer of the corporation, under the guise of shielding my assets from plaintiff-attorney's grubby hands. I figured the more layers, the more false starts, the more shells I could put around my illegal activity, which at minimum would be insider trading, money laundering and bank fraud, the better chance I stood of escaping the country and setting myself up abroad before anyone got wind of it.

My call night, though not a two-hitter, was tolerable. Two C-sections early, then a hot gall-bag at 1 am, then quiet until 6:30, when I got called to fix a few obstructed pain-med infusion pumps. A few hours of sleep were enough. I got back to my condo in Bethesda Tuesday morning at 8, napped until 10:30, checked my email and prepared for my meeting. Warren Tetley had been wrong; my LLC was already approved—it did not take until Wednesday. I looked the incorporation papers over and marveled at Wyoming's efficiency. In DC this would take twenty Wednesdays, I thought. I reviewed my brokerage account and scanned the news, gulping a quick lunch all the while. *Bloomberg's, CNN Money, The Wall Street Journal* and *Barron's* were all lathered up about the upcoming Fed meeting. The market had been volatile of late, and there was plenty in the news to make it so: geopolitical tensions, the pundit-parsing digestion of earnings reports, the weakening in commodities and petroleum, let alone the Fed meeting, compelled Wall Street to swing as much as 1 to 2 percent per day, up or down.

I got in my best suit at 11:45 pm and was reading *Golf Digest,* with sweating palms, in Devlin's K Street office by 1:15. I put down the golf magazine and noticed, among the *Vanity Fairs, The New Yorkers* and *Bethesda Magazines,* a dog eared self-help paperback, *Live Without Regret* by J. N. Hummel, lying among the journals. On the inside title page was the following inscription: To F. Devlin, Esquire. With gratitude, on our mutually beneficial conclusion to a thorny problem! Sig Thalberg.

I picked it up and thumbed through its pages. On page 29 I

read a series of phrases on change. They were: *When looking back doesn't interest you anymore, you're doing the right thing. You can't change what's going on around you until you change what's going on within you. One can't change the direction of the wind, but you can adjust your sails to reach your desired journey's end.*

Just then I heard the footsteps of Devlin's assistant approaching. Ms. Brownlee, Devlin's assistant, had that elementary school secretary look about her, with her pearls, finely starched suit, high heels, and glasses hung from her neck with a fine metal chain. I figured her for sixty but studying her visage and her physique—oval shaped face, full lips, turned-up nose, blond bob, long and slender limbs—nobody would blink if she said she was forty-five. In her day I bet she made the men crawl. And she had that "phone" voice, the type that on-hold prompts give you while they are not playing soft classical to ease the fact that they are too cheap to hire enough operators to answer your call.

At 1:30 she led me into Devlin's enormous office, my coffee in hand. There, in front of the trophy wall of Devlin in photographs with DC's and Montgomery County's sports stars, actors, politicians, TV anchors, activists, and the immediate past President of the United States, sat Devlin: 65-ish medium height, reasonably fit for a DC lawyer, with piercing ice blue eyes, a $2,000 suit and a $15,000 smile. As he stood and shook my hand, I noticed his right wrist where he wore what must have been a watch worth more than my car. We both sat.

"Thanks for seeing me on such short notice, Mr. Devlin. I know you are busy."

"The pleasure is mine, Dr Wren. May I call you Adrian?"

"Of course."

"Adrian, before we begin, are you related by any chance to Augustus Wren? There aren't many Wrens in the DC area."

I lied and told him I might be a distant cousin.

"Yes, his partner Dr. Weiss took out my late wife's appendix in, let's say, 1974, I think."

He was smooth as Crisco on hot tin foil.

I explained to him about the Wyoming LLC, the shielding of assets since my divorce, and concocted a story on the spot about Gail Force Holdings being a new venture of mine related to a medical device development opportunity that had been presented to me by a third party. I told him I had a non-disclosure agreement so that I could not discuss the details at that time, but that the device was soon to be approved for clinical use and showed great potential. One purpose of my visit was to see if it would be improper to ask him to serve as the registered agent for the corporation, as well as serve as legal counsel as an officer of the corporation. In my mind that could possibly shield me temporarily from federal investigators. I was imagining attorney/client privilege.

He looked down at his desk for a moment, scratching the back of his head. After what seemed an eternity, he looked up, his face a little flushed and said: "This is not the typical thing I hear in this office. Corporate law, certainly, is a lot of what I do. So is asset protection. So, in those areas, you came to the right place. And yes, I have served as a registered agent for those seeking to incorporate. And, assuming all your activities violated no laws, (he paused for a moment, looking me straight in the eye) in theory I could serve on your board as an officer of the LLC. It's not done frequently, but it is done. The laws in The District and Maryland have been, of late, muddy about an attorney serving as officer for another's corporation while simultaneously acting as counsel. (He smiled his platinum smile). Adrian, you must understand, however, I specialize in white-collar crime. I wonder why you've come to me as opposed to, say, Belkin in Bethesda, or Winston in Rockville or even Feinman in…"

"Simply put, you're the best there is."

He rubbed a long yellow pencil, eraser down, into his desk, looking me up and down.

"That's awfully kind. I appreciate the sentiment. I do have to warn you I'm probably more expensive than the fine attorneys that I just…"

"I'm sure they are all competent and capable. But I'd like to hire you. I have my incorporation papers here from Wyoming. I can designate you as an officer. Today, if that's alright."

"Well, slow down son. Before I agree to anything I need to know more about this, Gale-something.."

"Gail Force Holdings. I named it after a distant cousin and artist I admired and followed, Gail Wren. She was a pianist with a bright future until cancer took her at an early age."

"Ah yes! Gail Wren, the pianist. I remember now. *The Post* once did a piece on her in The Style section if I recall correctly. She was a young phenom. I'm so sorry. Talented young woman. Her parents, the whole family, must have been devastated."

"They were, from what I heard. Anyway, getting back to the LLC. I've surrounded myself with talented, sharp and well-informed people in all walks of medicine, engineering, business and finance. People at the SEC, like my friend Clete Shea, who gives me regulatory council, my brother Charles, my finance friends at Titus/Dixon and many others, here and abroad. We've put together a sound team of people, with a solid, cogent and conservative business and development plan. Besides, that's down the road. To start, I want the LLC to shield what I'm building. And of course, the registered agent."

I showed him a financial statement and a mock business plan from a template I had filled in from a website. Something I had fabricated to look impressive and official.

Devlin studied it carefully. I watched nervously to see if he was buying it. He looked up at me and back at the papers. He took off his glasses, placed them on his desk, took a long sip of water and cleared his throat.

"You know Adrian, I know a lot of smart people, people much smarter than me. Likely even smarter than you. You. You know medicine. You're likely a very fine doctor, to be at Hamilton for so many years and all that. The medical device gamehell any new venture related to untested products and servicesis not for beginners and, excuse me for saying, physicians are notoriously bad with money. The likelihood that you may lose a considerable amount of money is real."

I gave him my best rescue-dog eyes.

"I realize that. I've thought that through. That's why I'm not going to use all my money. Most of my savings and 401k will stay intact. I have some venture capital people who are interested. I can produce a letter from them in a matter of days if you so desire. Besides, there are other factors I have not mentioned. Other than the persistent fear of litigation, I'm tired of clinical medicine. It's wearing me down. A lot of my colleagues feel the same. But few ever do anything about it. "

The lies and bluffs came surprisingly easy.

"I appreciate all that. I do, Adrian. But why not get your friends or family to serve on your board?"

"For the simple reason that they say you should never do business with friends or family."

"You're right on that one. I've made that mistake too many times."

I sipped my coffee and looked down.

"Tell you what. Give me a few days to think this over. The registered agent part I can do. But the other thing; let me study it. You seem like a smart and diligent young man. Call me Thursday, say, 10 am? I'll make sure Ms. Brownlee will put you through."

"Can't ask for more than that! Thank you."

We shook hands and I walked out to the street. My feet felt so light that they felt as if they weren't hitting the pavement. I got in my car, opened the windows on the brilliant fall day and sped home.

Stopping at a red light on the corner of Woodmont and Old Georgetown I looked over to my left and saw a sign in the Glitz Camera and photo shop. "Passport Photos While U Wait!" I thought nothing of it and proceeded on the green light. Then suddenly, it hit me. I pulled the car into an empty parking space on Hampden and sat dumbfounded. Passport photos! I had a valid passport in my name. I was sure I could use it to get out of the country in time before the feds caught on to my crimes. But what about the foreign bank account? Even if it were registered under the LLC's name, I couldn't very well reveal or open such an account under my real name, privacy laws or not. I'd need a new name, and a new address, preferably in Wyoming, or even local on the Isle of Man, to establish the account. I pulled out of the space and headed home.

Once in my condo, I headed straight to the computer and googled fake passports. Numerous web addresses that dealt with people who wanted to vanish and "live off the grid" appeared. I had no idea that so many people wanted to be—well—*gone*. That search opened a new trove of information on how to live abroad, or even in The United States, under a new identity, with tips on your best shot at remaining unfound. There were plenty of warnings on how difficult it was to pull off. The authors were usually ex-military; some were right-wing nut cases or survivalist and civilian militia types. There was much talk of weaponry, how to handle money and how to steal and destroy cars.

During the internet search it dawned on me that, two years prior, I had had a patient, Horace Styles, who had some shady connections. I had done the anesthesia for his shoulder arthroscopy.

Surgery on shoulders, knees and hips hurt like a bitch, seemingly in that order, and I had made an effort to familiarize myself with the best pain blocks to treat these orthopedic miseries post-op. I remember Horace screaming in pain as he awoke from anesthesia, so I took out my 10 cc syringe, filled it 0.5 percent Bupivacaine and stuck a three and a half inch 22 gauge spinal needle in his suprascapular notch, where the pain fibers that innervate the shoulder emerge. He looked at me as if I was Jesus Himself. The pain was gone in less than a minute. Completely gone.

We got to know each other a little. He had gotten into trouble by forging his wife's signature on a home refi loan and she turned him in. He had had some minor priors, not serious stuff, but this was enough to put him away for eighteen months. Inside, he made some connections. It was connections I needed.

I called him up and he was pleased to hear from me. I told him "a friend" in a jam needed some fake papers. I swore confidence to him and he directed me to a Max Gimble, over on Pershing Drive in Silver Spring. I asked if he thought it was too late to call Gimble. He said give it a try. I thanked him.

It was just past 3 pm. I called Gimble. He picked up.

"Mr. Gimble. This is a friend of Horace Styles, Adrian Wren."

"Friend of who!?"

"Horace Styles. He said he knew you in…"

"Yeah. A friend of Styles? How?"

"Uh, I really can't say much other than he was a patient of mine."

"So, you a doc, huh?"

"That's right. At Hamilton in DC."

His Brooklyn accent started to creep out. "How do I know you're not a cop?"

"Well, you can call Mr. Styles, if you like. Or better yet, look me up on the Department of Anesthesia website at Hamilton."

"Waddya need, Wren?"

"Well, Horace told me you might be able to assist me in getting some documents for a friend. I…"

"He did, huh. What kinda documents?"

"Well, he said you could do passports, social security cards, drivers licenses; that kind of stuff."

"Waddya say your name is again?"

"Wren. Like the bird. Adrian.

"Well lissen, 'Wren-like-the boid', I don' do that kinda stuff."

"But Horace said.."

"Styles ain't seen me for years, besides I…"

"I got 5000 bucks.

"5000 bucks? Waddya think you can get for that? Lissen, Wren, what is it you need? I mean, for your 'friend'."

"I need a passport and a driver's license. That's it. Oh, and I might need you to come with me to sign some papers. And send me, by fax or scanned e-mail, papers I may ask you to sign when I'm gone and far away."

"Whoa! That's a lotta stuff! What kinda papers?"

"Well, I'm thinking, I mean, my 'friend' is thinking of starting a company and he put me in charge of getting some officers for the corporation. My 'friend' and may need to transfer some of our funds when we contact you. I…"

"What kinda 'company'?"

"Well, it's a medical device company. Anyway I…"

"Where ya live?"

"Bethesda."

"Figures."

There was a long pause. He went on, "Lissen. Tellya what. I'll do the passport, the driver's license and sign the papers, but I won't sign my name. I'll use another name that I've been working using cooked documents. We'll make it a package deal. 10 grand for the passport and ID, two grand to sign the papers."

"Done."

"Jus like that?"

"Just like that."

"Shoulda asked for more."

I arranged to meet him that evening at 6 pm 800 Pershing Drive, Silver Spring. I was able to stop by my bank before it closed on the way and withdraw 5000 dollars. The rest I'd have to get the next day; I didn't want to draw out 10 grand in one day.

His apartment was shabby, poorly lit and reeked of stale tobacco. It was a one bedroom, with a small kitchen adjacent to a small living and dining area. The living area had grimy, green shag carpet that looked like it had not been cleaned since The Monkees had their own TV show. He had a Philco TV that no doubt was black and white from the early 1960s. He was a silver-haired older guy, say 70, 5'9," 220 pounds, chewing on a Hoya de Monterrey cigar, unlit. He had the lightest blue eyes I had ever seen, a thick, tapered gray moustache, and was pink as a baby. He wore out of fashion double-knit slacks, a golf shirt, untucked, and red socks under his loafers. In the pocket of the golf shirt he had another cigar, still in its cellophane. He smelled of Brylcreem.

I sheepishly told him the services were for me, not a "friend."

He looked at me as if I had farted.

"How shall we begin, Mr. Gimble?"

"First, understand I called Styles on the phone. He confirmed everything you said. I also read up on you on the internet. Your hair's longer than your profile photo at the hospital. Anyway, step over here."

He took my photo on a white screen that he had pulled down. His moves were choreographed, quick and efficient. Over the next half-hour I looked on, rapt, as this virtuoso of forgery went to work. He pulled out a drawer of passports from different countries, all in different colors.

"Where ya wanna be from?"

"Sorry?"

He grew impatient.

"Where ya wanna BE FROM!? Ya know. What country?

"Uh, I guess the U.S."

"You're awreddy from the U.S."

"I know but I..."

"Speak any foreign languages?

"Actually, I do. I'm fluent in Spanish. I minored in it at Stanford."

"Okay then, you're from Spain now."

"Spain?! I mean..."

"Spain. You're from Spain! Good place to be from. Makes you less conspicuous. Plus, you can travel in the E.U. anywhere, easy."

"Spain it is. I guess."

He looked at a list of names from a file marked "Spain." The man had files from about twenty countries. I was dumbfounded."

"Okay, Juan, I'm gonna make you a nice passport. You see, the real Juan, may he rest in peace, left no relatives."

He spoke as if he were making a suit of clothes.

Juan. I shook my head.

I watched him craft the passport, excising the real photo with what looked like some hi-tech x-acto knife, applying the photo, sealing it under the barcoded plastic with a press he had assembled from a locked cabinet, checking the Spanish address against a master list in the "Spain" file. He asked me to look at the signature line carefully and advised me that, from now on, that's what my signature would look like.

"Mr. Juan de Nebra, from Malaga, here's your new passport. It's good for 10 years. I've never had one fail."

As I looked over the document, studying the already stamped pages and Spanish-language details of another country's passport, he got to work on a California driver's license. Evidently, Mr. de Nebra had spent some time in Ojai.

Passport and license in hand, I heard him say, "So, I gotta sign something?"

"Yes, tomorrow, if you'll come with me in the afternoon, I'll have you sign some papers at the Titus/Dixon office in Bethesda. I'll explain in the car on the way tomorrow. Do you have a suit you can wear, and a tie?"

"A suit and a tie?"

He shook his head.

"I got a suit and I got a tie. I also got a good ID I've been working for about eighteen months; a stiff in Wheaton named George Littleton. Got his address, email, everything. Been getting his Social Security benefits checks, too. A P.O. box off New Hampshire Avenue. Anything else?"

I stood in wonder how this man before me could possibly be able to do all these things. Gimble said

"Well!?"

"Yes, just wear a hat, bring sunglasses and the fake I.D. I'll need a copy of the I.D. before I leave here. You'll tell the lady there that you just had cataract surgery and you need to shield your eyes. I'll fill out all the paperwork. You will be asked to sign as an officer of the corporation. She'll ask you to make up a username and password. I'll write down that for you now, so you'll know what to enter tomorrow. Then she'll ask you to type a PIN number in a shielded box. Just before you enter that info, you will distract her. Ask her if she has a cigarette for after the meeting. She'll reach behind her for her purse and I'll enter the PIN. That way I'll only have access to the account. Understand?"

"Yeah, I understand. Now I also understand you owe me 12 thousand. "

I handed him the wad of 50 hundreds.

"I'll give you the balance tomorrow; I could not withdraw the full amount in one day or I'd raise some red flags. Can't afford to do that at this point in the game. Oh, and remember, you have to agree to sign whatever papers from the investment folks arrive when I ask you to. It's an 'authorization for transfer' form. Like I said before, they'll fax it or email, my choice, and you send it back, got it? Also, I'll need to attach your alias to my shell company; it's all made up fictitious. Once that's done it will mean that our business has been concluded."

"You mean sign under my 'George Littleton' alias?"

I nodded.

"I got no problem with that cause I figure that cow's been milked dry. But it's gonna cost you more, Doc. Like another 3 large, to make an even 15 grand."

"Okay Max. If I can trust you to do this, we're agreed. If you don't follow through, we'll both have a lot to lose. Like a lot of Social Security money."

Gimble took the cigar from his mouth and took a step back, tilting his head.

"Are you threatening me, doc?"

"No, not a threat. Just a fact. So, we both know where we stand, *George Littleton.*"

He said he would hold the passport and license until he received the balance. That would be tomorrow. I said that was alright. I told him I would pick him up the next afternoon about 3 pm. I asked him if he got it all straight. He said he did.

I left and sat in my car. Golden leaves fell on my windshield and the wind picked up. "Juan de Nebra." What the hell was I thinking?

I had the copy of Gimble's fake George Littleton ID and faxed it from the closest Staples to Mr. Tetley in Wyoming, along with instructions to add him publicly as "treasurer" of Gail Force Holdings. Included was a request that he fax the updated documentation to Tricia Porter's office at Titus Dixon on Wednesday between 3:30 and 4 pm Eastern time . I was sure to include a request to expedite the process so that all might be ready for my meeting with Ms. Porter. It was still before close-of-business in Wyoming, so I figured I'd also call Tetley from my condo just before 5 pm, Mountain Daylight Time, to make sure he received the instructions.

Wednesday in the OR was an easy day. I was not on back-up call, so I was able to get out by 2pm. I picked Gimble up at the appointed time. He was waiting outside 800 Pershing, an old Seersucker suit hanging from his stocky frame. He wore a white shirt with a stained and loud floral tie, white bucks on his feet that had seen better days, yellow socks and had a white fedora on his head. A large cigar was clenched under his moustache. He wore a pair of old Ray Bans.

We reviewed the plan in the car. Then my cell phone chimed, and it was Tetley, informing me that the name "Littleton" had been added to the corporation as Treasurer. I thanked him and asked if he would fax the updated documents to Ms. Porter. Her private fax number was on her business card on my car dashboard. I asked him to wait 15 minutes before doing so.

By the time we pulled into Titus/Dixon, I didn't know whether to go through with the meeting or just drop Gimble off and run like hell, writing off the 5 grand and the entire plan. I looked over at Max, who rolled down his window and threw what was left of his cigar onto the street. We entered the office and told the receptionist that we were there for Tricia Porter. We waited a moment and she came out. I rose slowly to my feet and took her in: her posture was perfect, she wore a sleeveless blouse and black skirt, to just below her knees. Her blond hair was pulled back in a ponytail. She wore silver, dangling teardrop earrings and a matching silver pendant, that nestled in the notch between her perfect collarbones.

"So, gentlemen, I understand we are to discuss trading on margin?"

"Actually, yes. And Mr. Littleton, along with my attorney, Mr. Devlin, who may join the board of a company that I've begun, is here with me to open a new account. It's for a medical device company listed in the State of Wyoming as "Gail Force Holdings." I want to open a corporate account for the company. Mr. Littleton is my Treasurer. I will have him as sole holder of this account. At least at the start. I trust him with my life."

Porter smiled, her lips perfectly symmetric and parted just enough to reveal two white, pearly incisors.

Gimble looked at her. He said

"That's right, miss. Treasurer."

Ms. Porter gave me a sideways glance. She went on, "Mr. Littleton, you might want to remove your glasses, it's a little dark in…"

Gimble pointed to his left eye.

"No, Miss. I just had the… the waddyacall, the – catarack soigery."

"Oh, I see. Well, in that case…"

She glanced at the papers again, looked up at us and with a blow of air from her mouth, took Gimble's fake ID and information. Just then her fax spat out the Wyoming corporate documents with Gimble's name as treasurer. Tetley had come through for me. She retrieved them and looked at me, puzzled. I explained the updated corporate papers and that Wyoming had been instructed to send them. With a subtle twist of her perfect head over her swan like neck she then told Littleton to enter a username and password, which he did.

"Mr. Littleton, since Dr. Wren has informed me you'll be the only name on the account for now, I'll need you to enter a pin number for all transactions to the account. Four digits, here in this little box."

She slid the box, facing him, with the protective cover so only he knew the code. I then stepped on his foot, under the table. Gimble turned to her and said, "Very well miss. Ah, by the way you got a smoke? I left mine at home?"

Tricia looked at him, then me, then back at Gimble. A small, vertical crease appeared between her eyebrows.

"Did Dr. Wren tell you I smoked!?"

She gave me a "How could you" look.

"I'd be happy to give you one, but you'll have to smoke it outside. No smoking in any building that's public in Montgomery County."

She turned, just as I predicted, to reach her Coach bag behind her desk. As she did, I quickly entered, without Gimble's view, the PIN, 0101, for Gail's birthday, January first. By the time she turned around, Gimble said, "Yeah, tanks so much. Marlboro Red! Just my brand. Oh, the number is entered, by the way."

With a snap of her head, Tricia blurted, "Wow! That was fast! Well, anyway. Do understand, gentlemen, that the account is not open until our research department vets the documents you've given me."

Turning to me, she said, "Dr. Wren, you've told me there was some urgency in opening this account. I believe you had mentioned something about a funding deadline in prior discussions. I know the people in research and, if they start this afternoon and work through tomorrow, your account should be active Friday morning. They owe me some favors, those folks."

"Ms. Porter, that would be great. Mr. Littleton and I really do want to get things going."

The three of us had a brief discussion on the logistics of margins, trading, and paper vs. electronic statements. We insisted we wanted only e-statements. I also reconfirmed with her that I, as president of the corporation, could transfer funds freely between my account and the corporate account, even though Littleton's name was on the account. She said that, as long as Mr. Littleton authorized it, that was the case. As we stood to shake hands, a sudden inner and hidden voice compelled me to act. Perhaps it was the life-changing significance of what I was planning, or a sublimated messenger telling me to see what was before me, instead of what might be. Perhaps it was stone-cold fear. I blurted

"Mr. Littleton, would you excuse me and Ms. Porter for one moment? This will only take a sec."

He shrugged, shook her hand, and shuffled out to the lobby, hoisting the cigarette as a token of gratitude.

I turned to Trish and began, "Listen. Thanks a bunch for all the help today. By the way, I know this is last minute but, are you free for dinner tomorrow tonight?"

The slightest hint of blush welled up from the tips of her revealed shoulders and spilled over her lovely neck, face, and ears. It was like the time-lapsed blooming of a flower.

"Why Dr. Wren. I never thought you'd ask me!"

"Well, if you're not busy, can I pick you up, say, 7 and we can go from there? Have you been to Old Angler's in Potomac, along the canal?"

She said she hadn't and would love to and gave me her address: 10115 Howard Avenue, Kensington.

"Pick you up then!"

As I rose she came from around her desk and shook my hand. My business end moved in my pants. She flashed me a brilliant smile and said she looked forward to the evening.

I found Gimble in the lobby, reading *Vanity Fair*.

"You seen the clothes these freaks wear? They're like fuckin' Martians!" he blurted, hoisting the pages in the air. He showed me a spread from some fashion week nonsense in Milan or Paris

"Crazy stuff! C'mon, I got to get by the bank and get you your seven thousand."

"Yes, you do. And, by the way; nice stems on that broad. You bang her yet?"

"Max! No, I have not 'banged her'."

But I was dying to.

We stopped at the bank, got him his money and returned to 800 Pershing. Once inside, he handed all the documents I had paid for. As I was leaving, I thanked him as he lit his cigar, saying, "Listen, Doc. I don't know what kinda crazy plan you got, but take it from me, if it's as kooky and nutso as I think it is, there's no comin' back. Ain't my business, but just sayin'."

He blew a large stream of pungent Dominican smoke in the air. The plume was thundercloud blue, the aroma a mixture of mahogany and cinnamon.

I told him I understood and lied that I had not made up my mind. I shook his hand goodbye and stepped out on to Pershing. The cool, crisp, October air kicked up some wet leaves. I stared across at the orange jack-o-lantern in the shop window. Everything seemed so sharp and enhanced: objects appeared more vibrant, smells more penetrating and sounds more acute. A sense of confidence and strength flooded over me. It was a feeling I had not had since my swimming meet days.

It was getting on 5:30 pm. I opened my car and sat, thinking of Ms. Legs and Shoulders. I reviewed what I had done and what remained to be done: I had a set of fake IDs, a new company, two board members (myself and "Littleton") and hopefully another on the way. I had access to my personal and LLC accounts, cash, leverage, and most of all, an insider's bet on interest rates come the 22nd. What I did not have was a ticket out of the country. I was going to have to handle that in person, with cash.

At home I made some dinner and headed to the computer. If the Isle of Man was my banking choice, then London would be my destination. Researching flights for Monday the 22rd, I found one departing Dulles at 6:10 in the evening, arriving Heathrow at 7:25 Tuesday morning. I could take the train to Liverpool, spend the night there and take the Steam Packet ferry to Douglas, arriving about 9 am. The trip from Liverpool, I learned, took less than three hours.

I had finalized my plans: I'd pool my money: the funds I borrowed from my 401k, my refi dough, my signature loan, my pawn and car sales and my Brokerage account plus the 50 percent margin. It came to a whopping 3 million and change. The ETFs I was eyeing allowed for a two or even three-fold bet to be placed on a single fund transaction. On Friday morning, I'd place all my bear-bets during my lunch break. After that, I'd do the unthinkable: I would tell Askin off and then quit, right then and there. I'd then drive out to Dulles, buy the British Air First class ticket in cash using my Spanish passport as ID, drive to CarMax to sell my car and head to my bank to deposit the car check. The bank closed at 7 pm on Fridays. Then, I'd Uber home and pack. I'd book, by phone, a night in Liverpool's Titanic Hotel and reserve the ferry ticket that I'd require once I entered the UK. I'd use a prepaid Visa card to buy those items.

Thursday I was the "out" person in the OR. That meant I supervised the nurse anesthetists, stayed out of the operating rooms proper, except for induction, emergence and any critical events that needed my attention. I ensured everyone got a 15-minute break in the morning, a half hour lunch and a 15-minute afternoon break. I also carried the code beeper, answered calls from the recovery room and made up the assignments for the next day.

At 10 am sharp, I took my coffee into the small private consultation room near the OR desk and called Ms. Brownlee at Devlin's office. She put me through.

"Adrian! Hello."

"Hello, Mr. Devlin. Is this a good time?"

"Good as any. How's your day?"

"Pretty busy. Have you given any thought to...?"

"I have. Yes, I have. I'll serve as the registered agent. And I've done my diligence on you and I've decided I'll join your little company. Any man who swam at Stanford, has been on staff at Hamilton this long and whose cousin's partner operated on my wife is OK by me. But I do have some conditions I want to run by you. In consideration of a 15 percent reduction in my legal fees, what I do in these types of arrangements is take a percentage of the company's annual gross revenues each year. That way I have some skin in the game. Notice I said gross; I know start-ups like yours may never make money and on the small chance that they do, there's often nothing left after expenses. Understood?"

There was a pause.

"Adrian, you there?"

"Oh, yes. Yes, I'm here. That sounds acceptable. Where do we go from here?"

"I'll send you a memorandum of understanding to sign. Ms. Brownlee can email it to you. And add me to the corporation as legal counsel; please let me know what documents you need to accomplish that. Sound good?"

"Sure. I can fax or email the signed forms to you this afternoon."

"Fine. And Adrian; call me Francis, OK?"

"Good enough, Francis. You'll get the necessary paperwork later today. Ms. Brownlee says she has your contact info and numbers. Look forward to working with you."

I stared at a fly on the wall and sipped my coffee. My pager went off, calling me to OR 5. I put the coffee down and took off.

Before I left work I had scheduled myself in an easy and not too busy operating room for Friday so that I could get out at a reasonable time to do some last-minute housekeeping. Thursday's workday ended about 4 pm and I was home a little before 5. That meant it was early enough in the day to call Warren Tetley in Wyoming and get Devlin's name on the LLC as registered agent, as well as an officer, my "legal counsel." Wilford Brimley was happy to oblige; to gild the lily I told him I'd be sending him a copy of Devlin's newly minted contract with me. Tetley asked me where I wanted the new LLC documents and all future correspondence sent related to Gail Force Holdings, LLC. I told him: Francis Devlin, Esquire, 112000 K Street, Suite 1750, Washington DC, 20009.

A little after 5:30 pm Devlin's MOU arrived in my inbox. I took pictures of it with my phone, signed it and forwarded them to Tetley's office in Wyoming. I then sent back a scanned copy of the signed MOU document to Ms. Brownlee. Looking at my watch, I had just enough time to take a short run, shower, get dressed and ready for my date with Tricia. While in the shower I ran my finger over the fogged surface of the glass sliding door and wrote the words "silent partner."

I picked Tricia up in Kensington on Howard Ave. at 6:45. The weather was unusually warm for late October, about 65 degrees.

She came to the door, a vision of loveliness: her hair was in a bob, the curve of which just hung over the left side of her face. She wore a deep blue pant suit, with black pumps and carried a small, black alligator clutch. The weather forecast had called for steady temperatures through the night, so she did not bring a coat. I opened the car door for her.

On the way to Old Angler's, she told me she had grown up in Silver Spring, attended Blair High School and went on to The University of Maryland, where she got a degree in finance. As a young woman, she had danced with American Ballet Theater, and made frequent appearances at The Kennedy Center. It was as a dancer that she picked up her smoking habit, a vice she had tried to solve many times. At Maryland, she quit dance and fenced, her blade being the foil. After school, she got an apartment, earned her Series 7, her General Securities Representative Exam administered by FINRA, so she could be a licensed equities trader. She had been at Titus/Dixon for eight years. She was eight years younger than I, 34, and had never been married.

We got to Old Angler's, an old stone inn founded in 1853 along the Chesapeake and Ohio Canal out the bend of MacArthur Blvd., about five minutes before seven. Our table was being set so we sat in the main level bar, which had a fire going. We both had prosecco. We briefly talked about my work, my hobbies and my family and at 8:15 we were led upstairs to one of the small, side dining rooms. The room was dimly lit, uncrowded for a Thursday night in October, and as the maître di pulled out her chair for her I noticed a graceful shock of blond hair that fell over her face, forming a seductive arc over her crimson cheek and corner of her mouth. She sat and smiled at me.

She asked what I liked to eat there, and I said the trout was always great. As she stared down at the menu, there arose that typical micro-moment where a companion can study the concentrating visage of his unaware companion; I was captivated by the way her mouth pursed, her eyebrows knitted, and her dimples became more pronounced. I ordered wine for us both, the Greek white Nykteri from Santorini. I watched her as the waiter took her order of endive salad, trout and acorn squash. I had the Caesar salad to be followed by the rockfish with sweet potato. She looked up at me.

"So, Tricia. Finally. Do you prefer Patricia or Trish?"

"Either is fine, but that's not my name. My first name is really Natalie. Patricia is my middle name. But Patricia somehow got started and stuck.

"Natalie! I like Natalie! May I call you that? It suits you so much more."

"If you like."

"Well, Natalie, I'm so glad we finally connected."

"I was wondering what took you so long."

"Well, I've been going through a lot lately; starting the new company, changes at work, dealing with my parents long distance from Floridathe usual adult things. It's so nice to have a chance to finally talk to you.

"Likewise. Work has been hectic for me too. It was a nice break to see you and Mr. Littleton, was it? Mr. Littleton the other day. He's quite a fellow."

"If you only knew." I thought to myself.

"Yes, he is 'quite a fellow'. Thanks for all your help. I don't want to talk business, and this will be my last question related to that, but do you think the corporate account will be open by tomorrow?"

"I do but bear in mind there's no guarantee. Monday by the latest."

"Great! Let's drop that. Anyway, you've told me a lot about yourself. You have any siblings?"

"Only child."

"What was that like?"

"Well, got lots of attention. And got to travel a lot. My dad took me everywhere he went. My dad was with a company that manufactured engine parts for aircraft. I got to see many different places."

"Only your dad?"

"Yes. My mom died when I was young. Breast cancer."

I felt as if she had punched me in the stomach. "I'm so very sorry!"

She touched the back of my hand and smiled ever so slightly.

Our wine arrived, and the waiter poured. I tasted itcrisp and light. Natalie took a sip, looking over at me from the rim of her glass. She said, "Wow! I've never tasted anything like that! It's delicious."

"Goes great with the trout. First tasted it in Santorini a decade ago. One of the wine world's best secrets."

"So, you—siblings?"

"Yes, I have an older brother Charles; he's a lawyer in DC. I had a younger sister, Gail, who died at 19 of… cancer as well."

She put her long fingers to her mouth. "Oh, that's awful! I'm so sorry!"

"My parents, all of us, are still suffering, in one way or another. "

"I'm so sorry. Terrible!"

"Yes, Gail was everything anyone could want. She was attractive, funny and sweet. On her way to a great musical career."

"That was your sister? I think I once read about her in the paper. The Metro section did a piece on her did they not? Something about a past local prodigy who played Carnegie Hall at a really young age?."

"Yes, that was Gail."

Our first course arrived.

"Gail had so much promise. Life's not fair. That's why, as I've gotten older, I've learned you must grab as much life as you can while there's time. Don't you think?"

"I do. But, you've got to have the money and time to do the grabbing. Few of us do. That's why folks come to me to plan retirement. To build something for later so they can live out their dreams."

"True. But often by then, aren't they old and sick. I mean, if you can, why wait?"

She slipped some endive in her mouth.

"Well, money and time, like I said, is the problem. People get so caught up in families and careers that they have no time to explore. They've also burned through so much money there's often not a lot left. Except for wealth transfer from parents. That's big in the past decade or so."

"Very true. But I once heard a phrase about consumerism, speaking of burning through money. It went: Consumerism is spending money you don't have to buy things you don't need to impress people you don't like."

"Can I use that with my clients?"

"Sure, for a price! Get my LLC account approved!"

She touched my hand and giggled.

Through the main course and rest of the wine, her allure grew. With each passing exchange I learned how smart, charming, and amusing she was. I wondered if it was the alcohol talking and, hoping not, asked her if she cared for dessert. With a cock of her head, she said

"We could have that at my place if you care to."

I cared to.

I paid the bill and we stepped out into the parking lot. She pulled a piece of nicotine gum from her clutch and asked if I minded. "It'd be better than me smoking, no?"

Traffic was light, and we were back to her Kensington bungalow by 10. Inside, I saw how neat and orderly things were, the antithesis of Gimble's dump, which looked like Dresden after the allied bombing in '45. She directed me to the couch in front of the coffee table and went to the kitchen. I looked around the room. There were pictures of her with what must have been her parents— pictures of her at all ages: dancing, fencing, one riding a horse and another of her with whom I assumed was a girlfriend, sharing some wine in Paris.

The house was simply but tasteful: natural woods and earth tones, framed authentic lithographs of classic European products; champagne, cognac, and motor cars. There were coasters on the coffee table of what appeared to be fake betting markers from the main casino in Monte Carlo, in denominations of 50, 100 and 500 thousand and 1 million francs. A clean ashtray, in the shape of a jet engine in profile, sat next to the coasters. Around the rim of the ashtray were the words "Pratt and Whitney."

As she was getting dessert and drinks, I looked around the place. On the wall was a photo with a plaque that read, above crossed fencing swords: "To Natalie Patricia Porter from the Goils with Foils. Thank You!" It was dated "Spring 2022." In the photo there was a group of teenage girls, of different sizes and ethnicities holding fencing foils with Natalie at the center of the group. She returned from the kitchen with a tray containing two slices of cheesecake, a bottle of Jameson and two shot glasses.

"I hope you like cheesecake. I made it myself. A low carb recipe."

"Oh, I do, I do. And I see you have a nightcap there."

"Just a little. I know we both have work tomorrow."

Turning to the wall, I asked her about the photo and plaque.

"Oh that. Yeah, that's a group I founded a few years ago. I teach fencing to kids in the District who would normally have no money for it. It's fun. And they like it."

"Wow. You do that and are a "Big Sister"?

"How'd you know that?"

"Saw the picture on your office wall. Remember? The picture?"

"Oh yeah, that."

I thought to myself: All this generosity of spirit and beauty and brains too. I could not help but think of Gail.

We ate the dessert and she poured me three fingers of whisky in the shot glass. She poured slightly less for herself.

"Are you trying to get me drunk, Natalie?"

"No, I just thought, you're a big guy, so…"

We clinked glasses. She said, "To Gail Force Holdings!"

I echoed her.

She moved closer to me on the couch and stared into my eyes.

"What time do you go to work tomorrow, Adrian?"

I finished what was left of the Jameson.

"I usually leave at 6:15. Patients are in the preop area by 0700. I…"

She put her hand on my knee. I looked at her and tucked the shock of flaxen hair obscuring her left eye back over her left ear. I leaned forward and tasted her mouth. A bouquet of alcohol, nutmeg and fresh flowers hit my nose.

She whispered: "Why Adrian…I…"

"Don't say anything. Just…"

She put her arms around me and kissed me like I had never been kissed. Her mouth worked its way over my neck and ear, as she whispered, "Do you want to go to the other room?"

"I really don't think I…"

For the next moment we melted together on the couch, the lights low, in a blur of muted colors, pungent scents and effervescent sensations.

Then, like some sort of organic machine, the two of us rose and she led me to her bedroom. She shut the door behind her and pushed me onto her bed.

CHAPTER 3
FRIDAY WAS MY DAY

Her alarm went off at 6:30 and she hit the snooze button. I awoke with a start confused. My clothes were in a heap next to the bed and her long, slender arm was stretched across my bare chest. My head hurt. I looked over at her, her make-up still on. Her lovely, dark lashes covered sleeping eyes. I cursed myself, heart pounding, and leapt from the bed. Pulling my clothes on, I knelt by the bed and shook her shoulder.

"Natalie, I've got to go! I'll be late."

She made a muffled, inexplicable noise.

"Natalie!"

She opened her eyes and smiled.

"Listen, I've got to go. It was a great night. I will call you this weekend, okay?"

She sat up in bed, one firm and lovely breast popping out above the bed sheet.

"Listen, it was great. You'd better get up! I hit the snooze button."

She pulled me by the collar and kissed me. There was the faintest taste possible of tobacco.

I bolted for the door and into my car. I knew I could not make it from Kensington to downtown in less than half an hour. I sped down Connecticut Avenue slowing for the speed cameras and gunning it in between. I turned on the news: more football chatter, local politics, and a piece about the upcoming Open Market Committee meeting on Monday. There was talk of a possible increase in rates due to an apparent rise in bond yields due to their worsening credit, linked to a falling dollar and inflation risks. Blah blah blah blah blah. There were also rumors of a growing friction that had developed between Chairman Silverstone and President Gabriel Stanton. The two had recently had meetings and issued statements in which there was disagreement, according to the press, over how best to handle the economy, which had been faltering under Stanton's watch. All eyes were fixed on Monday's meeting.

I pulled into the Hamilton lot at 7:10, knowing that if Fatso Askin saw me come in late he'd give me shit. I went in the back way and bounded the steps to the 2nd floor, where the coast appeared clear to the locker room. Only a few OR techs and a couple of orthopods were changing into scrubs so as I did the same, it looked as if I had slipped in under the radar. As I was leaving the locker room to head to my OR assignment, Askin appeared from the break room, his scrub pants pulled high and tight around his fat waist.

"Pushing the envelope, I see..." he said, smirking.

"Traffic was bad from Bethesda. An accident on Rock Creek Parkway."

"Funny, I didn't hear about that. Next time it might serve you to leave a little earlier."

Asshole. "Yes, prob-ab-ly. Listen, do you have ten minutes around midday? Perhaps the tail end of my lunch break? Like 1230?"

"Well, Adrian. My day is pretty full. Got to prepare for a medical staff meeting, but if you come around then I…"

"Thanks! See you then."

I rushed off to my room and set up the most basic of my equipment. Luckily, I was doing cataracts, so there was little setting up to do. After I signed out my midazolam and fentanyl, I headed to the preop area to interview my first patient. The other MDs and CRNAs were frantically buzzing around, pollinating the other patients and rushing gurneys under the watchful eye of the charge nurse.

Cataract patients usually don't require much attention. Most cataracts are oldsters, and oldsters don't need a lot to keep them quiet and still. Just a little squirt of the juice. Unless they've been boozers all their lives; boozers chew up the stuff we give them. Midazolam, fentanyl, propofol—doesn't matter. You can always tell a drinker. I was with Dr. Trone today, who took about 30-40 minutes to do what Drs. Wilcox and Feder could in 10 minutes. But that worked to my advantage. It gave me time to finalize my list of ETFs, the trades of which would be placed at lunch from my phone.

During my morning break, I asked Len Irvin, who was running the schedule, to get me a lunch break at 12:15. I had told him I was expecting an important phone call. He said he'd try his best.

At 12:05 Dr. Tran came in to relieve me. Tran was a Foreign Medical grad holdover from before Askin got the exclusive contract to provide anesthesia services to Hamilton. He was probably in his early seventies. Those Foreign Medical Graduates lived in fear; since many of them of the earlier generation never got board certified, people like Askin could use them. Tran was different; he got his boards when he was sixty! Talk about a rarity.

I gathered my stuff and headed for the private restroom next to the patient waiting area. I had written out the list of my short positions that morning, carefully reviewing and checking to see the ones most likely to rise in a falling market. I took the whole 3 million and change and bet it on 3 X shorts across the board, wagering more heavily on financials, energy, and high yield bonds. By the time I was finished, there were more bears on my trading screen than a Russian circus!

Then, I did something I had not planned to do—not then, anyway. I kept my meeting with Askin, but because of the culminating stress and pressure of the intense planning I had done for almost two prior weeks, emotion got the better of me.

I knocked on Askin's door. He said to enter. Sitting like some giant toad on a lily pad, pictures of his boat adorning the wall behind him, Askin extended his pudgy hand and directed me to a seat in front of him, which was set deliberately lower than his by about six inches. That old trick is used by many managers to project their authority. I was having none of it.

"Yes, so. Dr Askin. I've come to talk about the changes going on…the talk of salary reduction has got a lot of my colleagues concerned, myself included. Also, the EMR has been taking a lot of attention away from…"

He extended a small, greasy palm to my face.

"Let me stop you right there. If you're going to come in here with a laundry list of complaints, I don't have time for it today. We've discussed the need for salary reductions at our meetings and the compliance with EMR is something that the hospital instituted. You are well aware that Medicare reimbursements are down, and Medicaid has been…"

"Reimbursements are down?"

I pointed to a picture of his yacht on the wall and continued, "One wouldn't know looking at that boat. It's rather new, is it not?"

Askin looked at me with bugging eyes, his face reddening. He edged his large frame forward in his chair and folded his beefy hands on top of his desk. A bead of sweat dripped down his forehead. He wiped it away with the back of his hand.

"Dr. Wren. My boat!? What has that got to do with anything? The way I earn and spend my money is of no concern to you. For a person who showed up late today, you're speaking as if…"

"Let me stop you there. We grunts have been working our asses off, taking call, taking a falling salary, enduring spies who see how long we wash our hands after each patient, how we label our syringes, all for too long, while you…"

"Dr. Wren. Are you trying to get fired!?"

I could see the tiny red vessels cutting new rivulets in his muddy sclerae. "No, Askin, because I'm quitting! Now!"

He looked at me for what seemed a week and a half. He laughed.

"Quitting! Well! That's the thanks I get for mentoring you along! You're quitting! Well, you know that requires 4 weeks' notice and…"

"Yeah, but that's not what's going to happen. I'm leaving. Now!"

He looked at me in disbelief. "Now!?"

"Now, like right now!"

I got to my feet. He stood, shaking, and said, "You're abandoning your patients? Just like that?"

"No, not abandoning. You're a licensed, board certified anesthesiologist. You can get off your fat ass and take over my room! So long, Ask-hole!"

I turned to head to the locker room and heard him follow, speaking in a hushed and frantic voice.

"You realize I'll have you kicked off staff for this! Even your license! I'll have that revoked! I'll…"

"Do what you want. But if I were you, I'd lose some weight. You look like shit, Ass-kiss!"

I left him, with his pie-hole agape, staring at my receding figure. I opened my locker, changed into my street clothes, and walked out into the late October sunshine.

A pile of mail was waiting for me at home. Among the junk and bills was an invoice from Devlin's office for 800 dollars, representing a 15% percent reduction in his hourly fee. I immediately wrote out a check, addressed the envelope and found a stamp. I had to make sure to cement the attorney/client relationship before I had left the country. I was so exhilarated by my encounter with Askin that I picked up the phone and called Natalie.

"Hello, this is Dr. Wren. Is Ms. Porter available?"

The receptionist put me through.

"Hello."

"Hi Natalie. Do you have a minute?"

"For you I do."

"About last night, I hope you don't…"

"I don't regret a thing."

"Good. Neither do I. I know it's last minute but, can I see you tomorrow night?"

"Let's see…I might have to wash my hair. Then there's a special on the Accounting Channel about tax loopholes…then…"

"Very funny. What time shall I pick you up? We can grab dinner at Irish Inn. I hear it's going to be unusually warm. Ned can get us the corner table outside near the back."

"I heard too. They are calling for records this weekend. Even 80 by Monday. I love Irish Inn! 8 pm?"

"I'll get you at 8. And no more Jameson shots!"

"See you then. And uh, Jameson is out. But Bushmills?"

"See you at 8."

I checked in with the markets on the radio on the way to Dulles. Things had been choppy all week and this trading. Friday was no exception: tThe Dow opened 257 points higher by 9:35, only to sink back in negative territory by midday, and was now up 30. This market volatility boded well, I thought, for my chances to score big on Monday.

The British Air ticket purchase, as Juan de Nebra, went without a hitch. So did the CarMax sale. I had both accomplished by 3:30, more than enough time to get to my bank. I took $9,990 in cash from the account after depositing the checking, causing a suspicious look from the teller. "Buying a boat in cash this weekend," I told her. The rest I would withdraw Monday morning.

Returning home about 4:30, I took out the checklist that was wedged between pages 13 and 14 of my copy of *The Catcher in The Rye* sitting on my desk. Next to each item completed there was a red checkmark. Those items with red marks were:

-Get IDs.

-Form LLC.

-Buy plane ticket.

-Book hotel.

-Research train and ferry.

-Get F. D. and M. G. on board.

-Consolidate cash and execute trades.

-Establish LLC account with T/D.

-Research account, office space/virtual office for I. of M.

There were items listed that were yet to be completed. They were:

-Write mom and dad.

-Write Nat.

-Destroy all paper records.

-Destroy my laptop and cell phone.

-Start growing a beard.

-Cut my hair.

-Start wearing glasses.

-Put sell orders in midmorning Monday.

It was getting on dinnertime and I decided to give Cleesh a try. He picked up his cell.

"My brother!"

"Cleesh, listen. I know it's last minute but, you wanna meet for dinner?"

"What time? I gotta meet Audrey later for a drink. She got tied up for dinner. Some work fiasco. Always with her nose to the grindstone."

"Yeah. Anyway, how about Olazzo in 30?"

"See you there."

My feet took me to Olazzo where Cleesh had already gotten a table outside. It was freakishly warm–75 in late October. He was already past the first beer.

We ordered drinks and appetizers, and I got to the point.

"Listen, you're the first one I'm telling but, I'll be taking a sabbatical."

"Like a seventh day for an Adventist? What do you mean 'sabbatical'?"

"Well, I quit my job and…"

"You what!? Quit!? What the…"

"Listen; it's a long story. Anyway, I was getting burned out at Hamilton working for that douchebag Askin and slogging with the rest of the trolls and I decided to make a change. I'm doing a stint abroad."

"What kinda stint? Where?"

"Well it's still being worked out, but I've got something lined up in Europe and…"

I went on about some mythical teaching job in Switzerland where my skills would be more valued, and I could earn better pay in Swiss Francs and how I could see the world, the Old World, and do the things I had put off for too long and so on and so on. He appeared to buy it, most of it, and looked down at his beer.

"This doesn't have anything to do with that bet with Charlie and the interest rate question and the…"

"No, no. Well, not directly. I mean… no! "

"Not directly? I smell a lyin' rat. Are you playin' me? Cuz if you're playin' me…"

"No Cleesh. Just trust me. I asked you out tonight because I might not see you for a while, is all."

We finished our appetizers in silence.

"When you gonna be back? Who am I gonna cliché at with and…? The heart is a lonely hunter, you know…"

I laughed.

"Listen, probably six months. Perhaps a year.. Maybe, after I settle in there, you'll come visit. Whaddya say?"

He looked at his watch.

"Shit! I gotta pick up the ball and chain. Listen, can we talk tomorrow? You said you don't leave until Monday?"

"She's already a ball and chain? Wow, that was fast. Yeah, I'll call you in the afternoon."

CHAPTER 4
THE WEEKEND
BEFORE THE FALL

I was so tired from my frantic planning I hit the bed at 9. After a night of wild dreams, I awoke at 7, opened the blinds and saw the wind kicking leaves into the deep woods behind my building. The weather forecast called for continued warm weather, with a chance for thunderstorms in the evening. Thunderstorms in late October in Bethesda, I thought. Was God drinking Hennepin again, I wondered?

I went through the apartment and took out everything I planned to destroy, other than my laptop and phone. There were paper financial records, notes from my planning and old medical journals. I took all the books I wanted to recycle and put them in two large boxes, to donate later to the BCC High School Book Drive. By 9, I decided I'd take a stab at my therapist, Donna Shaw, MSW, to see if she had a cancellation. I had stopped seeing her a few months prior, but the great thing about Donna was, other than she was an MSW (the shrinks just pushed pills; few of them still did talk therapy) that she often took me last minute. One call and I found she had an 11 am free.

I was thumbing through a 5 month- old copy of *Psychology Today* in her waiting room when she extended her palm for me. Donna was 60-ish, tall, slender and a no—nonsense Catholic of Irish heritage. She'd been the inpatient director Glades Mental Health in Aspen Hill for thirty years and knew her stuff. Having lost a child of her own she knew, and had endured, her share of tragedy.

"Glad you could squeeze me in. Just wanted to say good-bye."

I gave her the same spiel I had given Cleesh. She nodded in sympathy. She then said

"Do you think quitting was wise? I mean, you had so much invested in the place; your career, the people, your finances…"

"I know. But I was dying there. There's more to life than grinding it out like that. I made good money, for sure, but things seemed so…so…empty. Routine. I'm 44 and divorced. I have no family of my own, save for Charlie and my parents. I miss Gail. If not now, when?"

"Yes, if not now when indeed. Have you thought this over with enough consideration? I mean…"

"I know it appears impulsive. But I feel so…I don't know! I've got to make a change, or I'll never forgive myself for waiting."

I was dying to tell her the truth. Maybe I was dying to confess to her, as she had told me she, at times, did to her priest. Maybe I needed to tell someone.

"I know that whatever I say here is protected. That is, of course, unless I intend to hurt myself or others, which I don't.

"Correct Adrian. Is there something else you want, or need, to tell me?"

I sat in silence and then smiled.

"Well, what I've told you so far only has partial truth. I'm not off for a sabbatical, in the strict sense. I'm off to change my life. There are things I can't tell you and things I can, but they don't involve hurting others or myself."

"Alright. But I will warn you. Be careful what you wish for."

"You're starting to sound like a friend of mine."

"How so?"

"He speaks in aphorisms. Kind of an old joke between him and me."

"Aphorisms developed often because they contain some kernel of truth, don't you think?"

I nodded. I glanced at the clock to her left. It was 11:55.

"Adrian, I hope you find what you're looking for. Please keep me posted whatever way you can."

"I will, Donna. Thank you for being there all this time. I'll see you when I get back."

I took Metro to Bethesda and grabbed a quick lunch. I called Natalie to reconfirm our date at 8. At home and gathering the books I had collected for the high school drive, I asked the doorman in my building, Santiago, for a dolly to roll the boxes up the street. I deposited the boxes in front of the sign that read "Student Book Drive Pick-up." A shredding party back home took me until 2:30 pm, where I bagged my destroyed documents in large trash bags and took them to the dumpster outside. I changed into my running clothes and took off down the Crescent trail. It was a freakish 80 degrees.

The clock read 3:40 when I hit the shower. I toweled off and, with the clock set to wake me at 7 pm, I got in bed and fell immediately asleep. Then the dream:

Natalie, or someone-like-her-but-not-quite-her and I are in a restaurant, but one I've never been to. She's looking at me with her chin tilted down and her head turned slightly sideways, a lock of hair over one eye. There are pictures on the walls of beaches, boats, exotic trees. We are drinking something. Suddenly, I ask her if the paperwork or forms or approval or something for the corporation has been approved and finalized. She whips back her head, pulls her hand from mine and accuses me of using her all this time. She stands and turns on a heel and one shapely calf later she is out the door and gone. I struggle to speak, to move, but I can't.

I awoke with a start, the sheets and pillowcase drenched in my sweat. I looked around. It was dark outside and light rain was spitting heavy drops against the windowpane. The clock read 6:55. I turned the alarm off and flipped the pillow over, dry side up. Staring at the ceiling, I followed a long, fine crack from the corner near my head to the center of the room. It looked like a long, meandering river, only with no tributaries. I spent the next minute imagining that the corner was its origin, or perhaps its delta, and that with time, long after I had left this living space for good, the river might traverse the entire length of the ceiling, looking down on some other occupant.

The weather report called for thunderstorms and more unusually warm weather, so I dressed accordingly: light slacks, a cotton button-down shirt and waterproof hiking shoes. With a small collapsible umbrella in hand I took an Uber to Natalie's. In twenty minutes, I was outside her Kensington house. She, dressed in a blue skirt, let me inside and asked where my car was.

"I sold it."

"Sold it?"

"Yeah, it's all part of what I'll explain at dinner. Do you mind driving?"

By 8:30 the weather was holding and Ned, the assistant manager from Ireland who sported a ZZ Top beard, led us to a table in the corner on the side terrace. We ordered drinks and appetizers. She locked her fingers in mine across the table, and leaned in.

"Natalie, I've got some things to tell you. None of them really bad."

She released her hands and turned her head.

"I'm going to be out of the country for a while. Europe actually. I'm going on a trip to meet with some people concerning my new business venture."

The fabrications flew. I was meeting people, some venture capital folks, to pitch my company. I was going to be gone for at least a month. I sold my car because someone offered me a good price. Then there was some truth. Getting to know her was the best thing that's happened in my personal life in a long time. I was taking a new direction with my life.

She looked at me over her wine glass.

"Well, I will miss you. Will you call me? Do you really think it will be a month?"

"At least a month. And yes, I will miss you too. A lot. If it runs longer than a month, I promise you this: I will let you know."

"If it runs longer than a month, maybe I can visit. I've not been to Europe since I was a teenager. Hey, what about your job?"

"You probably won't believe this, but I resigned. "

"Resigned!? Do you think that was smart?"

"I guess I'll be finding out. Look, let's order. I'm hungry."

We finished our meal and spent the night at my place. I told her I had no ash tray so smoking was out. She said she had not had a cigarette in three days. We fell asleep in each other's arms. By morning, with her beautiful back and mane of blond hair facing me, I crept out of bed and made breakfast: homemade oatmeal pancakes with warm syrup, coffee, fresh fruit, and mimosas. I gave her a pair of my old sweatpants, the bottoms of which she rolled up, and an old cotton Capital's jersey that had shrunk in the wash. We sat on the couch and ate, looking out at the fall morning.

"Look, it's nearly 11. I'd better be getting back home. You said your plane is tomorrow?"

"Yes, in the evening. I arrive in Geneva Tuesday morning."

"Can I see you before you leave? It will be a while until we see each other."

This seemed to only prolong the pain I had started to feel, a hurt that began when I started to have feelings for her. Had these sensations started earlier, perhaps, I thought, the whole plan would have been canned. But it was too late. I had planned and risked too much to turn back.

"Tell you what, can you do lunch before I go to the airport?"

We agreed that I'd meet her at the Titus/Dixon office at 12:30 on Monday. I told her to keep the clothes. She packed her dress in a shopping bag and I walked her to the door. She put her back against the door and I planted my face into her neck, just below her ear. I whispered, "I will miss you, Nat. I'll think of you every day."

"Do you really have to do this? Can't these venture people come here?"

"Nat, it's already been arranged."

I kissed her and kissed her again. She said

"Tomorrow."

"Tomorrow, 12:30. I'll call ahead for a table at Gabi's."

The door shut behind me and she was gone.

I had so much to do. I destroyed my laptop by drilling multiple holes through the hard drive, taking a hammer to it for good measure. (My cell phone was destined for death on Monday.) I packed the clothes I wanted to keep and put the rest in garbage bags for donation. Pictures I wanted to save went in a Manila envelope. I wrote my parents a letter:

Dear Mom and Dad,

By the time you receive this letter you may have heard all kinds of wild things in the news. Charlie will have, too. But don't believe everything to hear or read.

I've left the country, my job, and my life behind, at least for a while. My practice at Hamilton was growing stale. I'm not sure I really wanted to do any of it, the medical practice, anyway. It's just something I sort of drifted into, like so many other people. But I don't want to be so many other people; I want to be me, whoever that is.

I am not doing this to hurt you or anyone else. I've not hurt anyone, really, in what I'm doing. Those entities who profess to feel the hurt, if they do, will be able to sustain it. I'm not worried about them. I'm only worried about me and what I will do with the rest of my life.

Ever since Gail died the family has been broken. Dad, you've suffered and continue to suffer. Mom, you seem to do better, but I cannot fully know what you feel. You never really have shared that with me. Charlie is Charlie. He's busy with the law, his family and being Charlie.

You'll be happy to know I've met a woman I really like. It's early yet, but there's hope.

Please don't worry about me, but I know you will. I will be fine. I will let you know where I am and how I'm doing at the appropriate time. Please tell Charlie I say goodbye for now.

If an emergency ever arises, you can reach me this way, since I won't be carrying a permanent phone with a dedicated line abroad and I don't have a forwarding address as of yet:

Take out a classified ad in The International Herald Tribune for publication on any Saturday whose date ends in an odd number. I will be checking those days. Say the 'The shareholders of Gail Force Holdings will be holding its quarterly meeting In Bethesda, Maryland tomorrow', on such and such date. That will mean I will call Charlie by phone that day. I think it best, for the near future at least, that I reach you through him.

I know all of this sounds cloak and dagger but just trust me, there are reasons for this.

I can't repeat this enough: everything will work out. Love you both.
Adrian

I put the letter in an addressed envelope and put it with my travel things. I dressed for a bike ride, headed for the storage bin and took out my bike, putting in 22 miles along the Crescent Trail. Back by 4, I showered, dressed, made myself some dinner and turned on the old classic film "Metropolis" directed by Fritz Lang. By 9, I was in bed, took half a milligram of klonopin, and slept like a child.

CHAPTER 5
BLACK MONDAY

John Langford Silverstone, the Chairman of the Federal Reserve Bank of the United States of America and, arguably, the second most powerful person in the nation, sat at his breakfast table at his mansion at 9 Chevy Chase Circle and took two puffs of his albuterol inhaler. His mansion, named "Ishpiming" or "high ground" in Chippewa, became his, after a bidding war with a Hollywood producer, three years earlier, for a mere $21.5 million. The mansion was built by the late politico Francis Newlands, part-founder of the Chevy Chase Land company, the same conglomerate that built the suburb of Chevy Chase and surrounding subdivisions into one of the priciest towns in the country.

Silverstone was no stranger to wealth; he attended the University of Pennsylvania for his BA in Economics, then Harvard Business School, then served on Wall Street with various firms until his ascendancy to the top of Silverstone and Walker, an investment bank he co-founded in the 1990s. After he had made what some observers estimated to be close to $400 million, he left the private sector to serve as Fed Chief under the late president Timothy Doyle. With Doyle's death from heart attack two years prior, Vice President Stanton had assumed the office and Silverstone, naturally, stayed on. His relationship with Stanton, of late, had become strained, to a degree not since President Lyndon Johnson and his Fed Chair William McChesney Martin (who likened the role of the Federal Reserve Bank as a man about "to take away the punch bowl just as the party is getting good"), locked horns in the 1960s.

Next to Silverstone's erect figure at the breakfast table was the typed agenda for that day's Open Market Committee Meeting with all seven governors and twelve regional federal reserve bank presidents (five of whom had a vote) who comprised the committee. With his size 15 ox-blood wingtip shoes and slate grey suit with white starched shirt and blue and silver striped tie, the chairman looked every bit the part. His long silver mane was combed back neatly over his massive cranium, a pair of bifocals perched over an aquiline nose. Sipping his coffee and glancing at the clock in the kitchen, he noted he had fifteen more minutes until his car picked him up to take him the 25 minutes through Rock Creek Park and down to Constitution Avenue, where the meeting was scheduled to last from 8 am until 3 pm. There, as a first among equals, he would cajole, maneuver, and otherwise impose his will on a board apparently willing and even eager to do his bidding. There, the immediate monetary policy of The United States, without direct interference from Congress or the President, would be molded according to the basic economic principles of cash liquidity and the cost of borrowing. There, with an utterance and stroke of a pen, Chairman Silverstone would change millions of lives for months, if not years, to come.

I awakened at 7:30 am, ignoring the multiple calls that kept coming from the phones of former colleagues at work who, without doubt, were curious as to how, and mostly, why, my relationship with the Anesthesia Department at Hamilton Memorial had come to such an abrupt end. I got dressed, made a light breakfast, and turned on the news, whose lead story, I was pleased to see, was "What will the Fed do about interest rates?" Spending most of the early morning packing, arranging my documents and double checking my plans in my head, I nervously awaited the 9:30 opening bell. There was no telling when the committee would be issuing its statement on rates, so I had to wait just like the rest of the world. I did plan, however, to place my sell orders with my smartphone within minutes of the opening bell; I could not afford getting frozen out if trading were suspended due to massive losses, if that was to occur.

By 10 am the major indices, the Dow, the S and P 500 and the NASDAQ were relatively flat. Using my smartphone, I checked the weather report, checked the British Air website about my flight status and rechecked the train schedules from London to Liverpool and the ferry schedule from Liverpool to Douglas. I stepped into the kitchen to make myself another cup of coffee when, from the other room, I heard Neil Duckworth, of CBNC, say,

"And now this just in from our newsroom in Washington: In a surprising and what many observers are calling an unprecedented and shocking move, the Federal Reserve Open Market Committee has issued a statement that, due to what it calls 'the specter of inflation and a markedly overheated economy', the central bank has decided to raise the Federal Funds rate by a surprising 150 basis points, or 1.5 percent. Not since the days of chairman Paul Volcker under Presidents Reagan and Carter have rates risen so quickly by so much. Reaction on Wall Street has been nothing short of chaotic and catastrophic, with the major indices down anywhere between 3.0 and 4.0 percent at this time."

I looked on with a mixture of glee and disbelief, as the red signs signaling stock losses flashed across the screen. Scenes from the trading floor of the New York Stock Exchange were more like a war zone than an equity exchange. Unable to move, I watched as, by 11:45, the indices appeared to have temporarily bottomed out at losses approaching between 7.5 and 8.5 percent. It was as if the massive corpus that was the stock market, like a giant glacier calving gigantic floes of ice, was disappearing before the world's eyes.

By noon, the president had issued an emergency statement, questioning the political motivations of the Fed's actions and, all the while, sounding a calming tone that markets have sustained massive temporary losses from many causes untold times before and will certainly do so again. Bipartisan statements critical to the Fed's actions echoed the president's sentiments. Some pundits were even questioning the Fed Chairman's ability to lead, with some talking heads even citing his recent surgery and experience with anesthetic drugs as a possible reason for his apparently irrational behavior.

With a constant eye on developments in the markets, I headed over to Titus/Dixon to keep my date with Natalie, not even thinking of what awaited me. By the time I got there, the line was out the door; I could not even force my way in if I tried, and I tried. A mob of clearly worried and angry people, mostly retirees, were jammed into the entrance way. I stepped back onto the pavement and texted Natalie. By text, I said, "Are you OK? It's a war here!"

After what seemed like too long, she replied, "Adrian! It's horrible! This fed action is nuts! I'm drowning here!"

"Lunch is out then?"

"Lunch? I'll be lucky to survive the day! Call you this afternoon. Gotta go!"

I peeked through the window and saw the trading screen; the losses continued. If the trend kept up this would easily go down as among the single worst days for capital markets in American history. I felt like texting her again but thought twice about it. With regret, I headed back to my place to prepare for my trip to Dulles. On the way, I stopped at my bank to complete my final transaction there; the teller gave me a look. I withdrew the remaining $6,800 from my account, minus the fee to cover Devlin's bill and $100 to keep the account open. The teller asked if I'd like to speak to the manager about a larger credit line or a better interest rate, but I demurred. I had no time to deal with tellers and their intrusive marketing nonsense. I just wanted to get on the plane and get out of the country.

Back at the condo I changed into a suit with no tie, gathered my belongings and placed the letter I had written to my parents in my suit breast pocket. I took my med school, internship and residency diplomas off the wall and unceremoniously smashed each in the center, shattering the glass. I ordered an Uber ride to Dulles, took one last look at the place where I had lived the last fifteen years and headed downstairs. I handed Santiago, the day receptionist, a small envelope with nine $100 bills.

"Santy, I'm going to be gone for a while on business. Maybe a long while. I am trusting you not to open this until I leave and relying on you to evenly split what's inside with Jean Francois and Miguel."

"Sure thing Doctor Adrian. Have a safe trip. Where are you heading?"

"Asia for now, then Africa. Take care and all the best.

"Wow, Doctor Adrian. Be careful. It's crazy out there! Have you seen the TV?"

I told him I had and wished him well. During the ride on the way to the airport all the news channels were covering the economic story. Silverstone had issued a live statement at 3:30. He said,

"In conjunction with the Open Market Committee, I have decided that, for the welfare of our nation, a significant and swift interest rate hike is in order. Our economy, while strong, may be too strong. We have now, because of an unusual confluence of economic factors, the real risk of significant inflation and devaluation of our dollar, which of late has been punished by a host of foreign currencies. Our actions may be viewed as severe but are by no means unprecedented, and we feel that since inflationary pressures appear to be looming to an extent that far exceed our target, we must act and act now. The President and some members of Congress appear at present critical of our actions, but it is important for the American people to realize that we work not for them but for you, the people. President Stanton, while happy, I'm sure, to see an economy chugging along into an election year, must understand that, at times, fiscal austerity, however uncomfortable and even painful in the short term, may be the best medicine for our economic future. We will weather this storm together and come out the better for it. That's all I have to say on this matter for now. Thank you."

By the time I left the Uber driver at 4:15, I knew I was, on paper at least, well on my way to becoming a wealthy man. I grabbed my roller bag and backpack and stepped from the darkening curb into the airport, through security and headed to gate B 11 in Dulles's midfield terminal. I glanced up at the TV monitor on the way to the gate and saw the carnage: the Dow had fallen a staggering 9.7 percent, the S and P 500 10.8 percent and the tech-rich NASDAQ 10.7 percent. Passing gate B 9 heading for Tokyo, I spied an elderly Japanese woman who appeared to be travelling alone. I approached her.

"Excuse me, ma'am. Are you heading to Tokyo?"

She told me she was.

"I wonder if you might do me a favor? My friend collects

stamps and postmarks from around the world. Would you be kind enough to mail this letter from Japan?"

I handed her the letter destined for my parents, along with $20 to handle postage. She flipped the envelope back and forth, shook it and, with a shrug, agreed to my request. She refused my money, despite my insistence.

Before heading into the British Air lounge, I called Natalie.

"Are you still alive?"

"Adrian! Where are you?"

"Natalie, I'm at the airport. Dulles. My plane leaves soon. I'm so sorry I didn't get to see you before my trip."

"Adrian. I don't know what to say. Today, work, the markets; I've never been through anything like this! I just wish you were here with me and a bottle of something. Must you go now? Can't you take another flight? Like tomorrow?"

I felt sick to my stomach.

"Natalie. I can't. I've got meetings set up. Listen, I'll call you from Europe. I promise. I'll think of you every day. I've just got to go. Things will work out, you'll see. I'll see you when I return."

"But when will that be?"

"Soon, I hope. Listen, take good care. I will be in touch."

"Adrian be safe. Call me!"

"I will. Hang tough. Don't worry about the markets. They'll turn around. They always do. And don't worry about me. I will contact you."

With that, I stepped behind an empty ticket counter and crushed my cell phone with the heel of my shoe. I ground the heel deep into the electronic guts, took out a plastic TSA baggie and deposited the murdered device into the trash. I stepped into the BA lounge, poured myself a glass of champagne and watched the TVs as a sea of red stock losses roiled across the screen of the financial channel. All the news shows led with the same story: after the Fed's inexplicably draconian step, the financial gutting was spreading around the globe. Particular attention was paid to the failure, across the board, of the computer system that was supposed to halt trading after the losses reached a certain level. This in and of itself caused, it seemed, further uncertainty, and as everyone business-schoolboy knows, the markets loathe uncertainty. This, added to the fall of the markets themselves and the apparent flight of rational thought from Silverstone's brow, served only to stoke the fear, which had reached feverish levels.

After 30 minutes or so, they called for my flight to board. I picked up my bags and walked, head high, into the first-class cabin. The steward handed me a fresh stack of crisp newspapers: evening special prints of the *Wall Street Barometer*, *Barton's Finance* and *The Financial Times*. The headlines screamed in agony and writhed in pain:

"FINANCIAL 9/11 HITS WALL STREET!"

"MARKET MELTDOWN CIRCLES THE GLOBE!"

"SILVERSTONE DRIVES SILVER SPIKE IN MARKET HEART!"

"HAS THE FED CHAIR GONE OFF THE EDGE?"

I rubbed my chin, smirked, and took another gulp of the champagne. I waved the steward down and said, "Before you put that bottle away, I'll have another glass, thank you."

The first-class cabin seemed strangely empty. I signaled another steward, a beautiful brunette with bright red lipstick and said, "Where is everyone? First class, I hear, is usually near full."

She raised her eyebrows and said, "Not today, sir. The markets, it seems. I reckon the businessmen need to keep all troops close to home and available to handle the row and hullabaloo!"

I reclined in my seat, my feet up, propped my pillow and covered myself in a blanket, closed my eyes and regretted that Natalie was not in the seat next to me, her long, graceful fingers interlaced in mine.

That night, an emotionally burnt-to-the-crisp Natalie Porter fell back on the plush couch in her Kensington home, vodka martini in hand, and called Ann Desmond. Her friend, who lived close, picked up the line.

"Hey, are you still alive? I thought maybe you had died!"

"Oh Ann, this has been the worst day of my life! They train you for this kind of thing but this is ridiculous. No one has seen anything like it!"

The two spoke on about the trials of the day; the slaughter in the stock markets, the rush of the populace to banks, brokerage houses and wealth managers, the news venues all in spasms over the chaos of Wall Street and its reverberating repercussions.

Natalie then went on to tell Ann about Adrian's abrupt departure.

"I can't believe I'm saying these words, Annie, but I've fallen for him, hard!"

"You mean the tall, blonde, swimming doctor? The one whose picture you showed me from that medical magazine?"

"You know who I mean."

"I think you're just infatuated. You've only seen him a coupla…"

Natalie cut her off.

"I'm not infatuated! Well maybe I am, but there's more than that. He's different. He's not like the others. He's certainly nothing like Paul or Raul. He's so…so…well, he's this: he's gorgeous, strong, funny, artistic, sensitive and has the sexiest hair of any man I've ever seen. He draws portraits, he loves the music of some obscure eighteenth century Italian Baroque dude and when he talks about his late sister, you know the pianist I told you about, he gets a look in his face I've never seen in any other man."

She paused, biting her lip, and concluded

"Actually, I'm wrong. It just occurred to me. It's the look I see on dad's face when he's quiet."

"Wow, you really are besotted! So, be happy. When he gets back he's bound to…"

"Annie, he's gone! He's bound to forget me!"

"Gone where?"

"He had to disappear this afternoon on some sudden business junket in Europe–something to do with his medical device- thingy company."

Ann wielded her best mocking sarcasm.

"'Thingy-company?' Natalie, you're sounding like a child. From what you told me, he's crazy about you! And he should be. He'll be back. Business trips don't last forever!"

Natalie let out an audible sigh over the phone.

"I know Ann, but after the shitty day I've just had and him leaving so abruptly I…"

"Listen Nat, I know what. Let's you and me go out tonight. Get a few drinks and some Beijing duck over in Falls Church? I'll drive. You in?"

Natalie put her drink down and realized she hadn't anything to eat since breakfast.

"Why not, Annie? I'm starving! Come get me. But don't try to get me to go to Lizzie's baby shower this weekend. I'm sick of those affairs."

The martini had started to loosen the muscles in Natalie's neck. Her hands felt warmer and her mind was suddenly not so focused on the events of the day, stocks and love life included. She changed into her most form-fitting and flattering black jeans, put on a t-shirt and a comfortable oversized sweater and redid her make-up. With one foot toward the door and one eye passing the mirror, she caught a side view of a long flaxen strain of hair obscuring most of her left eye. She was out the door and into the late autumn air.

Waiting for Ann to come with the car, Natalie called her dad on her mobile.

"Dad, its me."

"Hey kid, what's up? Are you OK? The market moves must be hell on you today!"

"They were Dad. Listen, I just called to tell you I love you."

"I love you too, honey. Always. You sound so upset. Is everything alright? Is it the stock market and…"

"It's not just that, Dad. I think I lost something today and I…"

"Lost something? What was it?"

"Well, it's more than a something but…"

Just then Ann's car pulled up.

"Listen Dad, sorry. I gotta go. Ann's here. I…"

"Well, don't worry too much honey. I'm sure whatever you lost today will turn up soon. It usually does. Take care and call me tomorrow. Say hi to Annie for me."

"Will do, Dad. Love you. Bye!"

And with that Natalie got into the car and the two friends headed south to 495 and Northern Virginia, where cold Tsingtao beer, dumplings and the best Peking Duck this side of Hebei Province awaited them.

CHAPTER 6
FEBRUARY, 2024

Tim Armond, a tenth grader at Bethesda Chevy Chase (BCC) High School sat in the darkening afternoon light at his Chevy Chase dining room table. Having finished his math homework, he checked his cell phone for messages, looked up the latest NCAA basketball scores and took out his English homework. On the table was the assigned book, *The Catcher in the Rye*, by J. D. Salinger. He scratched the back of his head and laid out the piece of paper that had been folded between pages next to his notebook. His dad, Michael, an attorney at the EPA, came in through the kitchen door, home from work.

"Hey Tim, where's mom?"

"Still at the store. She'll be home in half an hour, she said."

"Homework? Good man. Whatcha' reading?"

"Some book about a messed-up kid."

His dad glanced over Tim's shoulder.

"Yeah. I read that too. Loved it. Great book. I remember my favorite part when Holden…"

Mr. Armond stopped talking and read the top of the folded page:

From the Desk of Adrian Wren, MD

He put his briefcase down and slowly picked up the note, scanning it from top to bottom.

"Dad, can we go see the Wizards on Sunday? They play The Cavaliers and…"

"Hold it Tim; let me read this."

The father pulled up a chair and stared into space. He snapped his fingers and arose, rummaging through the week's newspapers that sat in the cardboard box in the mud room. He shuffled through them until he found Monday's paper. He took out the Metro section and folded it to page C2. There, he started to read an article with the headline *District, Montgomery Police Baffled by Bethesda Doctor's Disappearance*

The article went on about how Adrian Wren, MD, an area native and longtime member of the anesthesia department at Hamilton Memorial had not been seen since the last week of October, when he had stated to friends and associates that he was headed to Europe on a business trip. He had apparently abandoned his Bethesda condo including its contents and destroyed his professional credentials and diplomas. Anyone with information on his whereabouts were asked to contact District or Montgomery County Police.

Armond loosened his tie, went into the den, and called the number. Within 30 minutes, detectives Spear and Bell of the Rugby Street precinct of the Montgomery County Police were at his door.

He ushered them in and told his curious son to wait upstairs. They all retreated to the den. Detective Ginny Spear began:

"You say your son found this note, folded, in the book?"

"That's right. He said the book came from the BCC book donation batch from last December. He needed the book for school. English class."

Detective Alan Bell said, "Mr. Armond, did you find anything else in the book? "

"No, just the note."

The detectives leafed through the book and found no other markings. Bell said, "If it's OK, we'll have to take this note and book for our investigation. Is that alright?"

Armond assented. The detectives thanked him and deflected Armond's queries about what they thought it all meant. Speer said, "Sir, we can't comment on an ongoing investigation, but we are grateful for this. It might lead us to a missing person. You did the right thing."

Once back at the station, the detectives presented the evidence to Captain Jack Montague, in charge of the investigation. Montague, who had been working the case since early in the year, had already been in contact with Washington, DC Police twelve days prior. DC police detectives had interviewed Sonia Stepanczyk, a nurse and former girlfriend of Wren's at Hamilton. She had come to the 9th district station of the Metropolitan Police to give information she thought was useful in the disappearance of Dr. Wren, having read, like Armond, in the paper about him. Ninth district detectives Adam Ware and Lenny Epps had questioned her after Stepanczyk presented them with a recording device she was using to monitor Wren's conversations. She had consulted an attorney about whether what she did was illegal, and the lawyer, Matthew Stein, had accompanied her to the station to help with evidence gathering and to protect his client. After receiving assurances from the police that she was in no legal jeopardy, Stein told his client to proceed. She had said, "I come because of what Adrian said that day."

Ware asked, "Which day is that, Ms. Stepancyzk?"

"The Tuesday that Mr. Silverstone had the surgery."

She looked over at her attorney, who told her to continue.

"You see, Adrian and I, we went out for many months. Between March and August of last year. We saw other people but we go out steady. He had dated other nurses before; this I know from talking to other girls, other nurses, in ICU and med/surg floor. Anyway, we go out and suddenly, in August, like middle of the month, he said he wanted to stop dating. He did not give me a reason why. I was very hurt."

She looked at the floor.

Epps asked her to continue.

"My brother, he is policeman in Warsaw. I was so upset, so jealous if Adrian had another girl that I had to know. So my brother, Jan, he told me if I really want to know what happened between us to get small recording device, a listening device. So I did. Online. Since Adrian often did anesthesia in my room, I put device under metal counter on anesthesia machine. That way, I could listen to Adrian talk on his cell, during cases and behind, what you call...'\ 'ether screen'. Many times he would call people during cases. So I listened."

She produced the device for the detectives, who looked at each other and offered Stepancyzk a coffee.

Epps then said, "Did you record these conversations?"

"No, I did not. There were so many. And they hurt me to hear them. But I remember what he say that day, because it was so strange."

Epps asked, looking down at his notepad, about what was said.

"He asked the tall man about 'rates'. He asked him 'where are they going?' And the man, he told him. He said they go up. 'Way up'. The man also started to say something about the president. President Stanton! I listened to all this later, but I'm not sure what it means. I erased it all, just like other messages, but I remembered what he said. I come today, with a lawyer, because my brother says it may be important to what happened. About him disappearing. That's all I know."

Epps then asked about Dr. Wren's personal and professional lifefriends, family, work. The nurse told him he had mentioned Charles, his lawyer brother, that she knew about his sorrow over his late sister and that his parents lived somewhere in Florida. About his work life, she added, "Adrian told me he was tired of taking calls and he was getting 'burnt out'. I was not surprised. Those docs, they work so hard. Too hard. And they all resent Askin, the chairman. Even the nurses know that and talk about it."

Ware thanked them both for coming in. He reassured Ms. Stepancyzk that she was in no trouble and asked her to be available for future questioning. Her lawyer told them she would. The nurse and her attorney left the interrogation room.

The two detectives looked at each other and smiled. Ware smacked the table with his open palm, hard. "A doctor disappears. He abandons his condo. Friends say he went on a business trip, after quitting a high paying job he had for a decade and a half. Nobody's heard from the guy. He just happens to talk to the fed chair less than two weeks before he vanishes, about interest rates. We got more digging to do."

Late October, 2023

After the exsanguination in the markets, with the blood running not only onto Wall Street but down the gutters and into the storm drains as well, I had turned my just-over-3 million-dollar stake into a 12.9 million-dollar fortune. My scheming, my gambling, my cunning had paid off. Now there was the issue of taking possession of the money. I did it like this: twenty-four the account values had been settled the evening of the crash (Exchanged Traded Funds, or ETFs, establish their daily Net Asset Value, NAV, after trading hours are completed, unlike individual stocks, which fluctuate in price during trading hours), I immediately reaffirmed, before my flight to London, all the sell orders I had placed that morning with the computer in the British Airways lounge. That meant by the time trading had closed in New York by 4 pm all my equity and other fund positions would be liquidated and converted to cash held in my money market account.

About 10:30 am on Tuesday morning, having collected my bag and cleared customs and immigration with my Spanish passport, I took a cab to the Titus/Dixon London branch on Lombard Street in the City of London area. There, I met with an account representative, a portly, middle-aged man with wire rimmed glasses, Mr. Anthony Warrick, identified myself as Adrian Wren using my United States passport and told him I was there to effect a transfer of funds, in kind, from my personal account to the Gail Force Winds corporate account. I showed Warrick the incorporation papers from Wyoming (that Tetley had sent me before I departed the U.S.), listing George Littleton as Treasurer and Francis Devlin as Counsel. I then asked Warrick if I might make a private call, phoning Max Gimble on his mobile. Max was none too happy to be awakened, but I told him, out of earshot of Warrick, that he needed to fax the authorization form, dictated by me, to the Titus/Dixon office in London approving the transfer, as per our prearranged agreement. I reiterated the importance of this and closed by saying, "Thanks again, *George Littleton*."

Within ten minutes, the desired form was ejected from

Warrick's personal fax line. It reconfirmed my intention to transfer, from my personal account, all but $10 to the Gail Force Winds LLC corporate account, where George Littleton was listed as the account holder. After perusing the authorization form, his glasses perched at the very tip of his upturned nose, Warrick turned to me and said everything appeared to be in order. He told me it would take twenty-four hours for the transfer to take effect and I told him that was fine by me. Since only I held the PIN number to the corporate account, Max Gimble could not then or ever know that it would soon contain just shy of $13 million. I thanked Warrick for his time and headed to Victoria Station to catch the London Euston 1:45 train to Liverpool.

After a satisfying meal in Liverpool and restful sleep that night, I awoke the next morning to take the Steam Packet ferry to Douglas, Isle of Man. On the voyage over I gazed out over the rough waters of the Irish Sea and contemplated all that had happened. I thought of so many things: Gail, my colleagues at work, my parents, and especially Natalie. It was hard to take in and digest the monumental changes that had occurred in so brief a time. The world seemed so open to me now. It was thrilling but also frightening.

Within three hours the ship had docked in port at Douglas and my first order of business was to find a place to live, any place at all, for it really didn't matter. In fact the cheaper and simpler the better, since my plan was to live on my boat the entire summer ahead. I picked up a copy of the Manx Independent at the ferry station and in it found a classified ad for a small flat to let, a one bedroom, close to the water on Market Street. Bags and belongings in hand, I took a cab to the address and within half an hour had charmed the land-lady, an older widow woman named Costain, into renting me the flat for six months, with an option to renew afterwards.

That afternoon, having showered, combed my hair and devoured some scones and coffee I had picked up at the small market next door, I put on a suit and tie, took my newly signed lease, along with my Wyoming LLC papers, Spanish passport and fax from Max Gimble and rushed over to the Manx Crown Bank office on Bucks Road. There I asked to meet Armstrong-Wicke whom I was told he was out for the day, but that a Grace Taylor would assist me in opening a new account in their Private Banking Division. Turning on the same charisma that had worked so well with my new land-lady, I saw that Ms. Taylor, an attractive young woman of about 30, with long dark hair, brown eyes and athletic build, was only too happy to open for me, under the name Gail Force Holdings Ltd., a corporate account, funded by the transfer of the entire assets of the Titus/Dixon Gail Force Holdings account. When she asked me the nature of the business I was in, I paused, looked at my shoes, raised my face with a smile and told her "yacht charters and excursions."

From her bank's computer, I was able to log in to the Titus/Dixon LLC account one last time and could not help but smile when I read the balance: $12,988,444.12, all in a money market account. To my extreme satisfaction, all my trades placed the day before had been flawlessly executed. Within an hour's time, all the paperwork had been put in place to transfer the entire sum into a new, private, foreign and solely personal hiding place. When the last signature was on the paper, I sat back in my chair, smiled at my new banker and kissed her hand. "The wonders of modern banking!" I said. I arose, thanked her again and headed out into the afternoon sun. I looked over my shoulder to see her standing and smiling, following me with her gaze as I stepped out into the darkening afternoon.

From my small apartment on Market Street in Douglas, I was now free to do as I pleased. My apartment served both as my European address for my Manx Crown account, as well as for the titling of my 2003 yacht, a 65- foot Viking Princess, which I purchased on the Isle with the single stroke of a check, for $475,000. Christened the "Gail Force Winds," my ship was in good enough repair to tackle most any seafaring expedition I might want to take. After a few weeks in Douglas, I was able to get a marine mechanic on the Isle of Jersey to get the vessel in top condition. It was mid-winter; I mapped out my course for the coming spring. My plan was to sail along the coastal ports of Portugal, Spain and through the Straights of Gibraltar, visiting Morocco, the islands of Corsica, Sicily, Sardinia, the southern Italian coastline, the Ionian islands, the Cyclades and then back out of the Mediterranean by summer's end.

To my continuing comfort there had been no notices in the International Herald Tribune, nor was there indication that any authorities were on to me back in The United States. Nevertheless, I thought it wise to consider moving at least part of my assets from Douglas to another attractive private-banking location, perhaps Luxembourg, in case I had somehow failed to cover my tracks.

I had called Natalie from a burner phone a few times, telling her I missed her terribly and that my meetings were going well. It was the fourth call, in mid-November, that went sideways. Things were clearly not the same. Audibly irritated, she had told me about a notice she'd seen in the paper about me going missing and was upset that I might have gotten her involved in something nefarious. She had every right, I thought, to feel that way. I tried to explain to her that my absence was all part of my business plan and that there should be no cause for worry but she didn't believe me. I told her to trust me, but I couldn't sway her anger. She told me that unless I explained everything about what was going on, I had better not call her again. I said I couldn't do that now, but that things were not as they seemed. She hung up on me.

I had no way of knowing how right she was to be concerned.

Missing her genuinely, but powerless to change my plans at the time, I checked into an internet café planning to write her an email. I was surprised and pleased to find my old Hamilton Memorial email address, <u>Adrian.wrenmd@hammemhosp.com</u>, still functional. I wrote:

Dear Nat,

That thing you saw in the news does not tell the real story. I did leave abruptly but I had my reasons. I keep thinking about the times we spent together and hope you felt the same feelings I did. I have not felt that way for anyone in such a long time. You are so important to me. You're different than anyone I've ever known, all in good ways. I find myself thinking of you constantly. After my work here is done I hope that I can get you over here to see me to spend an extended time with me. Maybe to stay. I say that because I plan not to return to the States for a long time.

I don't blame you for being angry. But know this: I did not and never could "use" you. That was not and is not my intention. What happened between us is real, at least from my point of view.

Please be patient, as hard as that is. Give me a little time. You are too important to me to ever forget what we have.

I know all of this is mysterious but you have to trust me. Please. It will be worth it to you, I promise.

With Love,

Adrian

CHAPTER 7
MARCH, 2024

Montague, who directed Bell and Speer from the Montgomery County Police, and Epps and Ware from the Metropolitan Police, were very busy come early spring. Cleesh had called my brother, Charlie, and asked him if he had heard from me. Cleesh knew Charlie from middle and high school as being my older brother, though they were never friends. Charlie said that he knew nothing about my absence, but neglected to tell him that, two weeks prior, he had received the copy of the letter I wrote to my parents. By the description of the alleged bet I had had with him for a mythical case of Hennepin, Charlie knew something was rotten.

Calvert and Crossland Mortgage's lien holder, Howell Capital, missed my November, December, January, February and March payments, as did my ex-wife for her alimony payments. The companies that offered me physician's signature-only loans were out $250,000 and were getting their people involved. This, along with my disappearance, started a chain of events that was to extend well into early summer. My mail was piling up at my condo, my monthly HOA fee had not been paid since last year, and Santiago had become beyond being concerned. The police had come to question him and he told them about the nine $100 bills delivered the day I left. This, in addition to the information that had been shared by the Metropolitan Police concerning Stepancyzk's statement and my barking creditors, was sufficient to get the FBI involved. Somehow, so was an unusual call from sources in the highest levels of government to the Bureau that finding me was now a top priority.

It didn't take long for the FBI field agent in charge of Fraud, Dana Thoreau, to pay a visit to the DC 9th precinct and Montgomery County's Rugby Ave. police station. Thoreau, 38, brunette and an avid martial artist, had been with the FBI for five years. A North Carolina native, she served in the Marine Corps and did two tours in Afghanistan. She obtained the proper authorization to access my phone records from last fall and winter. They revealed all my calls to Horace Styles, Max Gimble, Francis Devlin, Natalie, Cleesh and Tetley in Wyoming. Styles and Gimble attracted the most attention, being ex-cons. So Dana started there.

Gimble was first.

Thoreau arrived at Max's Silver Spring apartment on Pershing and knocked on the door. Gimble opened it, cigar in hand, wearing a stained blue polo shirt and wrinkled khakis.

"What can I do for you, young lady?"

Thoreau identified herself. Gimble did not blink.

"Please come in."

"Mr. Gimble, I'm here to ask you a few questions. Do you know a Horace Styles?"

"I do. We were in prison together, but you already know that. "

"Quite right. Do you know Dr. Adrian Wren."

Gimble sat in his chair and sipped his Cel-ray tonic.

"Wren…Wren…Oh yeah! The doctor! I've met him. He advised me about some pain problems I was having with my back. Styles sent him. Back in the fall, I think it was. Mighta been October."

"That's right, Mr. Gimble. Phone records indicate you and Dr. Wren had many conversations over a week or so in October. Why so many?"

"Well, my back, it was hurting pretty bad. I had to consult with him a few times."

"Why didn't you make an appointment with him?"

"Well, he don't have an office. He works out of Hamilton. He was doing it as kind of a favor."

"Then why didn't you use a pain doctor or see someone in an office setting. I assume you have Medicare?"

"Yeah, I got Medicare. But a lot of these docs, they just don't listen. Wren was different; he listened. And he helped me."

"What did he do for you, if I may ask?"

"Well, he looked at some old X rays I got, examined me and told me to take a muscle relaxant and Motrin every eight hours and do some back exercises he taught me. Sure enough, I was good as new in two weeks."

Thoreau looked at him long and hard and said nothing.

Gimble asked, as if to inquire about the soup of the day, "Anything else Miss? What's this all about?"

"I'm not at liberty to say. But you do know any false statements you make to me can put you in violation of parole."

Gimble displayed his palms.

"Who's made false statements?"

"Very well Mr. Gimble. One more thing. Do you know a Clete Shea?"

"Never had the pleasure."

"How about Charles Wren?"

"Nope.

"Francis Devlin?"

"You mean the big-time lawyer? I heard of him but never met him."

"How about Natalie Porter."

Gimble paused and shook his head.

"Definitely don't know no Natalies. Except Natalie Woods I know. She was a knockout, poor kid. I bet that bastard did kill her!"

"Well if you remember anything, please call me, especially if you hear from Dr. Wren. Here's my card."

"Oh, I will Miss. Have a nice day."

She smiled at Gimble. He walked her to the door.

"You too, sir."

Thoreau stepped out into the early spring air. In a few weeks, the cherry blossoms would be blooming. A warm breeze washed over her face, the smell of fresh grass in the air. She looked at her smartphone and reviewed the list of people, gleaned from my phone records of middle and late October, she needed to interview. She had yet to speak to Clete Shea, Francis Devlin and Trisha Porter. She chose Devlin.

Thoreau parked her car at the Silver Spring Metro station and took the Red Line downtown. She got off at the Farragut North Station about 11:45 and headed over to Devlin's office. One in his 14th floor office, she introduced herself to Ms. Brownlee, who called in to Devlin.

"Mr. Devlin, a Ms. Thoreau is here from the FBI to see you."

"Please tell her I already spoke to them about Vincent Marshall. Yesterday. I thought we had concluded our business."

Ms. Brownlee relayed the message. She called back in and said,

"Agent Thoreau says it is not concerning Mr. Marshall. It is another matter."

Thoreau entered Devlin's office and introduced herself. She showed her FBI ID and took a chair.

"What can I do for you, Agent Thoreau?"

"Mr. Devlin, do you know a man named Adrian Wren?"

Devlin cleared his throat and began tapping a pencil on his notepad.

"Why are you asking?"

"It seems that from our research that Dr. Wren and someone from your office shared a series of phone calls last October. Do you recall that?"

"I do."

"Then, I take it Dr. Wren is a client of yours?"

"Ms. Thoreau, is it? Ms. Thoreau, has Dr. Wren been charged with a crime?"

"Not as of yet."

"Then you know full well I cannot discuss anything about him."

"Yes Mr. Devlin, I'm all too familiar with attorney-client privilege. I'm merely trying to ascertain if…"

"Agent, all I can say is Dr. Wren and I had some business together. Other than that, you appreciate that I cannot discuss anything that went on between us. By the way, what brought him to your attention?"

Thoreau took out her notepad and scanned a list.

"Mr. Devlin, are you aware Dr. Wren has not been heard from since late October? "

Devlin began tapping his pencil faster on his legal pad, his eyes narrowing. Devlin answered, "My understanding was that he had had an extended business trip abroad."

"Did you also see the article in The Metro Section of *The Post* saying that a missing person's report had been filed?"

"When was this, Agent Thoreau?"

She told him. She also mentioned that some powerful people, alerted by *The Post* article and other unknown sources, had become very interested in the case.

"No, I did not see that article."

Devlin dug deeper with his pencil eraser into the yellow legal pad, wearing a hole clean through to the underlying page. In a hushed voice that took Dana Thoreau aback, he said, "I was in San Francisco for three days at a legal conference and then a leisure trip to Mexico during that time. And by the way, why is finding Wren suddenly so important?"

Thoreau looked aside, then back to Devlin, and told him she was not at liberty to say. She then remarked

"Are you also aware that Dr. Wren had left behind a series of unpaid debts, totaling well over a million dollars?"

Devlin shifted in his chair and brushed his hair back.

"No, how could I possibly know that?"

"Yes, it appears that his mortgage, which he had refinanced to the hilt, has not been paid since he restructured his debt. As well, he took out two large, physician signature-only loans from BMZ Capital and Prime Physicians Finance Corporation, both of which have gone unpaid. His former wife has not received her alimony checks since last fall. His HOA payments in Bethesda are in arrears and his mail, according to the doorman, a Mr. Santiago Perez, has piled up."

"Agent Thoreau, I was not aware of any of this. The last contact with Dr. Wren was the receipt of my legal fee in early November of last year. I assumed he was busy with his business endeavor. Yes, now that you've brought it to my attention the newspaper item you speak of gets me somewhat concerned, but I'm sure there is a simple and innocuous explanation. After all, the man did pay my bill."

"Mr. Devlin, this onion appears to have a lot more layers to it than I first thought. I know your hands are tied now but, as you can well understand, I'll probably be back."

She rose to her feet and extended her hand.

"Ms. Thoreau, unless you bring me a court order from a judge or a subpoena for records, I don't want to see you back in my office. Clear?"

Thoreau nodded her assent. She left the office and Devlin called in to Ms. Brownlee, "Bring me Dr. Wren's file."

CHAPTER 8
A NEW REALITY

My hair was now as long as it was in college, swept back and parted on the left, and my beard, which showed a disturbing array of gray and brown tones, gave me an almost biblical look. I got used to wearing glasses—zero diopter lenses—with 1.75 + bifocals for reading and to arising when I pleased, going to bed late and swimming in the middle of the day at the Douglas YMCA. I relished getting my boat outfitted and together to my very high standards, for I knew that for the next six months, at least, this would be my primary residence.

I carried only cash and prepaid credit cards, used burner phones a week at a time and enjoyed my visits to the Channel Islands of Jersey and Guernsey. I became known as "The Spaniard" to some of the locals around the pub I frequented, the Bell and Whistle, and was pleased to find the Manxies as among the nicest people anywhere. When they asked about my accent, I told them I had spent so long in America that my Spanish one had faded.

I made a conscious effort not to display my new-found wealth. I figured that after my spring and summer tour of the Mediterranean, I would then decide where to settle, at least for better year-round weather, and how I'd spend my time. I thought of Natalie often, and missed her, but was stung by the last phone conversation we had had. She had not answered the email I had sent and I reasoned perhaps it was best to let her cool off.

One Saturday in Douglas I picked up the International Herald Tribune on an odd-numbered calendar day and was taken aback by an ad in the classifieds:

The Officers of Gail Force Holdings will hold its quarterly meeting at the office of Charles Wren, Esquire, on April 22nd at 9 am. All share-holders are encouraged to contact Mr. Wren's office at the company's web address for the agenda and further details.

I immediately bought a fresh burner and called Charlie on his cell.

"Charlie? It's Adrian."

"Let me take this outside."

Pause.

"Adrian, where the hell have you been?! Do you realize what you've…?"

"Slow down, Charles. Take a deep breath."

"Don't tell me to take a deep breath! Do you know what mom and dad are going through? What were you thinking?"

"I was thinking I was tired of busting my ass for that pig Askin and paying my ex-wife alimony and I decided to take a chance and make a change. And it worked; in ways you can't even imagine.

"A change? Yeah, some change. If you ever get caught, *which you will*, you'll have change you never bargained for!"

"I won't get caught, Charles. It's all taken care of."

"Listen Adrian, if you care about mom and dad you'll…"

"Mom and dad haven't been mom and dad since Gail died. And what happened to Gail taught me a few things. First, life is never fair. Second, life is too short. And I was wasting my life grinding it out at Hamilton. Third, there's a whole world out there waiting to be explored. But you don't think that way Charlie, do you? Your law firm is your world. What happened to you, anyway? You used to be so adventurous…so…fun! I think the law and that big job of yours has changed you."

"Adrian, I think maybe you've lost your mind. If you'll only listen to me I think I might be able to…"

"Be able to what!? Come back and go to prison? Or if I'm real lucky, back to the grind? No thanks! No Charlie, I'm not coming back. Just do me a favor, tell mom and dad that I am just fine. Tell them I'll call."

"Listen Adrian. Wait! I…"

"Goodbye Charlie!"

Click.

I stepped into the men's room over at The Blue Anchor Bar and smashed the burner phone with the heel of my boot. Depositing the remnants into the trash, I left the restroom, stepped up to the bar, and asked the barman to pour me Macallan 25 year.

"That's 75 pounds a pour, sir."

I was about to break my rule of no careless displays of spending.

"In that case I'll have a double."

I took out my cash and paid the man.

* * *

It was February of 2003, and my first year of medical school in Boston. What a rude change from Stanford that had been; the

South End was about as far as one could get from that beautiful slice of middle California and still be in the same country. The school where my father and his father had gone had remained that barbed wire fenced enclave that had stood for decades among the poor of Roxbury and Dorchester. The gothic Mallory Institute of Pathology, across the street, stood like some time warped Victorian relic, and Boston City Hospital, with its leaking, subterranean passage-ways and open wards of urban poor—Irish, Black, Cape Verdean, Scandinavian—loomed like something out of a Hitchcock movie.

Gail had been diagnosed with Ewing's sarcoma six months earlier and had already gone through all the treatments ordered by the best specialists at Hopkins. Then the call came: Dad said she was fading fast and that I had better get home as soon as I could. I was in my OB/GYN rotation at BCH, and told my preceptor, a Cape Verdean doc name Will Fontes, that my sister was dying. "By all means, boy, don't think again. Get yourself there," he had said. By the time my plane had landed at National late the next night, Gail was gone. The last time I had spoken to her was four days prior.

Dad took it the hardest. He had enlisted all the best medical minds that he could find. In the end it did not matter. Mom was shattered of course, and Charlie, back from England with his girl-friend, put up a stoic front. He was not as close to Gail as I had been. I had taken a keener interest in Gail's music and her life in music. Charlie, well, Charlie had always been for himself. He knew from day one that he would be big in the law, maybe even politics. He saw the arts as something less serious, even less important, than what he thought he wanted to accomplish. Boy was he wrong. The politicians, the lawyersthey all swim in the same cesspool, if you ask me. Most of them, anyway. A lot like that blow-hard Askin: phonies just out for themselves.

I returned to school angry and bitter. But my view of my family had changed. What had once been a unit had come apart. Dad got really depressed, mom struggled hard with Gail's death and dad's undoing, and Charlie went on with his plans. So did I, after all, but I was left stateside to keep mom and dad as whole as they could be. I took as many trips home that year as time would allow, and it really did not allow much.

My parents thought retirement and leisure might ease things for them, but it seemed, at first, to make things worse. No amount of Florida sunshine, tennis or golf could bring Gail back. As time went by, things improved somewhat; some of my parents' friends moved down there and kept them busy. They did a lot of boating. That's where, the first summer off from school, I learned my way on the water, to keep and repair and maintain a boat. Boating was the only time dad appeared to forget what had happened, but deep down, I knew he was still suffering. The belly laugh was gone; so was the joking. He was not the man of so long ago who joked and chortled at the poker table. And the eyes, they changed. The eyes always tell.

* * *

The Gail Force Winds was almost ready to hoist anchor. I had refurbished the engine and outfitted her with a new bedroom, kitchen and head furnishings, including a new shower and bar. It turned out that the Isle of Man was not only a great place to bank privately, but also to register your yacht. I wanted to avoid registry under countries in the Paris Memorandum of Understanding, whose ships bore more scrutiny. It was the "Red Ensign Group," including the British Overseas Territories of Isle of Man, Gibraltar and Bermuda, that were most registry friendly. Almost like the "Wyoming of yacht registry."

I told my landlady, Mrs. Costain, that I would be travelling for six or so months and that, if she could, to please keep an eye out for the unit. I had paid her the rent up-front, all measly 1800 pounds of it, and remembered how she had smiled and kissed me on the cheek. Now it was an offer of some of her best Irish whisky. She asked why a swarthy, sexy Spaniard like me apparently had no woman, and I told her if I were twenty years older, she and I could make a go of it. She took a snoot-full of her drink, pinched me on the arm and snorted, "Why should that matter?" I think she was only half joking.

I'd leave Isle of Man early May and hit the major spots I had always dreamed exploring, like Gibraltar, southern Spain, Mallorca, Corsica, Sardinia, Sicily, Dubrovnik, Zakynthos, Paros, Naxos, Izmir and Bodrum. I'd set Cyprus as my end-point and return to the Manx Isle by fall. It was an ambitious plan, but one I thought I could handle. I'd need a crew, however, as piloting and maintaining such a ship alone was not feasible. Crew prospects were not hard to find, since the Isle is, after all, an island, and island people know a lot of seafaring. Some internet searching yielded prospects on competent hands who could be had for not much, and I made a list of places I might find them. After a few days and what seemed like too many interviews, I settled on and signed two men, both Irish and former Royal Navy low ranks, Colin Tynes and Michael McPhail. Colin and Michael were both single, strong and did not know each other, though they served in Her Majesty's Navy for much of the same time. Colin, tall, red haired, sinewy, freckled, and outgoing, was a competent cook, as it turned out. Michael, shorter, darker and standing to lose twenty pounds, was more introverted, but knew his way around a ship, as Cleesh might say, the Pope knew the Vatican. I commissioned them both for six months, at a generous 2200 pounds a month, including gear, grub and drink. They jumped at it. I let them loose on the ship on a Monday, and by Thursday, the Gail Force Winds looked like a new ship.

I had made a few friends on the isle, met some women, but had become close to no one. I missed my friends from home but discovered I was perfectly content, for the first time in a long while, to just be by myself, charting my own life, with enough money and time to make most anything I could want into reality. With my two crewmen ready to go, I began shopping for enough provisions to get us to the Azores if we wanted. I looked at the calendar: April 30th. Spring was here and it was getting warmer.

CHAPTER 9
PEELING ONIONS

Agent Thoreau reported back to her superior, Special Agent Mobray, on her progress. Interviews of Gimble and Devlin, she told him, were of little help, and subsequent discussions with Clete Shea, Horace Styles and Adrian's doorman, Santiago, revealed little, other than the fact that Wren had given his doorman an envelope full of nine one hundred - dollar bills, to be distributed evenly among all the doormen. And the mail had piled up.

Mobray instructed her to continue the questioning, this time with Shea, Charles Wren, Tetley and nurse Stepanczyk. The last additional name on the to-question list was Trish Portman. But after three days of Thoreau's beating the pavement, the only things of interest were these: the Shea interview revealed the "bet" Adrian had had with Charlie and a video review of nurse Stepenczyk's questioning by the DC police department in which Sonia discusses Adrian's conversation in the operating room with Fed Chairman

Silverstone. Tetley was evasive on the phone, saying Wyoming law forbade him to discuss any incorporation proceedings without a court order. The interrogation of Charles Wren was more involved.

Thoreau showed up unannounced to Charles Wren's office on April 28, midday. He directed his receptionist to let her in.

"Good of you to see me, Mr. Wren."

"I can't say I'm surprised."

Thoreau gave a startled look. "Why is that?"

"You're looking for my brother, are you not?"

"How could you possibly know th…"

"Because of this."

Charlie handed her a copy of the letter that I had sent my parents. Thoreau read it carefully as she sat, legs crossed, across from Charlie's desk. Charlie said, "And that's not all. Two days ago I received a phone call from Adrian. Most likely from a burner phone. Adrian's not stupid, you know."

Charles told her the details of our phone conversation. Charles continued, "Look agent Thoreau. The letter to my parents is vague. Adrian's phone call was belligerent and non-specific. He could be anywhere. I don't know what crimes, if any, he has committed, but I'm sure he's covered his bases well. I did not go to the authorities because I was not sure of what he's done. As I said, I don't even know what laws, if any, he has breached. I'm still trying to digest it all."

"Well Mr. Wren, it appears from my research, that your brother, at minimum, has committed any number of securities related crimes, as well as bank fraud, mail fraud, using a false identity to escape capture and a whole host of other federal offences too complicated to go into here. And while it appears no one has died or been physically hurt by his alleged actions, someone up high is really after his hide. Don't ask me why. In any event, I'll need to see the phone he called you on, as well as the master copy of the letter to your parents. Can you do that for me?"

"Of course. Anything you need. It's clear he does not realize the trouble he's in, does he?"

"No, he does not."

Thoreau left with Charles's phone and gave him her card.

"I'll return this just as soon as the lab gets through with it. If you need a replacement quickly, get a temporary and the Bureau will reimburse you."

Thoreau took Metro to her DC office and reviewed her findings with Mobray. On pure reflex he popped a Prilosec in his mouth and barked, "Find out what the hell 'Gail Force Holdings' is and who the fuck Warren Tetley is and what he knows. Also, pay a visit to this Patricia Porter, the investment lady, and shake her tree. Maybe some coconuts will fall out."

"Yes, sir."

"And Thoreau…

"Yes, sir?

Get me whatever you can on this Gimble character.

"Yes, sir!"

After lunch, Thoreau headed back to Bethesda, which was on her way home to Rockville, to meet with Porter.

At 3 pm sharp Thoreau entered Porter's office, coffee in hand. The two young women, both fit and stylishly dressed, one with a blond ponytail and one with a brunette one, sat across from each other. Porter was visibly nervous.

"I've never spoken to an FBI agent before. Do I have to…?"

"Ms. Porter, this is all routine."

"Do I need an attorney here?"

"I don't know, do you?"

"I haven't done anything wrong! I…"

"Then let's proceed. What was your relationship to Dr. Adrian Wren?"

Porter slicked her pony back and rubbed her ear. She cleared her throat and said, "I really think you need authorization to talk to me about clients. Our training clearly states that…"

"Is that all Dr. Wren was, a client?"

A crimson flush welled up from Porter's chest.

"Dr. Wren and I went out on a few dates. That's all."

"Did you handle his accounts here at Titus/Dixon?"

"You know I can't discuss that. Not without a court order. Dealings with clients are confidential."

"Then Dr. Wren was both a client and a friend?"

"Agent Thoreau, Adrian and I had a few dates and that was that. He told me he would be out of town in Europe for an extended time on business. As far as his financial dealings are concerned, I cannot discuss them. Now if you have no further questions, I have a lot of work to do."

Thoreau got to her feet and shook hands with Porter. Before she left, she said, "Ms. Porter, I feel it is my duty to remind you that if Dr. Wren has made you aware of anything that could be linked to a crime or crimes, that you could be charged as an accomplice. Just so you know."

Porter, frowning, linked her fingers together and asked Thoreau to sit down. "Adrian called me last week. He didn't say where he was or what he was doing. He maintained his story about his extended business trip. I told him how angry I was that he could not be more forthcoming with me about what he was doing. I hung up on him. I'd really like to help you but, without a warrant, I can't talk to you. You know that."

"Ms. Porter don't worry. We'll get all the warrants we need. In due time."

It was getting towards 4 pm and Thoreau stepped out onto Old Georgetown Road, in the heart of Bethesda's business district, and called Mobray in DC.

"Chief, I talked to Porter at Titus/Dixon but she won't discuss the business dealings Wren had. Not without a warrant. She said she and the doc had had a few dates. I'm gonna head home and see what I can dig up on Gimble and try to find out who this Tetley guy is. See you in the morning."

"Okay Dana but listen. This is getting too thick for one agent to handle. I'm going to bring in Locatelli. Meet me tomorrow at the office at 8 sharp. And be prepared to brief Pete on all you've found."

"Pete Locatelli? I thought he was ready to retire?"

"Nope. That's Lorenzo, not Locatelli. See you in the morning."

Thoreau called a girlfriend and met her at Bethesda Brew House. She'd had enough of the Bureau for one day.

At the same time, Max Gimble was preparing a move of his own. He had kept a mobile home at his friend's garage in Hyattsville and figured now might be a good time to leave his apartment for good in Silver Spring for a less conspicuous address. The way he figured it, it was only a matter of time before the FBI put the pieces together on his involvement with Adrian Wren and Gail Force Holdings. So too with his milking of George Littleton's identity and his bilking of the Social Security checks that had kept him with a steady stream of extra cash.

He forged one last driver's license for himself, a Samuel N. Perry of Bristol, Virginia, date of birth December 25, 1954. He emptied his safe, containing over $350,000 in cash, gathered his forging equipment and computer into an oversized canvas duffel, along with what little clothes he needed, and took a cab to where the RV was housed. By 6 pm he was on the American Legion Bridge, heading south and then west on I-66, to his late army pal's cabin in rural Virginia. By midnight, he had parked the RV way up the hill, among the darkened pines in front of the cabin, and sat on the porch swing, nursing a shot of Wild Turkey.

The next morning at 8 am, Mobray, Thoreau, and Locatelli met in the FBI conference room in downtown DC, along with agents from the SEC. Locatelli, 55, slender, with jet black hair swept back over an olive forehead, dressed in blue pinstripe with a gold and blue striped tie and sporting a large gold signet ring on the fourth finger of his right hand, sat between Thoreau and SEC agent Mark Timon, a man of about 30 who looked 15. Another SEC rep, Lucille Taft, sat next to Chief Mobray. Mobray recounted the details of the case to them.

Behind Mobray on a white board were taped pictures of the brothers Wren, Max Gimble, Horace Styles, Sonia Stepanczyk, Francis Devlin, Trish Portman, Santiago Perez, Clete Shea and a blank silhouette of Warren Tetley. Arrows linked the various pictures, and notations relevant to each personage were outlined in bullet points beneath the photos. Mobray added a few words about money to the doorman and calls to Natalie Porter and Charles Wren.

A discussion ensued about motive, ability, and Dr. Adrian Wren's recent behavior. The consensus was clear: Adrian Wren was fed up with his job, growing tired of salary reductions and increasing intrusions on his practice, and he resented paying alimony to his former wife. He acted on inside information gleaned from a sedated Federal Reserve Chairman. He leveraged his funds, in ways that were not yet completely clear, and made a substantial amount of money in the process. With the likely help of ex-con Max Gimble, he probably crafted a new identity for himself and could presently be anywhere in the world.

Mobray tightened his tie, looked out at his gathered agents, and proclaimed: "Let's go get us some subpoenas!"

CHAPTER 10
WATERWORLD

The Gail Force Winds was ready to leave Douglas by May 7th. I had firmed up plans with Colin and Michael, who had started calling me "Captain Juan." Michael was particularly curious as to why I didn't have a Spanish accent. I told him I had spent many of my young years in California, helping my father in the wine business, and that I had lost most of my Castellano dialect by age eight. My hair was now shoulder length, sometimes pulled back in a dull patina ponytail of gray and blond. My beard was similarly toned and neatly trimmed around the jawline. I wore a blue cap with white nautical braids on the brim and continued my ruse of needing glasses for distance sight. I doubted, perhaps naively, that even the most sophisticated facial-recognition software, wherever it might hide its prying eyes, would make me.

Colin and Michael, separated by only two years and in their mid-thirties, got on well enough. Both had never married, and both hailed from Northern Ireland. Colin grew up in Ulster, where his father worked as an assistant to the firebrand clergyman and politician Ian Paisley. Michael, less politically connected and inclined, grew up in Belfast. But the pair were raised in the tradition of, as history taught, the strongly Protestant and anti-Catholic Westminster Confession of 1646, the distillation of British reformed doctrine, which viewed Catholicism and the Church of Rome as the Anti-Christ. The economic hardships that had endured, due to The Troubles, from the 1960s to the mid 1990s, left both their families little capital to fund for higher education. By the time of the mid 1998 peace dividend, resulting from the Good Friday Agreements, allowed the Celtic Tiger economy to take shape, there was still not enough time for the boys to enjoy any fruits of the economic boom and leave their mean-streets roots. Eventually they both enlisted in The British Navy, Colin in 2011 serving on the HMS Iron Duke and Michael in 2012 on HMS Archer.

Once I first sought to hire seamen and they learned that I was (allegedly) from Spain, it took me a while to figure out their initial coolness and outright suspicion of my offer of employment. Once it became plain however, over beers and sandwiches at the Bell and Whistle, who they were and where and what they came from, I was quick enough to renounce my presumed faith, telling them I wanted nothing to do with Catholicism, or any organized religion. That, and the money I was willing to put out, seemed more than enough to satisfy them.

With the Gail Force Winds capable of doing 30 km per hour, my fantasy of covering the highlights of the Mediterranean in four or five months was doable. But mindful that the North Atlantic could be wildly unpredictable in Spring, I charted a course with frequent stops, both for safety and sheer desire to spend time exploring the back roads and people. I settled on a compromise course: I wanted to avoid Americans at all costs and keep the "touristy" stuff to a next to nil level. That meant the big cities were out. The Azores were good, but Lisbon was not. Rabat, Algiers, Formentor, Corsica, Cagliari, Zakynthos and Paros made the cut; Naples, Athens, Istanbul did not. I was comfortable with that kind of itinerary; so was the crew. We shoved off the Monday morning, May 7th.

The first night in my cabin, after a fine dinner with the boys of beef stew, a California red zinfandel and some homemade brownies, I laid back in bed and stared at the cabin's ceiling of finely polished mahogany. Back home, the chumps at Hamilton were slaving away for the Fat Fuck. Here I was, worth almost 13 million bucks, free for the first time in my life. Free to wake when I please, explore the world, drink scotch at noon and swallow the world. Free from alimony, malpractice attorneys, insurance companies, Medicare audits, continuing medical education and obese patients who never took care of themselves. It was the last point that particularly stung and I was glad to be free of it. People who destroyed their lives. And I had to clean up their messes. Gail never had that chance, I thought. None of her illness was her fault. Here was this pearl, this rare gem, beautiful to beholda light, a genius, a burning bulb of raw talent and power, all compressed into this gorgeous sinewy slip of speed, lightness and power. A modern-day goddess. A Venus of the piano.

I thought back to her New York debut. Mom and dad and I were in the third row, keyboard side. Charlie was "too busy" to make the trip. I was bursting with anticipation, waiting for her to appear—and then she did—after the concertmaster had tuned the orchestra up to the middle A on the monstrous Steinway, the black battleship waiting to be commandeered.

The house lights went down, there was a hush and she came out, followed by Rebroff. She wore a blue, form-fitting gown, her hair in stunning blond shocks, a simple string of delicate white pearls around her neck. She smiled, and I could see her dimples. The conductor led her to the front of the stage, the audience sensing something truly special was to happen. She gave me that look, the look that meant we shared our joke, the joke about how the conductor, during certain passages, would shake his big Russian ass in time to the beat. She died laughing telling me of it on the phone during rehearsals the prior week. After the brief orchestral introduction, she came in, unleashing a torrent of ferocious chords, her posture perfect, her attention laser-like. She poured everything out that a human could that night; how a mere teenager could have the artistic maturity, let alone the technical talent, to unleash her singular brand of passion and fury that evening still amazes me. Even from the medical and psychiatric standpoint. Young people aren't supposed to be able to do that.

A few short years later she was gone. Part of me died then, too.

The sailing those first few weeks was unusually smooth. It took us about a week to click as captain and crew, and once we hit our stride, there appeared no limit to the places we could go. I found it easy to spin my fiction about growing up in California, the son of a winemaker. The boys got inquisitive however, as to why a Spaniard, whose nation was known for producing great wines of its own, would travel halfway across the world to make wine. I said, "Boys, look at the Italians. The Gallos and the Mondavis did it. My dad was trying to replicate their model. And he did, in a sense. Only not as big."

I was fortunate Colin and Michael knew too little of the wine world to know what was bullshit and what wasn't. Irish whisky and beer, they knew. But wine? They couldn't pick a dime-store plonk from a vintage Bordeaux.

Mealtime was really the only time, next to drink time, that

we got to know each other. Colin had come from a large family in Ulster—five boys and three girls. He was the fourth child. A good athlete, he played soccer for the local upper school team, before his naval stint, and had had plenty of girlfriends. But when the economy in Northern Ireland was just starting to gel, he had neither the education nor training in a trade to make a life for himself. He was outgoing, a joker of sorts. Quick with imitations, especially of my American accent, and puns.

Michael was the opposite—introverted, even brooding. The only time he really revealed himself was after a whisky, and then, watch out. The words came too fast and too loud. His late father had been an alcoholic and had abandoned the family when he was ten. That left him and his two older brothers to help support his mother, who had developed severe rheumatoid arthritis and could no longer work as a dispatcher for the police.

Neither of them had ever been to America and they were full of questions: did people really carry weapons openly in the street? What was a real American hamburger like? Why did the United States feel it had to be the world's policeman? Had I ever been to Hollywood? Did President Clinton really have sex in the Oval Office with an intern?

Before our first stop in the Azores in late May, I had decided on a set of rules: each man could go ashore, one at a time, alone and for overnight, taking turns. I would come and go as I pleased. If any of the two got drunk, in trouble with the law or brought anyone back to the ship, he'd be fired then and there and left in port. I would always have the keys to the ship. My cabin was off-limits. I would keep track of how many nights ashore each man got. On the 20th of each month that we were away, each man would earn two full nights ashore. They could go at the same time, together or separately. I had full say about how long we stayed in each location, whether we sailed or waited out bad weather, and what was for dinner. What they did ashore, barring breaking the law, was their business. My business ashore was my business.

Our first stop was Horta, the port capital on the volcanic island of Faial. I told the crew that I was going on a seven-hour hike to the Caldera, the highest point on the island at about 1000 meters. The joke in the Azores was that if you didn't like the weather, wait ten minutes. Boy, was that true. It could be 80 Fahrenheit and sunny down in Horta town, and raining sideways and 50 up at the top of the Caldera, with a visibility of 20 feet.

They flipped a coin to see who was going ashore that day, to do as he pleased. Colin won. I set out about 8:30 and Colin left with me, only to turn off as I headed toward the path to the volcanic rim. Colin said he was heading to the main town to explore, grab lunch, take a hike of his own and buy some wine and a bottle of port. I told him I'd see him at dinner.

In a cafe in Horta town I hooked up with a group of Germans, just out of university. There were three men and four women, all fit and intelligent. I couldn't tell if any were couples, but I envied the men. The girls were beautiful and obviously athletes. Their English, for the most part, was quite good. They came from Dusseldorf and had all graduated together. One of them, Murat, was a Turkish German. The rest appeared to be native born. I spoke with Murat about the "Doner Murders," a series of National Socialist Underground murders perpetrated by the Neo-Nazi group of the same name between 2000 and 2007, in which ten ethnic Turks, Kurds and a Greek, all green-grocers and doner-kebab vendors were brutally cut down.

I couldn't help but think of Gail when I met these young people. They were smart, cultured and cared about their health. Three of them played instruments. Five were multilingual, speaking, among them, German, English, Italian, French, Turkish and Swedish. A few were scientists; one was a computer engineer and two were heading on to medical school. One was going to study law. They let me tag along with them, exploring the rim of the caldera and the spectacular view of the island from 3/5 of a mile up. We lunched together along the crater, marveling at the wonders before and beneath us. I made a connection with a tall, slender brunette, Petra, who seemed to have taken a liking to me. Her English was impeccable. She had spent a summer abroad in San Francisco, studying marine biology at San Francisco State University. Petra asked me if I would join them for dinner that night in Horta town. I told them I would.

I got back to the boat at about 6 pm. Michael was sitting on deck, drinking a beer and reading a copy of Rugby League Journal. He put his paper down as I approached.

"Mike how goes it?"

"All good, Captain Juan. Just catching up on the rugby."

"Where's Colin?"

"Not back yet. Should be in soon though. Looking forward to dinner."

"About that. Dinner. It seems there's a change of plan. I'll be dining in town with a group of friends."

Michael looked as if I had kicked him.

"If you'd like, you can go grab some sandwiches at the restaurant near the bait shop just up the road. Or call Colin on the mobile to do that. Either one, your choice. Just for tonight."

Michael took a long swig of his beer and placed the bottle next to his chair on the deck. He folded the paper neatly and said, eyes narrowed,

"Yeah, either way, like you says, Captain. Either way."

He scratched his stomach as I edged past him to head to my cabin. I could feel his eyes following me.

By 7 I was showered and in a pair of white jeans, a burnt-orange University of Texas t-shirt with the longhorn logo on it and a pair of blue Keds on my feet. Colin was back and talking to Michael aft. They appeared to be whispering when I told them

"Don't know when I'll be back. See you boys later."

They nodded their assent as I stepped past them and on to the dock.

At 7:30 I was at Restaurante Canto da Doca on rue Nova. The Germans were already through their first round of drinks. Petra flashed me a big smile, patting the vacant seat next to her. I slid beside her, and she placed her wine glass, lipstick on the rim, in front of me to take a sip. Under the table I felt her squeeze my knee. She smelled like lilacs.

The dinner went on for hours. Vinho verde, fresh prawns, lobster and homemade bread and a variety of cheeses. The talk was all over the map: world politics, soccer, computers, movies, American music. The students were eager to know about my shirt. Did I attend that school? (No.) What was Texas like? (Big.) What was a "longhorn"? (I told them.) Was my horn long? (Peals of laughter.) After coffee, five of us went to the B Side nightclub to dance.

After two caipirinhas, I let go of my allergy to dancing and consented to let Petra take me out on the dance floor. I hadn't danced with a woman in a club like that for probably 25 years, I thought. But Petra could dance. She was wearing white, tight jeans of her own, with a blue and white striped tank top and Converse sneakers. After three fast numbers, the DJ chose a slow one, and she pulled me toward her, the top of her head along my jawline. Her hair smelled like honey. She whispered,

"Let's get out of here!"

My heart skipped and beat and without hesitation I took her hand headed to the street. Her friends were busy dancing and drinking. We caught a cab to the dock, and ten minutes later, we got out. She appeared puzzled.

"Where is your hotel?"

"You're looking at it."

"A ship?"

"Yes. My ship. The Gail Force Winds."

She looked at me with wide eyes. The deck was dark and quiet as I led her to my cabin. The ship's clock read 12:30. Once inside her wet, glossy lips met mine, the taste of cachaça on her tongue. She inhaled and took off her top. She mumbled something in German and eased out of her jeans. She peeled mine off and sat at the foot of my bed. She tucked her chestnut hair behind her ears and said

"Now, let me see a real Texas longhorn!"

The night passed too quickly and I awoke with Petra lying next to me, my Texas longhorn t-shirt covering her shapely frame. I heard a loud knock on my cabin door and looked at my watch: 10:05! Petra turned and sprawled over my chest, her hair a nest of tangles. The knock came again, louder. It was Colin.

"Captain, you OK in there? It's nearly 10:15! Breakfast is on!"

Petra rolled over onto her side and I got up, putting my shorts and shirt on.

"Colin, give me 5 minutes. Be right out! Overslept!"

I heard him step away.

I went over to the other side of the bed and knelt next to Petra.

"Petra. Sweetheart. Time to get up. It's late."

She opened one squinting eye, raised her head, and looked around. She then fixed a smile on me. Her German accent now stronger she said, "Oh, Captain Longhorn. What time is it?"

"Past 10:30. It's late. Come, let's get dressed. "

I helped her negotiate her way back into her jeans and handed her bra and top. She grabbed me again and kissed me. I felt like telling the crew to leave me alone for another hour but thought better of it. I helped Petra to her feet and peeked out through the crack separating the door from the frame. Colin and Michael were sitting at the breakfast table, drinking tea. There was no way of getting her out unnoticed. I came above deck, Petra in tow.

"Boys, I won't be but twenty minutes. Help yourselves to anything there; biscuits, toast, cheese, and there's ham in the fridge!"

Their eyes followed me in silence as I led Petra off the ship and onto the dock. I looked back over my shoulder, their eyes fixed on us. They didn't say a word—not to me or each other. Both wore faces bereft of expression.

I got in a cab with Petra and headed for her hotel. She asked, "When will I see you again?"

"Soon I hope. I don't know how long we'll be in Horta. But I will see you. I've just got to get back to the crew now.

Petra purred like a cat.

"Tell me you love me."

"Now Petra you know I…"

"Go ahead, say it!"

I humored her. In a mocking voice, I said, "Petra, darling. I love you!"

"I knew it! You can't resist me, can you?"

Part of that was no lie.

"Petra listen, here's your hotel. I've got to go. We'll see each other again. How long will you be here?"

"Til Friday. This is Tuesday. We have plenty of time. Now I know where to find you!"

She kissed me again and got out. The cab started back towards the dock, her figure receding in the rear window. She turned on her heel, blew me a kiss and then shot me a smile, her white teeth in contrast to her coffee-colored face.

It was early afternoon when I returned to the ship, and Colin and Michael were clearing the table from lunch. They spoke not a word, nor looked up as I passed on my way to my cabin. I went below deck, changed into fresh clothes, and took out my map. Pulling my long hair back and tying it into a ponytail, letting the tail fall over my left shoulder, I sipped a leftover iced coffee, now diluted and warm, and drew a rough course on the map with a red pencil. I figured if we did 30 km per hour for a full day's ride we'd be able to make the coast of Portugal in less than a week, easy. I was startled to hear a knock on the door.

"Captain, it's Michael."

"Yes Mike, what is it?"

"A word, if you please."

I got up and went above deck. Michael stood, legs apart and arms folded over his chest."

"I believe it is my turn to go ashore tonight. I was wondering what time I could leave?

I looked to see if Colin was about but saw no sign of him.

"Has the ship been washed down, the engine checked and the provisions list been made?"

"All done, Captain."

"Well, how does 4 pm sound?"

Michael scratched his chin and tugged on the brim of his cap.

"4 o'clock sounds okay, Captain. "

He smiled.

"Then 4 it is. Where's Colin?"

"He's in the galley, going over the provisions list one last time."

"Please tell him I'd like a word."

"Aye aye."

After a few minutes, Colin appeared.

"You wanted to see me, Captain?"

"Yes. The provision list all done?'

"Here it is."

"Very well. I'll head into town and hit the market. Did you finish the clean up?"

"I did."

"Fine, I'll return about 3 then."

Colin looked at me for what seemed like too long. I said "That's all."

"She's pretty."

"Who's pretty?"

"That girl from this morning. German is she?"

I narrowed my eyes at him and stepped forward.

"She is pretty. And, yes, she is German. But that's my business. Only my business. Understood? "

"Aye, Captain."

Colin turned his back to me and left.

I stood thinking about my relationship with the crew. On the one hand, they were employees, not friends. They were being paid, and paid well, to help me run a ship I could not run myself. However, I knew that I was, at heart, a social animal. I had never been a loner. I also knew that being on the run, my making friends was risky. I had to somehow balance the discipline of an employer with my desire to maintain human contact, in all its forms. Clearly, this early into my new life, I hadn't found the key to pick that lock.

It was an "odd" Saturday, so I decided to look at the international Herald Tribune for any Gail Force Holdings notices. To my relief, there were none. I picked up some ham, cheese, fresh bread, Portuguese white wine, and beer, along with some fish and fresh fruit, and made my way back to the ship. I told Colin that since Michael was heading out about 4, dinner would be at 7. I put the provisions away and headed to my cabin for a nap.

I woke at 6:30 and went to the galley, where I opened a beer. I took out the fresh tomato and washed it, slicing it thinly. I took the fish out of its wrapper and cleaned it in cold water. I took out the three cheeses, an Evora, Nisa and Sao Jorge, and put them on a plate. I called out to Colin and told him to set the table. In a frying pan, I poured olive oil, crushed garlic, and a cup of white wine. I placed the fish filets in the pan, the sizzle sighing and the aroma of pungent garlic hitting the air. I flipped the filets over, poured some capers over them and stuck a fork in one. When the meat was tender, I transferred the fillets to the plates and called for Colin.

"Bring these to the table. I'll bring the rest."

There's nothing like food to lubricate a conversation. Colin started eating like it was the first food he had ever tasted. He took a gulp of his wine, and pinch an end off the crust of bread, mopping up a portion of the olive oil/wine and garlic reduction. He rolled his head with delight.

"Captain Juan, I had no idea you could cook like this."

"Not hard, Colin. Just common sense. That and balance. Keep it simple. That's why the Italians and the Portuguese have it all over the French; peasant food. No need to be complex. Kind of like life, don't you think?"

"I do think if it means eating like this! Mike doesn't know what he's missing!"

"Taste the cheese."

He did. All three. You never saw a man eat with such gusto.

"Bet you never ate like this in Northern Ireland."

He laid down his knife and fork.

"Those were tough times. At least in the navy we knew we were getting fed. You have no idea, I don't think."

"No, I don't. In California, it was much like Spain. Everything was fresh. And my dad could cook, too."

The bullshitting came so easily to me.

We finished the meal in silence. I looked at my watch. It was 8:15. Back home at Hamilton, it was 3:15 on a Saturday, and a day where I could have easily been taking 24 hours of call, making money for the pig. Instead, I was on my boat in the middle of the Atlantic, almost 13 million in the bank, and plotting my course for a summer in the Mediterranean. I looked on as Colin cleared the table and began on the dishes.

I watched the sun set, alone, from the prow of the ship. I could see beautiful Mount Pico on Pico Island, across the straights, a sublime collar of pink and gray clouds encircling its neck. There was no question in my mind that if I had to do it again, I would not change a thing.

CHAPTER 11
THE THICKENING

At FBI Headquarters in downtown DC, Agents Thoreau and Locatelli reviewed their list of interview subjects and the documents and devices to be confiscated. They had obtained the proper court orders from federal judge Milton Stanley, who, acting on information from Montgomery County and DC Police, as well as information submitted by Wren's former wife, Calvert and Crossland mortgage, two medical-practice loan companies and others, felt there was sufficient evidence that a crime or crimes had been committed. The whiteboard at headquarters was filling up; more extensive interviews and seizure of records were yet to be realized on Titus/Dixon and Natalie Patricia Porter, Clete Shea, Francis Devlin, Charles Wren, Horace Styles, Max Gimble, and Warren Tetley.

Their attempts to locate and interview Max Gimble were fruitless. Their visit to Horace Styles was likewise worthless since he stuck to his story, despite warnings about parole-violations should he be lying, that he sent Max Gimble to Dr. Wren for "medical" purposes. Clete Shea's interview also added nothing of value; nor did Charles Wren's. The focus then turned on three objectives: finding out where Gimble had escaped to, what involvement, if any, did Porter have in all this and, why was Francis Devlin, well known criminal defense attorney, involved?

They started with Porter.

It was early in the afternoon when Natalie Porter, along with branch manager Deborah Stallings, Titus/Dixon in house counsel Adam Fleet and outside criminal defense counsel Mort West sat around a conference table at FBI headquarters. Chief Mobray watched from a remote location, accompanied by two other FBI agents. Porter was clearly nervous.

The interview was conducted in a non-threatening tone by Thoreau and observed by Locatelli, who was taking notes. The attorneys present were assured that Ms. Porter was not, at this time, the subject of a criminal investigation; this was merely a fact-finding mission. Natalie's hands were shaking, to the point where she could not easily control her cup of coffee, and she conferred often with her attorneys. After the bare bones of her story was laid out, Thoreau began to dig deeper.

"So Ms. Porter, it seems you had more than a professional relationship with Dr. Wren?"

"As I said before, he asked me out on a few dates, and I went out with him."

"Alright. I have the records here of his personal brokerage accounts, as well as a corporate account that you said he set up with a George Littleton. For the record, we cannot locate Mr. Littleton, despite the fact that someone has been cashing his Social Security checks. We are looking into how that is possible. Can you tell me about this corporate account for a company called Gail Force Holdings?"

Natalie looked over at her attorneys, who nodded for her to proceed.

"Yes. Before Adrian and I—I meanDr. Wren and I—started to date, he brought in a man to open an account. A corporate account. He asked some unusual questions."

"What kind of questions."

Natalie licked her lips.

"Well, he asked if he could, after the account had been set up, freely transfer money between his personal account and this corporate account, even if his name was not on the corporate account. I thought that a bit odd, but I said he could, with Mr. Littleton's permission."

"Could you describe the man he was with, Mr. Littleton?"

"Well, he was odd, too. He was about 65 or 70, medium height, heavy set, wearing sunglasses indoors as well as a hat. I asked him about that and he said he had just had eye surgery and needed to shield his left eye. He had a grey moustache and wore kind of a shabby suit. He spoke with an accent. A New York kind of accent. He had some cigars in his front pocket but asked me for a cigarette. I thought that was strange."

"You are very observant, Ms. Porter. We like that. I'm going to show you some photos and would like you to tell me if you recognize any of these people."

Agent Thoreau laid out, one by one, photos of Styles, Shea, Charles Wren and Gimble. She denied having ever seen them except for Gimble, when she paused, tilted her head, and said

"That one sort of looks like Mr. Littleton. "

She picked up the photo and stared at it.

"It is! That is Mr. Littleton! "

Thoreau looked over at Locatelli, who had paused his note taking to look at Porter. Mobray leaned forward in his chair from the observation room.

"You're sure you've seen this man before?"

Porter nodded her assent.

"What did this man Littleton say?"

"Nothing much. He let Dr. Wren do most of the talking. I do remember that when it came time for the PIN number to be set up for the account, Mr. Littleton asked me for a cigarette. I got him one from my purse I kept behind my seat and told him he'd have to smoke it outside the building. Then, we all said good-bye and Dr. Wren asked Mr. Littleton to step outside. That's when Dr. Wren asked me out for our first date."

Just then Mobray's phone rang. He picked up.

"Mobray. What is it?"

"Chief, just a quick word from the fellas in Cheyenne. They spoke to this Warren Tetley dude and slapped him with the subpoena. He was resistant at first—hell you'd have thought by what they said he was ready to draw down, but bottom line, he coughed up that Gail Force Holdings was set up by none other than Adrian Wren, although his name is not listed in the corporation. The only names are, get this, George Littleton and Francis Devlin. Devlin's name was actually public record."

Mobray leaned back in his chair and stared at the calendar on the wall.

"Chief, you still there?"

Mobray rubbed his eyes.

"Yeah. I'm here. Good work. Thank the guys in Cheyenne. Out."

Mobray hung up the phone and called Locatelli on his cell, telling him to wrap up the interview and get to the observation room ASAP. Locatelli leaned over to Thoreau and whispered to her. Thoreau stood.

"Ms. Porter, you've been most helpful. Mr. Fleet, Mr. West, we have the financial records and the transcript of the conversation your client said she had with Dr. Wren when he called. We will have to review those items again. Ms. Porter, if there are any further items you or your attorneys would like to add, or if you have any questions, you know where to reach us."

The group from Titus/Dixon left the conference room and Mobray opened the door to the observation room. He directed Thoreau and Locatelli to take seats.

"Word from Wyoming is that Wren set up a corporation with Littleton and Devlin as officers. Now that we know that Gimble has been posing as Littleton, that explains his disappearance. I still don't get Devlin's angle though. Doesn't make sense. We need records from his office. Turn the place inside out."

The FBI had a field day in Devlin's office: client files, computers, phone records, whatever they could find in drawers, closets, cabinets, whatever was not nailed down. Three days later, Devlin sat in his office, along with his counsel, Daniel Carmi. Locatelli and Thoreau were sipping their coffee, across from the conference table. Carmi began.

"Agents, my client has been through the indignity of having his office disrupted, his records and computers confiscated and his phone records examined. There is not a shred of evidence to suggest he has been involved in anything illegal or untoward. I'd like to know..."

Locatelli interrupted.

"Save it, counsellor. We're just trying to understand what's happened. "

Locatelli bounced his crossed leg as he reviewed some items on his notepad. He turned to Devlin and remarked

"Mr. Devlin, did Dr. Wren mention in your meetings that you, along with your then law partner William McBride, litigated his father for malpractice in the 1970s? "

Carmi looked over at Devlin with wide eyes. He hunched forward in his chair, his eyes fixated on Locatelli, and said, "Francis, you never told me that you…"

Devlin held up his hand.

"Listen. Wren never mentioned anything about that case. In fact, he misled me. I should have trusted my goddam instincts! He led me to believe that Augustus Wren and he weren't father and son. Son of a bitch! I'll bet he was not even born when that case had been litigated. Besides, that was almost forty years ago. I was just starting out. My partner made me take that case. And it was a shit case at that! I don't even do med-mal anymore. "

Locatelli looked over at Thoreau, who toyed with the stirrer in her coffee cup. She looked up and said, "Mr. Devlin, your records indicate that the young Wren hired you to represent him in his new medical device venture and to serve on his board as legal counsel. We discovered documents listing you as his registered agent for something called 'Gail Force Holdings LLC'. Was that your understanding?"

"It was."

"Can you explain to me how you were to be compensated?"

Mr. Carmi started to tell his client not to answer the question; but Devlin waved him off. Visibly trying to compose himself, Devlin went on, "Daniel, it's OK. I've got nothing to hide here. Agent Thoreau, it's unusual but not unprecedented, here along K Street, that lawyers of my standing and caliber sometimes will take compensation in the form of equity in a business venture or entity that they feel might hold promise. Dr. Wren's credentials, along with his manner, his claim of backers and obvious ambition, led me to arrange such a deal with him."

"Do you think he had another motive, Mr. Devlin?"

"Now I do. I see it. He's trying to tie me up in whatever criminal activity he's involved in to get back at me for what I thinks I did to his dad in that fucking malpractice case almost a half century ago. That way, can't you see, he not only evened the score but bought himself some time and cover when he went abroad?"

Devlin pinched the flesh of his brow between his eyes, head down, and said, "Look, have only myself to blame for this. I failed to do my due diligence. This doctor, this Wren fellow – he's smooth."

Locatelli fixed his eyes on Devlin. With his Montblanc pen in hand, he pointed it at Devlin and exclaimed, "I agree. He did try to divert attention from himself. And buy himself more time to escape. And get even with you in the process. Why else would he go to the trouble of getting you involved? He didn't need a lawyer on his 'board', or anyone else."

Carmi, like Devlin next to him, sat back in his chair, a look of relief washing over his face. He began

"Then you are not seeking to prosecute my client?"

Thoreau answered, "Mr. Carmi, we don't prosecute anyone, as you surely know. We investigate. And our investigation, so far, gives us no indication that your client was behind any criminal activity. It appears he was just being used. That, and being paid back for what Dr. Wren believed was an alleged wrong perpetrated by Mr. Devlin on his father. Mr. Devlin, the Bureau, at least at this time, regrets any inconvenience and is prepared to return your records and computer. But we do ask that, if Dr. Wren contacts or attempts to contact you, you will let us know immediately."

Locatelli and Thoreau left Devlin's office and stopped at the Eagle's Den Diner on H Street for a bite. In a booth, with their sandwiches and iced tea, Thoreau began, looking down at her notes, "So, it all is falling into place: the good doctor learns where rates are going from sedating Silverstone last October. His former girlfriend, the Polish chick, records the conversation and goes to the DC Police about it. A man in Chevy Chase finds a note in his kid's book, belonging to Wren, with some cryptic stuff scribbled on it, clearly related to the planning of the crime. Before that, Wren sets up a dummy corporation in far-away Wyoming, with Gimble, the forger posing as Littleton, and Devlin as a dupe. He wines and dines his broker, all the while using her to set up a corporate account where he can transfer the money. He borrows up to his eyeballs and bets everything on his market play. When he scores big, he skips the country, likely with ID made for him by Gimble, and transfers the money to the corporate account. Then, and this is the crucial part, he moves the money over to a foreign account and, voila: He's got it made! He leaves everyone else behind holding the bag!"

Locatelli chewed on his pastrami and rye. He put the sandwich down and smacked himself in the forehead. Thoreau looked at him in surprise.

"Are you OK, Peter?"

""Foreign account"! Dana, gimme that copy of Wren's note found in the book from that Chevy Chase kid."

Dana pulled up a copy from her phone. She handed it to Locatelli. He scanned it with intensity, mumbling as he went down the list.

"Goddammit! How could we be so stupid!? How come nobody's picked up on this sooner? I of M! Isle of Man! That's where the fucking money is! Look!"

Agent Thoreau looked over the list, biting her lip. She looked up slowly at her partner. Locatelli inquired, "Remember that seminar from the SEC and Treasury people last summer about off-shore laundering, given by that (fingers snapping), that Thompson or Thompkins lady? You know, the one with the short skirt and cleavage? Isle of Man was big on that list!"

Thoreau rolled her eyes. She said, "I know the folks in forensics and research have looked this over. I can't believe they didn't consider that…"

"Yeah, well Dana, the forensic and research people don't always have the big picture. We need to get to Mobray about this."

Three days later, in early June, Charles Wren called Clete Shea at his home at 7:30 pm, where he was just finishing dinner. Clete was putting the dishes in the sink.

"Clete, this is Charles Wren. Do you have a minute?"

"Yes, I do. Glad to hear from you. Penny for your thoughts?"

"Fine. Listen, did the FBI come talk to you about Adrian?"

"Why do you ask?"

"I'm trying to learn everything I can about what he's up against."

"To be frank, two agents came to see me at the SEC two days ago. A hot brunette and an older, slick guy. The lady did most of the talking. She was focused on the Hennepin 'bet' you allegedly had with Adrian about interest rates. She was all hot and bothered to know about the meal I had had with Adrian at Da Marco's—what was said, how Adrian was behaving, stuff like that. "

"Okay. Did they give you any indication about where he might be or the nature of what he's done? I guess I'm trying to say: did they tell you anything about what crimes he's committed and what his plans were?"

"Well, yes and no. Yes, in that they believe Adrian used inside information to make a shitload of money in the market when it took that huge tumble last October. But, no in the sense that that's all they'd say. They were as quiet as church mice when I asked if they knew where he was, who he did this with, why he did it and so on. Have you heard anything on your end?"

"Actually, I have. Adrian called me a few weeks ago."

"You're shitting me! From where?"

"I don't know. All he had to say, and he kept it quick, was that he had this chance to make the money, and he wasn't going to miss it. I tried to impress on him the enormity of what he did, crime-wise, but he just got angry and hung up. The only other piece of information I got was a letter he wrote to my parents, a couple of days after he disappeared, postmarked from Tokyo. "

"What did the letter say?"

"It was basically a short manifesto on how he had to seize this opportunity, that mom and dad shouldn't worry about him and that everything will turn out. That's about it."

"Well if anyone could pull this off, it's Adrian. To be able to plan this, to escape the country, if he did, unnoticed like that and hide enough money to have made all this worthwhile, he must have been as busy as a one-legged man in an ass kickin' contest. And that would be vintage Hadrain Wren MD, don't ya think?"

"Well, if you know anything else that might help me locate him and talk some sense into him, let me know."

"Well there is one small thing. You may or may not be aware that he was dating a new chick the weeks before he left. Said her name was Natalie. I think she was his broker."

"Broker!? Huh! That's interesting. Listen—good to talk to you. Thanks for the help. We'll keep in touch."

"Sure thing. Good luck."

Charles hung up the phone and took a sip of his scotch. He looked out from the back porch of his Potomac home, where the water in the pool was gently lapping against the sides. His wife and kids were at his in-laws' house in close-by Avenel, and Charles had the house to himself. Somewhere in this wide world, he thought, Adrian was having the time of his life. Placing another ad in *The International Herald Tribune* would be useless, he thought. Adrian would never stay on the line long enough to get the call traced.

Unless, he figured, he could make the bait tempting enough. He put his scotch down and began writing some ideas on a legal pad.

In the forensic lab at FBI Headquarters, the technicians had confirmed that Adrian's fingerprints, gleaned from multiple locations in his apartment and workplace, were all over the note found in *The Catcher in the Rye*. The fingerprints left on the book itself, as well as on the envelope containing the nine one-hundred- dollar bills Santiago had saved in the drawer at the condo reception desk all matched Adrian's prints. The note had been enlarged and put up on the whiteboard in the area where Thoreau, Locatelli and Mobray were working the case. The three of them sat before the board, putting the pieces together.

It was now clear that M. G. was Max Gimble, F. D. was Francis Devlin and that I. of M. was, without much doubt, the Isle of Man. The case was coming together. There was nothing at that point to indicate that Charles Wren, Clete Shea or Natalie Porter were accomplices in the scheme. With Gimble's prior convictions for forgery, it was apparent that he assisted Wren in obtaining papers good enough to get him out of the country. It was more likely than not that Devlin was just a stooge for Wren, a man whose set-up as a potential collaborator was based on a grudge the attorney did not know Wren had harbored. Styles was a non-entity, as was Warren Tetley.

Mobray sucked his cold, black coffee between his teeth, touched his stomach and addressed Locatelli and Thoreau.

"'The Isle of Man'. Even if we know it to be the place where the money is, it's not going to be easy to find it. Those places hold on to their privacy like a doe holds a fawn. We're going to have to work with Treasury and even the State Department to see what kind of tricks we can pull. In the meantime, there's enough evidence, in my mind, to go to the prosecutors and get a grand jury to issue some indictments. Once that's done, it's time to turn up the heat. Go to the press, Interpol, Scotland Yard directly, and make it difficult or at least uncomfortable for Adrian Wren, or whoever he is since October, to go about his business."

Thoreau pulled her hair back and tied a scrunchy around the tail.

"Chief, what if the money's been moved? He's smart enough to do that."

"Yes, he is. But first things first. Once we can squeeze the Manx cat as tight as we can, maybe it'll howl. There are paper trails to these things, you know. But let me talk to Treasury and State, and I'd like you and Locatelli to get our legal people in touch with the right prosecutors to get the ball rolling. I'll get Wiggins to get on Interpol and Scotland Yard. Oh, and another thing: we need to see the passenger manifests from the day Santiago the doorman saw Wren leaving for his "business trip" last October. His three likeliest air options, as you know, were evening flights from Dulles or BWI out of the country, probably London, or Reagan National to New York, Philly, Boston, Atlanta or Chicago and then out of the country. Get Wallace and Byrd on that. They can cuss me out later.``

Just as the agents were rising from their chairs, Mobray snapped his fingers.

"And get a warrant for a team to bust open Gimble's old apartment. He must have left something behind."

The next day from just outside Bristol, Virginia, Max Gimble took a burner phone and made a call.

"Horace is that you?"

"Max? Where you been?"

"Gone, Horace. Gone. Heat's on, you know. No more Silver Spring and Hyattsville. What can you tell me?"

"FBI's come to talk to me. Asked if I knew Wren, you, and some other folks."

"And?"

"And nothing. Just stuck to the story that I sent Wren to you for your bad back. House-call and all. Denied knowing anything else. They bought it and left. I think you owe me, you bein' gone and all."

"Horace, I think you're right. How does a thousand sound?"

"Two thousand sounds sweeter."

"You always were smart, Horace. Let's split the difference and make it 1500. Deal?"

"You the man, Max. I just know the man. 1500's a deal."

"I'll get a friend in LA to pop it in the mail. Don't want any tell-tale postmarks, ya know."

"True that, Max. Oh, and Max, I'm done referring docs, understand? Can't go back in, you know."

"I understand Horace. You take care."

Gimble looked out on the rolling lawn beneath his cabin, a glass of Wild Turkey on ice in his hand, a cigar resting on the edge of the rocker's arm. He ran his thick fingers through the oily coat of his golden retriever. "Nice Winnie, nice Winnie. Now, go get me my slippers…"

Mobray was able to get Interpol, as well as Scotland Yard, involved. He had a dossier sent out, complete with Wren's most recent hospital photo ID, fingerprints, and information on stateside banking and brokerage relationships. The Department of Justice was equally helpful; federal judges from the District of Columbia and Maryland charged Wren in absentia with bank fraud, insider trading, mail fraud and a handful of other federal crimes. The review of passenger manifests from the day Wren disappeared was long and tedious, and the combing through thousands of names, nationalities and passport numbers was going to take time.

The decision had been made from offices higher than Mobray's that, since Wren had been gone now more than eight months and millions of dollars of illegally gotten money was at stake, it was time to start pressuring the runaway doctor. A senior FBI official leaked to the press the basics of the story, and Mobray had given an interview to CNN, ABC News and other major media outlets regarding the details of what was now being referred to as "The Case of the Deadbeat Doctor." The press ate it up. *People Magazine, Time, The Economist, The National Enquirer,* as well as *The Washington Post, The New York Times, Barron's* and *The Wall Street Journal* had taken the story and run with it. There were ugly rumors that Natalie Patricia Porter, the attractive blond broker, had been complicit in the doings, as might have been the slick K Street lawyer, Francis Devlin. There were news trucks outside Adrian's parent's house in Delray Beach, Florida. The senior Wrens had their whole existence disrupted. They called Charles for advice who, as well, was being besieged at home and at his office with questions about his brother's motives and disappearance. Even Clete Shea's link to the SEC was called into question.

Something had to be done to take the heat off Adrian's family, and that attempt started with a meeting arranged between Charles and the FBI. Charles was told in a June conference at FBI headquarters with Mobray, Thoreau, Locatelli that the most promising way for him to assist in getting the press off his family's back was to lure Adrian into another phone call. Charles began, "You know from the letter Adrian wrote to my parents the means he wanted to use to communicate in case of emergency. But, the problem is, he must be using a burner phone. He's too smart not to.

Mobray nodded to Thoreau, who said, "Mr. Wren, we appreciate your cooperation and assistance in helping to catch your brother. We too believe that Dr. Wren uses burner phones. But that does not necessarily mean we can't locate him, roughly at least. You see, I'm sure you've heard the term "triangulation." And while we can't exactly trace from where the call emanates, by synching the call with simultaneous signals from two nearby cell towers, we can deduce the approximate location of the call. That way, we'll at least get a general sense of where he is, so we can concentrate our efforts there."

Charles leaned forward in his chair and wiped the grit from the inside corners of his eyes.

"Do you want me to place the notice?"

Locatelli answered, "Yes, but we'll write it. The next odd Saturday is three days from now. We will set up a trace on your office phone and mobile. "

Locatelli handed Charles a typed sheet of paper. It read, "The Officers of Gail Force Holdings will be holding a special sharehold-er's meeting on Monday, June 15th at 10 am at its headquarters. All interested parties are asked to contact Charles Wren, Esquire, at 240 300 9700 extension 100 with any questions."

Charles was told the FBI would send technicians to his office that afternoon to set up the trace. He was issued a new phone with his mobile number. Charles was to place the ad the next afternoon.

On Monday morning, June 15th, at 10:15 am Charles' office phone rang. Charles kept Adrian on the line for as long as he could, telling him how upset his parents were and how he might mitigate his legal troubles by turning himself in. Adrian would have none of it. Charles kept his brother on the line long enough for the tech-nicians to triangulate coordinates—Adrian was now somewhere between Gibraltar and Malaga, Spain. The agents called Mobray. Technician Austin White told his chief the approximate where-abouts of the call.

Mobray was elated. Two hours later, at 12:15 pm, Thoreau and Locatelli sat at the conference table. Mobray said, "He's on the southern Spanish coast. I'm contacting our International Operations Division and legat in Madrid. I want the two of you on a plane tonight. Our legat in Madrid is Mercedes Soler. As our legal attaché in Spain, she will have already coordinated with Interpol and Spanish Police re what we know about Wren, where he's likely to go next and how. We've also been authorized to issue a reward of $300,000 for his capture."

Locatelli and Thoreau glanced at each other with a "are you shitting me?" look. But both had worked for the Agency long enough to know how things worked. Mobray said, "Your flight is from Dulles at 8. Here are your tickets and instructions. You are to meet Soler in our Madrid office at 3 pm tomorrow afternoon. You arrive in Madrid at 9:30 am. That will be enough time for you to get to your hotel, take a rest and change. Your car leaves here for Dulles at 4:30. That leaves you ample time to prepare on the flight. Here are some pills that you can take, if you need them, at 11 pm tonight so you get some sleep on the flight."

He handed each of them their dossiers and travelling papers, as well as blister packs of sleeping medication.

"Any questions?"

Locatelli said, smiling, "No Chief. Just wondering how Dana and I got so lucky…"

Pete Locatelli went back to his home in Alexandria and told his wife not to expect him back for a few days.

Dana Thoreau went back home to her cats to gather her things and set the feeding timer for the next few days. She called her ex-Marine boyfriend and left a message on his voicemail: "Dinner's off tonight, gotta go to fucking Spain for a few days! Later."

CHAPTER 12
FALLOUT

In the months leading up to my departure on my sea voyage, I had been following the incredible story of the professional destruction of John Silverstone. President Stanton had been able, for the first time in US history, to sack a sitting Chairman of the Federal Reserve Bank of the United States of America. In what had become a highly politicized move, the president took it upon himself to punish the banking leader; it wasn't without cause. And cause was what he needed.

In my own research that I conducted online after Silverstone's fall, I learned that only the president, under article 10.2 of the Federal Reserve Act of 1935, had the power to oust the chairman from his post for "cause," and Stanton used every weapon in his arsenal to make sure Long John was gone. By instituting his draconian monetary moves the prior October and allegedly abusing the power of his office, Silverstone had crossed the line: he issued inappropriate, politically charged statements from his fiscal bully pulpit and took, in the eyes of the president, actions designed to destabilize the economy and derail any chance of Stanton's retention of the presidency in the next election. And many in Congress, the press and the general public agreed: Silverstone had, by far, crossed the line. Many questioned his sanity, even postulating that it was possibly a stroke or brain tumor that caused him to act so capriciously. In fact, it wasn't until almost a year after Silverstone's momentous gaff that he suddenly lost sight in his left eye. Three days later, after a neurology appointment and an MRI at Georgetown University Medical Center, it was announced to the press that the former Fed chair had been diagnosed with multiple sclerosis, and had quite likely suffered from the initial signs of that disease that fateful October morning.

By April, President Stanton had used his clout to enlist members of Congress, as well as Cabinet members, to his cause. By the time I left the Azores and was off the coast of southern Spain, Silverstone was history and it did not take long for the Senate to confirm a new Fed Chair from one of the existing Fed Board of Governors. In a matter of months, one of the most powerful men in the world was out of a job, ridiculed and marginalized. It was a spectacular descent.

I could not possibly have known at the time that the very actions that led to Silverstone's demise ran parallel to efforts to catch and punish me, for no less than the FBI, the SEC, the U.S. Marshall's Service and a growing force of international intelligence and policing agencies were on my trail. My first inkling of this came as a rude shock I received in Cartagena, Spain in the third week of June. I was enjoying a beer along the waterfront with a young woman from New Zealand when I got up to use the restroom. On the way back to my table I saw a man reading a copy of the tabloid paper *World Wide Witness*. On the front page was my picture, below a headline that read "Wren Flies the Coop with Millions." I felt like I was going to throw up. I got up, apologized to the woman that an emergency had arisen and left her sitting, mouth open.

I immediately went to the closest newsstand and bought a copy. With sweating palms and trembling fingers, I sat on a park bench and read with growing apprehension about my escapades; how I had abused my power and trust as a physician for personal gain, how I devised an elaborate scheme, using my friend at the SEC, an alleged girlfriend at a brokerage firm, a former ex-con patient and possibly my own attorney brother to abscond with millions of dollars. Some people, the article went on, even expressed the thought that I was involved in some larger conspiracy to ruin President Stanton's election in November or wreck the career of a formerly well-regarded Fed chairman. Or both.

The picture in the article was a reproduction of my Hamilton photo ID. There I was, clean shaven, short haired and smiling, in my scrub top and without glasses. I was described in the article as, according to witnesses and unnamed sources, a "smooth-talking charmer" who "made a habit of using people and discarding them like so much tissue paper." The article outlined the steps that had been taken thus far to catch me. The FBI, according to "undisclosed sources," had sent a team of agents to southern Europe to scour the region, coordinating with Interpol and local authorities in "concentrated efforts." Worst of all, the article mentioned my parents, who were quoted as being "devastated" by the events.

Then the shitstorm reached an apex: the article closed by mentioning the $300,000 reward for my apprehension and conviction. A shock of electricity ran through me. For an instant, I thought that Charlie might have been right. Maybe I didn't consider the gravity and enormity of what I had done. Maybe I was the conniving monster portrayed in the article. Maybe I deserve to be caught and punished for using my friends, business associates and patients, for God's sake, to achieve my selfish and hedonistic ends.

I crumpled the paper in tight fists, the ink staining my drenched palms. I looked around to see if anyone was watching me. Indeed, suddenly it was as if everyone was staring at me. I looked all around me—out onto the waterfront, behind me in the park, at the bar to my left and over at the mini-market to my right where I had bought the paper—with an uncomfortable suspicion and urgency that had been nonexistent merely an hour before. My entire life, it seemed, had changed in the passage of mere minutes. I was frozen, unsure about what to do first. My thoughts raced. Do I turn myself in? Try to cut a deal? Ditch my crew and ship? Call my parents? Call Charlie? Call Natalie? My heart beat faster, my breaths quickening. I broke out into a cold sweat. I decided to lie down on the bench, the crumpled paper still in my hands, and concentrate on my breathing. A seven count on the inhale and an eleven count on the exhale. I did this for three minutes, but it seemed like a decade. I got back to a sitting position, hoping to feel calmer, but I didn't.

With a new-found vertigo, I looked at my watch. It was 3:20 in the afternoon. I arose on trembling legs, threw the crumpled paper into the nearest trash receptacle, and leaned against a railing. A passing man asked me in Spanish if I was alright. I told him everything was fine. I started my walk back to the ship, about a mile's distance, my mind a jumble of images, none of them good. Then I stopped in mid-stride and made a conscious effort to reason things out. I told myself that all tabloid newspapers were sensational and unreliable. That exaggeration was the norm in their reporting. Besides, my crimes were not violent; no one had been harmed physically. And in the scheme of things, why would the FBI and other agencies, who were busy catching violent criminals and preventing terrorist attacks, throw immense and expensive efforts at me? I was small potatoes in the grand scheme of things.

Then I deluded myself into thinking that perhaps my ex-wife, that bitch Katherine, concocted this whole story and sold it to the tabloids. That's right she was pissed-off and full of revenge because I had stopped paying alimonyand was trying to capitalize on my disappearance.

Suddenly, I was feeling a little better. My dizziness abated and my legs felt stronger as my stride grew more confident and energetic. I began reflecting on my wealth, my cunning and my skills. I was still worth almost 13 million dollars, was I not? I still commanded a yacht and crew. My wits had enabled me to realize what 99.999% of human beings could only dream of. I had a new identity, with new papers, a new look and new history. My chances of being caught, with my long hair, beard, glasses, hat, and workable Spanish identity were so remote as to be laughable.

I returned to the Gail Force Winds at 4 pm to find Michael and Colin above deck, putting away some engine tools. Colin addressed me.

"Nice lunch, Captain Juan?"

"It was Colin. Thanks. Whose night off is it?"

Michael stepped forward.

"Mine, Captain. I have my eye on a jazz club, the Blue Alley."

I tried my best to avoid eye contact with the men, but the more I did so the more inquisitive they seemed. Colin asked

"Somethin' wrong, Captain? You look a little pale."

I blurted out, "I think I might have caught a bad prawn at lunch. I think I'll go lie down and take a rest. Mike, have a good time."

I felt their eyes follow me across the deck. The silence was awkward. I turned to them before heading below and said, without much thought

"We shove off tomorrow. Early. 8 am. I'll give you details in the morning."

The men looked at each other and then back at me. They knew something was not right. I just hoped they had thought it was a prawn.

Back in my cabin, I took out my map, a pad of paper and a pencil. Tapping my pencil on the map, I ran my eyes over the North African coastline. I swallowed and dug the eraser into the first "o" in Morocco. I raised my head, looked straight ahead, and told myself the truth: my former wife didn't sell any story to the tabloids, the FBI was not disinterested in me and it didn't matter whether my actions had physically harmed anyone. The truth was that I was now in deep shit from my own deeds. The concentrated efforts of law enforcement, despite my forged passport and changed appearance, would likely catch up to me. Reason told me that they almost always do. I knew then I needed to make a radical shift in my plans.

After debating the options in my head, I concluded that I had two choices: negotiate a deal with US authorities or get myself to a country with no extradition agreement with The United States. The former meant all my wealth and dreams of independence would be dashed. The latter allowed me to maintain my new-found wealth, but at a price. I'd always be looking over my shoulder, worrying if the next person around the corner was there to cause me trouble.

My two best immediate options for non-extradition nations were relatively close: Algeria and Morocco. I knew that because I had compiled a list last October for just such a contingency and stored it underneath a flap inside my shaving kit. Other than Northern Cypress, Lebanon and Saudi Arabia, there were no other viable choices accessible from my location. I chose Morocco for many reasons: a relatively stable government under its monarch, Mohammed the Sixth, a modern banking and financial system, religious tolerance and, because of its former colonization by the French, an eye for fine cuisine and alcohol. Morocco, with its vibrant cities, beautiful beaches, deserts and mountains and cosmopolitan nature was the right choice. Also, I'd seen the country before.

With such a place to spend my wealth, there was no way I was going to turn myself in.

I came above deck and asked Colin and Michael to sit down.

"Colin, I'll start preparing dinner. We shove off for Morocco in the morning. Mike, that means you must be ready to go early. Clear? "

"Aye. Always wanted to see that place, Captain. Heard many stories."

"Yes, I know it well enough. Spent three weeks there during college. Alright Mike, off you go. Don't stay out too late. Colin, I'm heading to the market for dinner. Any requests?"

"We haven't done steak in two weeks."

"Steak it is. And salad. And fruit and cheese for dessert. "

Michael and I left the ship, him turning right and I left off the dock. I headed to the outdoor market near the collection of bars and cafes off the waterfront. It was nearing the end of siesta and things were starting to get busy. Passing a group of American tourists nearing the market, I sensed their collective eyes crawling over me. I pulled the brim of my cap over my brow and kept my head down. I caught a snippet of conversation from the fat lady in the group, who said in a Southern twang

"…and they said it was a lot of money! Imagine, leaving your family and friends behind like that! And a doctor, too!"

The group passed by and I hurried to do my shopping, my insecurities growing again. Walking past The Anvil English Pub I glimpsed into the bar, where many patrons were sitting, chatting, and watching the soccer matches on television above the bar. I saw the New Zealand woman, Carol, sitting on a barstool, drinking some wine, and trying to ignore the man to her left. I started to walk in but, hesitating, thought better of it. Then I saw it.

Between periods in the soccer match the bartender had switched the channel to Sky News. There was my face, for the world to see, on the right of the screen, above a caption that read,

"FBI Seeks New Leads in Case of Missing Doctor"

I stepped into the back shadow of the bar, well behind the counter and looked up, like the rest of the patrons, at the screen. The commentator said, "In a developing story of the American doctor who apparently acted on inside information after treating former American Federal Reserve Chairman John Silverstone, the FBI has announced a $300,000 reward for the apprehension and successful prosecution of this man, Dr. Adrian Wren. Wren has not been seen since last October, when it is believed he fled the United States with almost $13 million in funds that were accrued after trading in stocks on information learned from his encounter with Chairman Silverstone. Anyone with information regarding Dr. Wren's whereabouts are encouraged to call the toll-free number at the bottom of our screen.

In continuing news, the American Secretary of State…"

The continuing words were drowned out by the pounding of my pulse in my head. I pulled the brim of my cap down further over my brow and, careful not to catch the eye of Carol, hurried out of the bar. I didn't know what to do next. Do I shop for dinner or just rush back to my cabin and think this out? I caught view of myself in the mirror in a window of a dress shop. There I was: long haired, heavy bearded, clunky-thick black glasses over my eyes and a mangy old baseball cap on my head. Even I had to admit, in my simmering state, that I looked nothing like I did eight months before in Washington.

I sat on a bench next to an ice cream shop and tried to calm myself. If I don't shop for dinner, I thought, and returned empty handed, Colin will wonder why. And arousing anyone's suspicions at this point, I reasoned, was not a good idea. I got up and looked again into the shop window mirror. My face was paler than I'd ever seen it. I pinched my cheeks to redden them up, looked around, and started towards the market.

After my shopping, I returned to the ship, the whole while keeping my head down and my cap-brim close to my forehead. Colin was setting the galley table. With a voice that was being commandeered by an odd, fluttering falsetto, I got out the words

"Just going to get these steaks seasoned. Won't be a minute. S-see if you can get the grill going. And also, I'll get these veggies washed. "

"Aye, Captain." Colin looked over at me and said, "Captain, can you even see with your hat pulled so far down your face?"

I tried to keep my increasingly unsteady hands from his view. "Trying to avoid this woman I met last night. New Zealander. The clingy type."

" I see."

I took the steaks out of the brown paper wrapping paper and laid them on the cutting board. I cut the fat from around the edges, sprinkled some salt and pepper over them and laid them aside. I put the vegetables in a colander and washed them with cold water. I snapped my fingers, reached into the fridge, and opened a bottle of cold vinho verde, left over from our time in Portugal. I poured myself a suspiciously large amount of wine in a wine glass and took a big gulp. I raised my head to find Colin staring at me. I said

"W-would you like a glass?"

CHAPTER 13
MADRID AND THE SOUTHERN COAST

An unrelenting heat wave had settled over Europe that early summer, and Spain was getting hammered. By the time Agents Thoreau and Locatelli, their suits drenched in sweat, arrived at legat Soler's office, the temperature had risen to 96 degrees, with a heat index of 104. Once on the 5th floor of Soler's building, they were greeted with a merciful blast of cold air from the legat's air-conditioned office. Soler, short, 50-ish, plump, dark-haired and all business, directed them to a conference room.

Soler began.

"I trust the heat is no different than in Washington? I hear it can be brutal there, as well. The 'swamp', I believe they call it? Anyway, let's get to it. The call that was traced to Dr. Wren put him on our southern coast as of a few days ago. But since you left

Washington there have been new developments. One of our profilers came across this."

Soler slid a folder containing a thin stack of papers over to the two agents. It was a manifest of ship registries that had been collected in The United Kingdom and Europe in the past few months. There were hundreds of names on the list, but on page 3 there was one row highlighted in yellow: Douglas, Isle of Man; Viking Princess. Gail Force Winds. Gail Force Holdings Ltd., April 22, 2024.

Locatelli looked at Thoreau, and she back. Thoreau said, to no one in particular

"Gail Force Holdings. That's the name of the company that was formed in Wyoming, and the same name on the Titus/Dixon corporate account. Littleton's account and Devlin and Littleton's company."

Locatelli interjected.

"You mean Wren's company, with Littleton and Devlin as the frontor as the patsies."

Locatelli looked over at Soler and leaned forward in his chair.

"How in the world did you get this information?"

Soler smiled.

"We have an agent here with, shall I say, 'no life'. By that I mean he gets his entertainment swimming in suspect profiles. It's like a pool to him. An ocean, even. He finds it comforting, even refreshing. Anyway, our agent Torres constructed an algorithm of Wren's interests, activities, and talents. The short of it is he ran a cross-reference search using information ranging from Wren's social media habits to his hobbies to his family member's names to his associates to the clues in the case thus far. Don't ask me exactly how he does it but, believe me, he does it. The Titus/Dixon account, his late sister's name, Wren's personality, his postings on Facebook and Twitter—all information forwarded in his file and dissected by Torres—and the most recent ship registries, got us to the name of this ship."

Thoreau sat back in amazement. She said to Soler, "You said 'Wren's personality'. What bearing did that have on Torres's search?"

"That's the incredible part, I think. Torres has Wren pegged as a guy who's intensely loyal, especially to the memory of his late sister. There were no less than 32 total references to Gail Wren on Wren's Facebook feed. It seemed that every year on her birthday, and on the anniversary date of her death, he posted comments, more like lamentations, and videos of some of her concert performances. His musings lead one to believe that he was unusually close to his younger sister, and the tone of some of his postings were tell-tale, according to Torres."

Thoreau shook her head.

"'Tell-tale' about what?"

"Well, for one thing, there's a certain anger, according to Torres, that comes across in many of the postings. Some of them border on the literal, while others just plainly are so. A bitterness that pervades the remembrances: it's almost like he's saying, 'What kind of God could take away such a beautiful talent?' or 'My patients slowly kill themselves with bad habits while Gail, who never did anything wrong in her life, gets robbed from us with a cruel cancer.' That kind of stuff."

"So all this led Torres to The Gail Force Winds. Astounding. That's remarkable police work."

"We think so. And, given that Wren is on our southern coast-line, as of a day or two ago, his ship is likely somewhere in that area as we speak. The coastal patrol of the Civil Guard has been alerted and is searching the area now. We've alerted the Civil Guard units and Spanish Navy in Gibraltar, as well, and put out a request for assistance from the Moroccans. But we don't count on them: they still think that most of The Straits are theirs, as well as Ceuta, which, by the way, Spain has owned since 1668."

Locatelli asked, "Has Washington been made aware of these findings?"

Soler clicked her tongue.

"Of course, Agent Locatelli. While you were freshening up in your hotel this morning. Mr. Mobray is up to date. And oh, has he not told you?"

Thoreau and Locatelli gave each other a "what now?" look.

"Your plane to Malaga leaves tonight at 8:15. Captain Lorca of the Civil Guard will have you picked up from there. His people will direct you to your hotel, and tomorrow you will meet with Lorca to assist the Agency in its search. Any questions?"

The agents registered a resigned look between them. Soler concluded, "And another thing. You must know what Torres thought was important: Wren is fluent in Spanish, so he may be attempting to impersonate a Spanish national. Also, Wren spent an extended time in his younger years travelling through Morocco. We feel he is likely to take refuge there. We have, as you may be aware, no extradition arrangements with that country. That makes it a particularly attractive target destination for him."

Locatelli and Thoreau returned to their hotel and got their bags together. In the car on the way to the airport, after grumbling and complaining about the whims of The Bureau and their last-minute schedule changes, they discussed Wren's likely next moves and the probabilities that he was in fact on the Gail Force Winds and in the area of Malaga. Locatelli feared that this might end up another dead-end, with Wren either not on the ship or with no intention of heading to Morocco. The Mediterranean was too big a pond, he thought. There were too many other places for Wren to disappear, both inland and by water. Also, Wren was perhaps too smart to head for a place he knew the authorities were, in their research, wise to. Morocco was, albeit briefly, a part of Wren's travelling past. Still, Locatelli thought, Wren could be close enough to make a dash for it. If Wren was as close as Marbella by now, the Moroccan coastal area of Ceuta was a short hop.

The Spanish jet touched down with Locatelli and Thoreau on board in Malaga at 9:30 pm. They were in their hotel by 10:30 and Locatelli was asleep by 11. Not Thoreau. She looked over Wren's file, a tumbler filled with two-fingers of minibar scotch in her hand, with the valuable information that Torres had collected. Examining Wren's hospital ID photo, reviewing the extensive training he had had on the water, she convinced herself that he was indeed on the Gail Force Winds. Why go to the expense and trouble of buying and registering the boat if he wasn't going to use it? Also, with the doctor's travel history, she felt there was no coincidence between Wren's last known location and his proximity to Morocco, a country that afforded a newly wealthy man like Wren untold opportunities for luxury and the exotic. Sure, he could have ventured to Algeria, but that was unlikely. Too unstable and not wealthy enough. Tunisia and Egypt were out of the question. Tunisia's too poor and backward, and Egypt too unstable. No, it had to be Morocco.

At 11:15 she got a text from Mobray in Washington, which was cc'd to the sleeping Locatelli. A German university student, Petra Richter-Haaser, had met a man weeks ago in the Azores who fit the description of Wren and reported it to authorities. She had seen a news report on television about Wren and was confident it was he. More importantly, the student confirmed that she had seen Wren on The Gail Force Winds and spent time with him on the boat. An attachment to the text included a composite made using Wren's photo and the enhancements as described by the German student: long hair, thick beard, glasses, and a baseball cap.

The next morning at breakfast Thoreau handed a copy of the composite, printed from the hotel's business center earlier that morning, to Locatelli. She said, in between bites of her toast, "This is what our friend probably looks like now. I'd never pick him out on a street corner."

Locatelli gave the composite the once over and agreed. "That is an ongoing problem. He's smart and has talents. Problem is, for him, he'd need a crew of some sort to float a ship that size around. He's likely not travelling alone. And that means, sooner or later, the person or persons he's travelling with, if he wants to run fast and out of suspicion, will have to be jettisoned. That's not always easy. I'm not sure Wren is the liquidating type. He doesn't strike me as a killer. He's never been violent, as far as we know. But once he's alone, things will start to happen. You'll see."

Thoreau took one last gulp of her coffee and the two made their way to the hotel reception area, where one of Lorca's men was waiting. The Civil Guard station was a mere ten minutes away. Once there, Captain Enrique Lorca greeted them and directed them to his office. Thoreau was struck by him. Here stood the most handsome man she had ever put eyes on. Lorca was just over 6 feet tall, had piercing brown eyes and a mane of brown hair, with blond highlights, swept back over his high forehead. Under his uniform, Thoreau surmised, lay a body of chiseled muscle. His features were perfectly symmetrical, with an aquiline nose that sat poised over a perfect set of lips and a slightly cleft chin. He was the kind of man who might seem to wear a perpetual 5 o'clock shadow. His posture was that of a dancer. He smelled like rich tobacco. Locatelli took note of Thoreau's reaction and subtly stuck an elbow in his partner's rib as they sat down. Lorca began, "May I offer you some coffee? Something to eat, perhaps?"

Locatelli declined for them both and began the discussion.

"We understand that you have put out alerts for Dr. Wren's boat, the Gail Force Winds. Here is a composite from Washington of what we believe Wren may look like now. The German girl, Richter-Haaser, gave a description."

Lorca gave a glance over to Thoreau and then back to Locatelli.

"Yes, those alerts have been issued. Our patrols are paying special attention to the docks, harbors and our coastal areas of Malaga and Marbella. We can distribute this composite in those locations as well. We also can send this to our stations just inland in case your subject of interest decides to abandon the sea route. How long does your Agency anticipate your presence here?"

Thoreau smiled and tucked her hair behind her ear.

"We never know. We serve at their pleasure, as I'm sure you do to your superiors. But our job here is to coordinate with you and any other relevant authorities on actions that give us the best chance of apprehending Dr. Wren. You are aware there's a reward on his head?"

"I am. I was surprised that your government, excuse me, the FBI at least, is so intent on his capture. After all, it's just money he stole, is it not? He did not injure or kill anyone, am I correct?"

Locatelli sensed his partner's growing interest in their host. Peter said, "That's true, but our government appears to be taking a, shall I say, atypically intense interest in apprehending him. Perhaps it was the way he gathered and acted on the information he extracted from a top American official that has caused this. Indeed, the honest and smooth function of our capital markets is of vital importance, as I'm sure it is here in Spain. We don't know—we just do as we are told."

After a twenty -minute discussion of logistics and coordination of efforts, the meeting concluded, but not before Thoreau reminded Lorca of the hotel where she and her partner were staying. Looking Lorca in the eye, she stood, extended her hand, and said, "You know where to find us if you need us, Captain."

Lorca turned her hand over and kissed it. Locatelli grabbed his partner by the elbow.

"Thank you, Captain, for your assistance. Agent Thoreau and I will stay in touch. We can show ourselves out."

In the car Peter had words for his partner.

"What was that about? You were practically drooling all over him!"

"I was not drooling! And besides, I am human, you know. Back off, Peter. We've been working this case non-stop since the Agency put us together...You may be past your prime but I'm..."

"Who's past his prime?"

Locatelli smiled at her. He went on

"Alright, alright. I think I know a nice lunch spot; read about it on the plane. I'll take you there after we change. "

I had finished cleaning up the dishes from dinner and brought back to the table the one fourth full bottle of red that was left over from the meal. Colin was picking the remnants of the steak from between his teeth with a toothpick and scratching his stomach. The bottle of Portuguese white, now history, and the red at dinner, had done their job in taking the edge off my nerves. It was getting on 10:30 pm and Michael, I thought, had better be getting back to the ship soon if we were going to set sail early. Colin had told me what he had done in The Royal Navy, which was a seaman specialist navigator. He contrasted his work to Michael's, which was as a member of the Royal Navy Police. In truth, Michael actually outranked him, a fact of which Mike frequently liked to remind his countryman.

Colin started to steer the discussion to my alleged days spent in California and, before I went on about it, I was careful to ask him if he had ever visited. He said he had not. I trusted him. With that, I was able to comfortably spin more bullshit about how my father started in the wine business, how he taught me everything he knew about winemaking and my exciting life as a youth in California. I surprised even myself with the depth and breadth of the nonsense I could spew. Evidently, I was a proficient surfer, owned a green VW beetle when I got my license and had a tall, blond California girlfriend when I was 17.

By 11:30 I was in my cabin and heard someone step onto the deck. I spied Michael in the crack of the door jamb, a smile on his face and heading to his quarters. I was feeling much better than I had earlier that afternoon, confident in my plan. My money was plentiful and easily accessible, I told myself. My disguise was solid, my ship fast enough to make it to Marina Smir, just south of Ceuta, to get out of international waters and do what I had to do. That included telling the crew that their services, once I was safely in Morocco, were no longer needed. If I provided them with a generous bonus and travel funds to get back to The Isle of Man, I reasoned, they'd go without too much fuss. Then I'd be free to set myself up in the country I had grown to love from a time long ago. My priority was to get out of Europe as soon and as quietly as I could.

Before retiring, I logged into my Crown Bank account and checked my balance. Mr. Juan de Nebra, of 127 Foster St, flat #4, Douglas, had on deposit 12,333,822.77. I logged off, brushed my teeth, and turned out the light, my alarm set for 6 am.

CHAPTER 14
ELECTION YEAR

President Stanton looked out on the green lawn of the White House from the Oval Office. The Democratic National Convention was less than two months away, and polls had indicated that his race against Republican challenger Audrey Toliver, Senator from Nevada, was too close to call. The brawling New Englander, himself no stranger to bitter political fights, felt up to the challenge from the west. But he was still concerned. At 11 am sharp his campaign team, led by campaign chairman Thomas R. Murray, entered the office, and took their seats, with Murray sitting directly in front of The President.

Stanton began, "You'd better be here to give me good news, Tommy. My stomach's upset this morning."

"Mr. President, all I have is good news. We've secured the endorsement of all the major police groups, including the National Association of Police Organizations. We're close to getting the backing of the automakers and the IBEW. For a Democratic president, you're getting some pretty diverse support. The Association of…"

Stanton leaned back in his chair and put a large, black winged-tipped foot on his desk.

"Tell me something I don't already know, Tommy. "

Stanton had taken over as president when the sitting president had died in office. He was, before becoming vice-president, the Governor of Massachusetts, who ruled on a firmly right-of-center platform in The Bay State. Before serving as governor, he was the Mayor of Boston for four years, and before that, the speaker of the state legislature. Tall and imposing, he cut a very Lyndon Johnson-like presence, his sheer gravitas compelling his minions to do his bidding. Much like LBJ, he twisted all the arms, oiled all the machines, and courted and cajoled all the operatives he needed to affect his will. And he was, like the tall Texan, a very much "in-your-face" politician.

Despite his efforts in civil rights and pay and employment equality for women, he was a proponent of the death penalty, solely from personal experience. Back in the late 1970s, when Stanton was a teenager, his beloved father, Wilson Stanton, had been gunned down during a robbery of the latter's liquor and convenience store in Boston's tough Roxbury section. On a warm and clear night in June of 1979, the future president rode his bike to his dad's store, laying the bicycle in front of the narrow doorway of the establishment as he took off his backpack. Just then, two teenage thieves and killers, the white 19-year old Sean Magrum and the soon to be 16-year old black youth Chet Dalton burst out of the store, guns and money in hand, and tripped over the bicycle. As they regained their footing, Gabriel got a clear look at their faces, enough of a look to later identify them when they were apprehended by Boston City Police.

(Magrum got forty years in prison and Dalton, who was supposed to be tried in Juvenile Court, was tried as an adult and served twenty-five years, after Magrum had confessed to being the shooter.)

After the teens had fled, Gabriel found his bleeding father on the floor behind the register and summoned, with the help of a passer-by, an ambulance, and police. Despite extensive efforts by the Trauma Team to save his father's life, Gabriel Stanton, his mother and his two sisters lost Wilson four hours later in OR 7 of Boston City Hospital's surgical suite. The crime left the junior Stanton forever changed; no matter how liberal he could be on other issues, he was, from that moment, adamant in his support of capital punishment. And the anger over his father's murder had never left him. It seemed only to intensify as the years passed.

President Stanton asked Tommy that morning where things stood in the election regarding his continued support of the death penalty. Although protesting it to be a relatively unimportant campaign issue that season, Murray demurred that support appeared to be rising in the wake of a growing number of high -profile killings in the recent years. One particularly heinous incident had taken place in New Jersey a mere two years before where a man had killed his wife and four young children while they slept and then attempted to throw their bodies from a lifeboat into the sea off of Barnegat Point. He presently sat awaiting execution on New Jersey's death row, made possible by the governor's overturning of a 2007 law in that state that ensured the last person to have been executed there was, and remained, in 1963. His appeals and legal maneuverings were making national and international news, and Stanton bristled at it. But what angered the president almost as much as the killing itself was the growing news coverage of botched executions.

There appeared to be little progress made since the series of mangled executions in Arkansas in 2015. The medical profession, the very people best equipped to deal with the administration of lethal injections, would still have nothing to do with it. And Stanton knew he could not compel doctors to participate. So too with the drug companies, who supplied many of the pharmaceutical ingredients necessary to carry out the task. Even the European Union instituted an export ban. Stanton wasted his leverage on them, he thought. All his efforts in Congress, in meetings with governors, trade organizations and even secret liaisons with representatives of the manufacturers themselves, had come to nothing. It didn't help that the papers and advocacy groups continued with their steady stream of "propaganda," as the president called it, from states as diverse and geographically distinct as California, Florida, Missouri and Oklahoma. To anyone who would listen, Stanton loved to point out that even the $800,000 San Quentin facility for lethal injection remained dormant due to that state court's ruling that the California Department of Corrections and Rehabilitation ran afoul of the California Administrative Procedure Act when it tried to block oversight into new lethal injection methods.

Stanton was stymied. He knew he could not bulldoze his way on this issue. Not at least, until the "cruel and unusual" nature of the punishment, as so many death-row inmates and so many papers and other media venues had portrayed it, was altered. There had to be some way around this one, he thought. He could not have known at the time that his eventual answer was, incredibly, thousands of miles away in the form of a fugitive on Europe's southern coast.

My first draw of presidential attention came a mere four days after Stanton's Oval Office meeting with his campaign manager. President Stanton had taken the day off and had booked a tee time at Burning Tree Country Club, a mere two miles from where I had grown up, for 9 am. There, along with Governor Price of Texas and

Senators Tillman of Georgia and Brewster of Alaska, they enjoyed a round on the rolling hills and manicured fairways in unusually mild weather for that time of year in Bethesda. With Secret Service riding along, they concluded their round at 12:15 and headed for the clubhouse, which had been closed for their private use.

Over Bloody Marys, beers and BLTs, the politicians had told war stories and joked. By 2:45 pm the senators and the governor made the excuses that time was running late and signaled for their respective cars to be brought around. Stanton, despite the disparaging looks of the Secret Service agent in charge, ordered himself a third Bloody Mary and scanned the day's paper. Eagerly accepting the drink from the waiter, the president growled to no one in particular, "I wanna read the goddamn paper like any other American male on a Saturday afternoon!" On the Sports page, the Nats were making a mid-season run for the NL East, and the Dc football team was due to open camp in a few weeks. On the Style Page, to which the president gave a cursory glance, the Real Housewives of Potomac were at it again. The president balled up that section in a tight spheroid and tossed it to the floor next to his seat, loudly sucking the bacon remnants of his sandwich between his back teeth. He took a quick look at Metro, flipped to the obituaries, took a gulp of his drink and loudly chewed on the liquor-infused stalk of celery. Turning next to the main section of *The Post*, he saw a story below the fold that caught his eye. The Headline Read: "Authorities Closing in On Runaway Doctor." He began reading the body of the article.

"FBI and other domestic and international law-enforcement officials stated yesterday that they are confident about the imminent apprehension of Adrian Wren, MD, the DC anesthesiologist who last autumn appeared to have acted on inside information from his then patient and former Chairman of the Federal Reserve Bank

Jonathan Silverstone and realized millions of dollars in stock gains. Agent Charles Mobray of the Washington office of the FBI stated that Wren, a former long - time member of the Anesthesiology Department at Hamilton Memorial Hospital in Northwest Washington, had been last sighted in the Azores Island Archipelago and had been traced, from phone communication analysis, to Spain's southern coast. He is thought to be travelling in that area aboard his 55 -foot yacht the Gail Force Winds, a Viking Princess make that had been previously registered in The Isle of Man."

The president put the paper down and stared into the red-flecked tomato juice debris on the ice in his drink. He scratched the back of his head and sat silent for a full two minutes. He looked around, caught the attention of his agent, and blurted, "Get me Charles Mobray of the DC office of the FBI on the phone—now!"

It took a full thirty minutes to get Mobray on the line, for he had left his DC office at 11:30 that morning to attend his son's baseball game at Landon Summer Day Camp in Bethesda that afternoon. By the time the surprised agent got on the phone with his president, it was the bottom of the seventh inning, and he was out of breath.

"Yes, Mr. President? You wanted to speak with me?"

"Yes, listen Mr. Mobray…by the way, have we met before?"

"Uh, I don't believe so, Mr. President."

Mobray suddenly felt as if his own voice was coming from one of those old tape recordings between American presidents and any number of official Washington underlings, of the kind one might hear on documentary TV shows.

"Anyway, about this Dr. Wren thing…"

"Yes, sir? I'm surprised you are familiar with that …"

"How close are you folks to catching this fella?"

"Well, Mr. President, from our agents on the ground and the

assistance of the local authorities, The Spanish Civil Guard and Interpol and so on…"

The President barked, "How close, Mr. Mobray!?"

"Well, sir, I'd say days; a week at the most."

"Well when you do get him, the instant you get him, I want to hear from you. Got it? You call me, I'll be sure you get through. Is that clear?"

"Why yes, Mr. President, it is. But may I ask why…"

Mobray regretted the words as he spoke them.

"No. You just be sure I talk to you the moment Wren is taken into custody."

"Yes, Mr. President, I will sir. Is there anything else?"

"No. Enjoy your weekend."

"Thank you, Mr. …."

The line had already gone dead.

Mobray stood in the Landon bleachers, holding his cell phone like it was a slimy fish. He looked back among the moms and dads in the stands, who were oblivious to the fact that the man sitting next to them had just been on the phone with the world's most powerful person.

Mobray stepped away from the noise of the game and called Thoreau. It was six hours later in Spain meaning 10 pm in Europe. Thoreau was startled to see her chief's number light up on her mobile, especially since she was not at her hotel, not with Locatelli and not alone. No, Agent Thoreau was nowhere near her hotel, because she was in Captain Enrique Lorca's seaside condo, half dressed and drinking her second cold glass of cava, as her dark-featured host was lighting a Cuban cigar.

She put her index finger to her mouth and motioned for Lorca to keep quiet. As she brought the phone up to her left ear, the Spaniard placed his large, warm hands around her neck and shoulders and began massaging. Thoreau was frozen in panic.

"Yes chief"?

"Any new developments with Wren? I've just had the strangest phone call."

"Well, chief, the locals are all over it. As I emailed in my report we've got the name of Wren's ship, should he be on it, distributed the composite everywhere he's likely to be or gonna be and Locatelli is working on the contacts we've made to beat the bushes here." She could hardly contain herself from laughing. She continued, "And what strange phone call was that chief?"

"Never mind that for now. I'll fill you in later. Anyway just be sure that…are you alright, Agent Thoreau? It sounds like you're in a tunnel or something. What's that noise?"

Thoreau turned to Lorca and gave him her "how could you!" face, holding the mobile in the crook of her neck while using both hands to remove his hands from her neck. He backed off, sat next to her on the couch and cleared his throat, placing the big toe of his bare foot in the crotch area of her plush bathrobe while he flicked the growing cigar ash into the ashtray.

Her Chief asked again, "What was that noise? "

"Just me moving the chair. It slid along the floor of my hotel room. Yes, my hotel, they have…uh… beautiful hardwood floors here in Spain. You know, uh, Spain is known for, uh, its hardwood flooring."

"Never mind that, Dana! Just keep me closely in this loop. I want to know about any developments, anytime of the day or night. Is that clear?"

"Yes, sir."

"And that goes for Locatelli, too! You tell Peter, tonight. Got it?"

"Yes, sir. Tonight."

"You'd better get some rest, Dana. You sound tired."

"Yes, sir. Rest. Right away. "

She cut the line and Lorca let out a soft chuckle. Dana snapped, "If you weren't so fucking handsome and sexy I'd cut your nuts off."

"Agent, I'd love to see you try. By the way, you're not missing your Marine boyfriend now, are you?"

"Hell no! Not him or the Bureau, for that matter!"

The same Saturday that President Stanton was enjoying his round of golf, Natalie Porter had arranged to meet her friend Evelyn Thatcher for dinner in North West, DC. Thatcher, a mutual friend of fellow University of Maryland alum Ann Desmond, and the daughter of one of the founders of Kelsey, Thatcher and Broome, a DC law firm specializing in lobbying, public relations and other areas relative to the machinery of the federal government, had been one of Natalie's roommates the last two years of their time at school. She had gone on to Georgetown University to get her law degree and was an associate in her father's law firm, which was thick with clients that inhabited the length of K Street, clients whose leases on office space kept the landlords in their Lear jets and condos in St. Bart's.

It was 7 pm when Evelyn found Natalie at Lambrusco, a trendy new bar and restaurant on N Street. The place was just starting to get busy, though not as busy as in fall and spring, due to the town's flight of people to Rehoboth Beach and Ocean City on summer weekends. Back in late fall, the two women had discussed Natalie's excitement at meeting Wren and dating him. Evelyn was married to a man who she met at Georgetown U, a lawyer who was out of town on a golfing trip with his buddies.

"Hey you, long time no see. You look great!"

She gave her friend an air-kiss and sat across from her at the high two-top. After some small talk of marriage, work and the summer, Evelyn started in on a sore subject.

"Can you believe the news about Adrian?"

"Please, don't remind me. I'm just gaining acceptance to the fact that the feds don't suspect me anymore. I still can't believe what they say he's done. "

"Say he's done!? Natalie, you've got to get over him. The evidence seems pretty damning."

Natalie looked over at her friend, who had put on a good 25 pounds since college days. She suddenly appeared much older, too.

"Evelyn, you don't understand. Even if Adrian did half of what they say, he's still the most exciting man I've ever met. And with what I've met in the last six months, I'm beginning to think what he did was not so bad."

"Natalie! He used you!"

Irritated, she said, "Actually no, I "don't see." Why would he call me? Why would he tell me everything was going to work out? True, I only went out with the guy a few times. But I can't help but think that what started as a professional thing, his help with the accounts and all, turned into something else. I don't see him as using me. Just don't see it."

Her voice trailed off as the waiter reappeared. They ordered their dinners.

They drank their drinks in silence. Then Evelyn said brightly, "Anyway, did you know I'll be attending the Democratic National Convention in Los Angeles in August? Our firm is heavy into Stanton's election bid. You want to come? I can probably get you in."

Natalie mulled over the thought of spending a hot week in Los Angeles with K Street lawyers. She looked over at her friend, busy devouring her Caesar Salad, and shifted her mind to the few times she spent with Adrian. No matter what trouble he was in, she thought, it would probably be preferable to where she was in her life right now. Suddenly, she felt like she'd drop it all and find him, somehow, and take on anything that came their way. Her reverie was interrupted by the arrival of her second prosecco.

"You sure you don't want to come? They'll be plenty of single men! "

Natalie could not help but notice the piece of lettuce stuck to the corner of her friend's mouth. With her index finger, she motioned to her. "Um. You've got a little, uh, little lettuce, uh. Yeah. That's it…"

On Tuesday morning President Stanton sat in The Oval Office with his Chief of Staff, fixer and longtime confidant and advisor Izzy Rappaport. Rappaport had grown up with Stanton in the dicey Boston suburbs, near Roxbury and Dorchester, and their parents had been friends. But Rappaport, like Stanton, attended Boston Latin, over on Avenue Louis Pasteur near The Harvard Medical School, instead of public school. His parents had saved enough to get him through; after all, he was an only child. Izzy was devastated when Stanton's father was murdered in the robbery, and he stood by his friend, and his family, in the tough times that followed. Stanton never forgot him for that. The bond that he and the president shared could not be breached.

Izzy took a seat across from the president and took out his notepad. Rappaport had a medium build, dark complexion, and a long thin nose, dark eyes and a full head of black hair. Miraculously, he had not started to grow gray, a fact not lost on his boss who constantly asked him when that process was going to begin.

Stanton told Rappaport about the plan he had formulated over the weekend should Wren be apprehended. It involved leaning on his own Attorney General, Otis Scoggins, not to get involved in any potential prosecution of Wren, in return for Stanton's remaining silent on all the dirt he had on the nation's top law enforcement official. He knew Scoggins and all his weaknesses and was confident that something could be worked out. His idea was to arrange a deal for Wren, once he was caught, to exchange his avoidance of prison for, if it could be secretly structured, a scheme to employ him as the government's executioner for states that use the lethal injection method. After some initial discomfort and wonderment on his old friend's cunning and creativity, Rappaport started to come around.

"Gabe, do you really need this kind of risk?"

"Izzy, you know as well as I do the deals that go on. This is a nothing, in the scheme of things. Besides, if it ever got leaked, which it won't, we'll deny everything. We'll get Wren prosecuted and put away. Look, we're just improving on a service that's already legal. Legal in a lot of states, anyway. Besides, there's no rush. There's not enough time before the election to do anything about this anyway. So, don't worry."

Rappaport gazed across at his boss. "Same old Gabe. Always thinking 'outside the box.'"

Before their meeting concluded, Stanton got to his feet: "One other thing, Izzy. Get Ed Driscoll on the phone. Tell him I want to see him, here, in the Oval Office. See if he can come this week. Or at least next Monday! Tell him we'll fly him in."

Driscoll was a childhood friend of them both of them, a Boston Latin classmate. He was also Chairman of The Department of Anesthesiology at Chappell Memorial in the suburbs of Boston, a private, upscale hospital in Brookline.

"What do you want with Eddie?"

"Got some questions for him, Izzy. Don't worry, I won't leave you out."

CHAPTER 15
TROUBLE

I couldn't fall asleep after Michael returned to the ship. It was already almost midnight and I knew if we were going to get an early start, I'd have to open the "candy-box," my stash of emergency drugs. I located and opened the bottle marked "benzos" and took out a white, scored 2 mg clonazepam, breaking it carefully in half along the straight ridge running the center of the pill. I put it back among the non-narcotic pain killers, antibiotics, and other sundry pharmaceuticals that I'd collected in case of emergency. I took the pill with my bedside water and waited for 30 minutes until the drug washed over me. After a night of vivid dreams, I awoke to the alarm at 5:15, eager to get at the white paint and roller brush I had left over from the ship's renovation.

I had planned to paint over the ship's name the evening before because things were clearly getting too hot for me. It would have been better to do it last night, but with Colin hanging around and

Michael returning at any hour I decided to wait. I opened my cabin door to find the sun just coming up and everyone asleep. I reached into the supply closet next to the galley and got the small can of paint and roller. By 6 am I was done. I figured if the crew had asked me what happened to the name, I would make up something about how I didn't like the name anymore or how I wanted a different style of script or some other nonsense I seemed so able to turn out. I wasn't too concerned about it.

It was about 150 nautical miles to Ceuta, my first stop to refuel and re-stock before heading down to the quieter coastal towns south of there. Once safely in Marina Smir, where we'd be refueled and the galley supplied, I would make the boys a nice dinner, get them happy on some drink and tell them that the plans had changed. Their bonuses and return money to the U.K. added to their normal pay would soften the blow, I reasoned.

I told Colin to take the helm while I went below for a good part of the crossing. I didn't want to take the chance of being spotted by Spanish Navy ships or the marine forces of The Civil Guard. I reckoned with good seas and gunning the engine we could make Ceuta well before nightfall. I was feeling betterbetter about my plan, my money, and my ability to pull this off. Then, the unthinkable happened.

It was about 1 pm when I received a knock on the cabin door. It was Colin telling me that Michael wanted to speak to me above deck. I came out directly and found Michael at the helm. We were in wide water by then and the weather was clear; you could see the distant coastline of North Africa across the straits. My spirits were lifting. Michael called for Colin to take control of the ship and he directed me to the rear, out of sight of Colin. Then he asked me to sit down. I didn't know what to think.

I knew something was amiss by the way Michael had carried

himself earlier in the day. He was unusually fidgety, even for him, and wasn't shaven. That was not like him. He shaved every day. Couldn't stand any stubble of beard, he had confided in me. Just as I was about to speak, he said, "Listen Captain. Let's make this as easy as possible, OK?"

"Make what as easy as…?"

At that juncture, he produced, from the back of his pants tucked under where his shirttail hung, the largest handgun I had ever seen. It was a .44 magnum Smith and Wesson, like Clint Eastwood carried in his *Dirty Harry* days. He pointed its monstrous barrel directly in my face and began saying, in a low voice, "Now listen carefully, Dr. Wren. You're going to be very quiet."

My head snapped. I nodded. I started to say, "But I'm not…"

"Quietly, Doctor. I know exactly who you are. Saw you on the telly last night in town. You're quite famous now, you know?"

"But, like I said, I'm not…"

"Shh. This is what we two are going to do. We're both going above astern where I've arranged something for Colin. You are going with me."

With that he directed me up and we both walked, my heart pounding and my head full of pressure, to where Colin was calmly piloting the ship. In a sing-song voice, Michael said, "Colin, would you stop that engine for a moment?"

I looked around at the open sea. We were entirely alone on a brilliant summer day. Colin cut the engine and came back to us. Michael brandished the gun and the look on Colin's face was, at first, amusement.

"What are you doing with that thing, Mike? Put it away; you'll be liable to…"

Michael interrupted him. In a low, calm voice he said, "Don't ask me questions. Just do as I say."

We swayed, the three of us, out in the open ocean, a few seabirds cawing overhead. The peacefulness of the sea stood in stark contrast as to what was transpiring.

Colin turned to me, as if this were some big joke: "Has he lost his mind?"

Michael pulled the hammer back on the pistol. The sound clipped the air. "Colin, do you see that container next to the ropes there? In it are three days' supply of food and water, a sweater and jacket, plus bedding, a tarp, sunscreen and a medical kit. What you are going to do is take the life raft down, put yourself in the water with the supplies and start heading to your closest bit of land. The captain and I need to be somewhere. Don't ask me questions—this is all for your own good."

Colin looked over at me and then back to our captor. Just as I was about to speak, Michael directed the gun in my face muttering, "Not one more word."

Colin slowly got up and did as Michael said. He was shaking, and had difficulty getting the raft unsecured from the ship. With Michael following with his eyes, Colin took slow, deliberate steps in carrying out the directions. In less than ten minutes he was in the water looking up at us, clearly scared and bewildered, as we left him in the gentle wash of our wake. I was driving the ship, with Michael and the big black gun behind me.

Soon Colin was out of sight. Still consumed with trembling, I stated in a reed-like voice,

"I think you are making a big mistake. I'm not who you…"

"I know exactly who you are, Dr. Wren. I've lived with you for weeks on this ship. There's no mistake. Your hat, hair and beard may have gotten you by, but time is up. We're returning you to Spain, where I'm going to collect a lot of money over you."

Deciding that denial was futile, I thought quickly. If I offered to pay him off, maybe he'd let me go. I offered that up.

He turned me down. "Too risky," he said. He said he'd rather "take the bird in the hand."

"Besides, what am I going to do? Guard you while you go back to Europe to withdraw all that money in some European bank? You'd be recognized before that, and I could be out everything. No, I'll take what I can get here. Now look, shouldn't take us but a few hours to get back to Marbella. When we get there I'll…"

Just then, I decided if I didn't act now, I was through. He was right; we'd be back to southern Spain by night fall. He was standing a mere foot behind me, his left hand holding the .44 and the right clamped on to the polished wood that surrounded the helm. On pure instinct and adrenaline, I wedged my right foot firmly against the corner of the joint between the lower side wall of the helm and the floor and hooked my left foot around the base of the captain's seat. I gunned the engine, turned violently to port, spinning the wheel leftward with both hands. I lurched starboard, securely against the side of the helm's hard plastic interior, as Michael spun to the right, flipping over the partition that separated the helm from the side gully. The nauseating thud of his head hitting the metal guard-rail sounded like the report from an air-rifle. In what appeared to be one horribly choreographed instant, both the .44 and Michael, heels up, went flying into the foaming sea. Instantly I cut the engine, my hands and legs still shaking from the cortisol rush and leaned over the side for any trace of him. In my haste and carelessness, I almost laid my hands on the fresh crimson smear of blood he left, so bright and ugly on the brilliant white surface of the ship's interior edge. After what seemed like a long and desperate search of the opaque waters for any sign of the former Royal Navy sailor, I decided to restart the engines and head back in the direction of where we had left Colin.

It took me about fifteen minutes to find Colin and when I did he wore a look of confusion and astonishment. After I had gotten him, the raft and supplies aboard, I told him Mike went overboard: Mike had gone mad, probably from some repressed PTSD from his time in the navy. My mind worked quickly, spinning new fantasies:

"Mike had confided in me many times, when you had gone ashore, that he'd been bothered by nightmares. He said he was starting to hear voices. Some of the voices, being transmitted from a secret signal installed by The Royal Navy aboard The Gail Force Winds told him that I was an enemy agent, probably a Russian, posing as a Spaniard. It was his job to save you from me, and then turn me over to the authorities in Spain. Just after he left you in the sea, and before we made it a few miles, he abruptly leaned over the side of the ship and shot himself. You can see some of the blood there."

I pointed over to where Michael had hit his head before he careened overboard.

"You know, Colin, I've heard heavy drinkers like Mike are more prone to mental disease."

Panting and wide-eyed, he swallowed the whole story. I told him the best thing for us was to continue to Ceuta, where I would pay him his balance for the summer, a bonus and transit money to return home. "Today's disaster makes me feel like I don't want to continue this voyage" I lied. "I'll contact the authorities and file a police report, since I was witness and privy to all of what happened."

Colin was so shaken that I could have told him anything and he would have done it. Taking control of the ship, I told Colin to go below and take a rest. Take a drink if he needed one. I would take care of everything. Thanking me, he took a bottle of whisky, a glass and went below. I re-charted my course for Morocco, feeling better than I had felt in days. The turbulent events of recent times, I thought, were finally over.

By the time we pulled into the dock in Ceuta the sun was just setting. Colin had come above deck an hour before, still tired and stressed. I sat him down and explained that it would be best if we split up. Before he could register a protest, I handed him a manila envelope full of the money I had taken from my cabin safe. He opened it, and with a pained expression said, "This is more than generous. Are you sure you don't need me to talk to the police with you?"

"No, I saw most of what happened, so I'll handle it. Besides, you've been through a lot. You could have drowned out there in the middle of nowhere. Take your money and find yourself a nice hotel. There are plenty here in town, or just north of here. I'll phone you in a few days once you're back in Douglas. Did Mike have any family you're aware of?"

"He had a sister in Ireland. Elizabeth. Elizabeth Melton, of Ulster, last I heard. That's the only family I heard him speak of. Both his parents are dead."

"I'll see if I can contact her. Or have the police do so."

We said our goodbyes and an enormous sense of relief washed over me. I decided I would try to sell the ship, or just live on it for a while, and use it as a base to find a more suitable residence in Morocco. I'd call my banker in Douglas, transfer some of my funds to a local bank and buy a car. Once I had gotten settled in and esti-mated, using the internet and a search of the press, how the search for me was progressing, I'd likely have a better idea of how much traveling outside the country I might do. Things were suddenly looking up.

I decided I'd write Natalie a letter, and pay a stranger, just in case, to post it for me in another country, just like the Tokyo letter I arranged at Dulles Airport. After a light dinner and a glass of wine, I pulled out some paper and wrote

Dear Natalie,

By now you've no doubt seen me in the news, and from what I've seen and read and heard, the press is painting a pretty accurate picture of what I did. I did use information I gleaned from Silverstone to make a lot of money. So what? I consider it is a victimless crime.

But explaining my "crime" is not why I'm writing. I'm writing to convince you that what I did, and how I structured my plan, had nothing to do with you. You were an innocent bystander. It could have been anybody in your position.

The times we spent together were some of the best I've had in a long while. I think of you often. A lot of the time I wish you were here with me. But I know that's not likely to happen. Not likely, but not impossible.

I'm consolidating my money and starting a new life somewhere where the police can't get me. I see a much better life for myself than in the States. Grinding it out for someone else was just not me. At the risk of sounding arrogant, I'm just too smart to do things the "traditional" way. There's so much more to life, and I intend to find it.

If there is some way for you to see clear to join me, if you want to, I'll figure it out. But I need time; and time is in abundance now.

I hope you understand. I hope you think of me and I hope you want to see me again.

Yours always,
Adrian

I folded the letter and placed it in the envelope. The wine finished, I took a drink of scotch, turned out the light and immediately fell into a deep sleep.

On a Monday morning in early July, Attorney General Scoggins, the first of the President's two meetings that morning, sat across from President Stanton. At the back of the Oval Office sat Izzy Rappaport, scribbling in his notebook. Scoggins was Southern-fried fat boy. A former federal judge in Georgia he had attended The University of Georgia as an undergrad, majoring in political science, and went on to Emory's law school, where he wrote for the law review. After law school, he took a position as in-house counsel for the Coca-Cola Company, spending almost twenty years in that capacity. He was nominated and confirmed as Attorney General by Stanton after serving in the Georgia statehouse.

Sweating and looking back at the calm Rappaport, Scoggins crossed one stubby leg over the other, grabbing his pasty-white calf in the area where his sock hadn't covered it, and listened as the president dropped uncomfortable hints about Scoggins's checkered past. He made oblique references to the affair Scoggins was carrying on with one of his office staff, the no interest loan he had received when he was briefly in the Georgia state legislature and the ridiculously low rent he was paying for his daughter in the U Street corridor apartment she rented. Scoggins twisted and squirmed, dabbing his brow with a white handkerchief from his breast pocket, as the president droned on and concluded

"Now, Otis, I have something I need you to take care of, if the situation arises."

Otis gave an awkward smile, uncrossed his leg and shifted forward in his chair.

"How can I help you, Mr. President?"

Stanton smiled and took a sip of his iced tea.

"There's a guy a few thousand miles from here who's about to be caught by the FBI. Never mind for what. Thing of it is, Otis, I need this fella for a project I'm working on. That's where you come in."

"Yes, sir?"

"As you know, I'm up for re-election, or election, anyway. As such, I need to thread the needle on some issues. And this guy is going to help me thread one of them. Not soon, mind you, but down the pike. However, I need to tell folks where I stand on this issue and how I'm going to make things better."

Scoggins appeared confused. Pulling his tight collar away from his thick neck, he remarked, "I'm not sure I understand. What issue are you…"

Stanton announced, in a voice too loud for Scoggin's comfort, "The death penalty, Otis! The death penalty, and how it's carried out. This guy, this Dr. Wren, is going to, if I can work it out, help me get inmates executed quietly. Quietly, you hear? He's got skills I need. Talents!"

Scoggins turned around to see a passive Rappaport, reading a magazine. With a look of bewilderment, Scoggins muttered, "Where do I come in?"

"Well, Otis, for starters, it's like this: when this Wren gets caught and brought in, I'm going to get him out of the FBI's hands as soon as possible. Never mind how. Once that happens, there's going to be a push for him to be prosecuted, if word gets out about his apprehension. That's where you come in. You see, he's not going to be prosecuted. I have other plans for him."

"What sort of plans, Mr. President?"

Stanton narrowed his eyes at Scoggins. "Don't concern yourself with that. That's between me and some other folks. Buy where you come in is this: there is to be no grand jury, no indictments, no investigation into Wren. I don't want you or any other DOJ people involved. No talking to him, no subpoenas, no contact, no nothing! Is that clear?"

"Yes, Mr. President, it is. But how are you going to…"

"Leave that to me. I'm going to make some arrangements. Cut some deals. You know how to cut deals, don't you Otis?"

"I do. Sure I do. I know exactly what you mean."

"Fine. Then we're all set. By the way, how's that son of yours, Dusty?"

"He's just great, sir."

"Cameron enjoying life in DC? Her apartment, and all?"

Scoggins rubbed his chin and lowered his voice. "Sure is Mr. President."

Stanton got to his feet. "Fine then, Otis. I'll have Ms. Dembley show you out. Be sure to say hello to your wife."

Scoggins rose, shook the president's hand, and walked past Rappaport, who barely lifted his gaze from the magazine. The president's smiling assistant guided the Attorney General out of the office. Rappaport got to his feet and asked, "Think he'll play ball, Gabe?"

"Of course he will. I know where he lives."

Stanton put himself behind his desk and asked Izzy. "Is Eddie here?"

The assistant announced that Ed Driscoll was on his way into the Oval Office. After five minutes, the three childhood friends, the President, the fixer and the compact, stout and balding Anesthesia Chairman were altogether, sitting in a neat circle in front of the President's desk. Stanton began, "Eddie! Great to see you. How are Marie and the kids?"

"Fine, Mr. President. Will is…"

"Stop with the 'Mr. President' stuff, Eddie, we're all old friends here.

Driscoll chuckled. "Ok, *Gabe*. Will is at Stanford Medical School and Eva is at Harvard Law."

"Great! Smart kids. Takes after their Ma!"

The three chums talked some about the old times in Boston—golf in Brookline, playing basketball in the Fens, Sox games at Fenway Park. After the small talk, Stanton got to it.

"So, Ed, the reason I got you here, in case you were wondering, was not only to shoot the shit about old times. I need your advice. Your good counsel."

Edward Driscoll, Boston Latin 1974, Yale BA 1978, Harvard Medical School 1982, Anesthesiology Residency Columbia Presbyterian Hospital 1986, Fellowship, cardiothoracic anesthesiology, NYU Medical Center 1987, was only too pleased to oblige.

"What is it, Gabe?"

"For my own reasons, and this may seem strange, I need you to tell me about why it has been so goddamned hard to get drugs to carry out lethal injections."

Driscoll was flummoxed. Why on Earth, he thought, would the president fly him down on a private jet to talk about this, of all things?

"Well, Gabe. I didn't expect that question but, as I am a chairman in the field, and do know something about the topic, I'll tell you what I know."

He discussed the ACLU lawsuits that were filed in Nebraska to reveal the source of the drugs used for execution. He spoke of Virginia's efforts to shield the identity, in 2016, of the pharmacy that provided such drugs for lethal injection. He went on about the European Union's ban on exporting sodium thiopental to the United States, for fear of diversion to executioners. He said that in 2011 the sole makers of pentothal, Ubicra Pharmaceuticals, stopped their domestic production of the drug and how they tried, unsuccessfully to get the agent made in India. The Indians, out of fear of liability, said no. He concluded by mentioning the Missouri "Black Hood Laws" that protected the identities of everyone involved in lethal injection executions, and how *The Guardian* and the *Associated Press* filed suit in that state against such laws. He was a font of information.

The President was impressed. Izzy took notes.

Stanton said, "Ed, thank you for this. It really helps me."

The true purpose of the visit now became clearer to Driscoll who hesitated and then asked, "Gabe. I sense this has something to do with your late dad, god bless him. Am I right?"

Stanton hung his head.

"Listen, Ed. You know me. You've known me since we were kids. You know where I stand on this issue. It's important to me. I just needed some facts from someone in the know. Just facts, that's all I'm after."

Driscoll sat silent. There was an uneasy quiet in the room. Izzy, trying to move on and brighten the mood, said, "Well! I hear the White House chef has made us all a great lunch. Maine lobsters with coleslaw, fresh tomatoes and ice cold Narragansetts! Come on fellas, let's get going!"

I had spoken to my banker in Douglas. All was well. There had been no efforts by anyone to inquire about my accounts at the Manx Crown Bank. Besides, any attempts in that regard would have been fruitless. The Isle of Man was still the best place in the world to hide money and still have easy access to it. I had been on the boat in north Africa for two days since I had let Colin go, taking trips to the market, taking in the water, the weather, and the food. At noon on the third day there I was on deck searching in the papers for a home, after my refreshing hammam, or Turkish-style bath in town, when I noted in the distance the Spanish flag snapping in the breeze next to the post office. I thought it strange that the Spanish flag would be displayed so prominently outside a government building here in Morocco. It then dawned on me that most of the people I had encountered spoke to me in Spanish, not Arabic and all the street signs were both in Arabic and Spanish.

Then, with a sickening feeling, I realized it: I was not in Morocco at all. I was in Spain. Yes, I was on the African continent, but turns out Ceuta was an autonomous Spanish city. It had not been under Moroccan, but Spanish, rule since the Treaty of Lisbon turned it over to them from the Portuguese in 1668. In the turmoil and tribulations of the past few days, I had committed a crucial planning error. I threw the newspaper below deck and scrambled to loosen the ship from the dock, eager to sail the few miles down the coast and into Morocco proper. I wasn't thinking how one man could pull this off on such a large ship; my priority was to get the hell out of Spanish-controlled north Africa.

I scrambled to unmoor the ship, my heart pounding in my throat. Just as I went aft to tend to the lines I witnessed, with a profound sinking feeling in my gut, the abrupt conclusion of all my work and planning: two Spanish Civil Guard ships, the Rio Belelle and the San Phillipe descended on me, trapping me to the dock. I dropped the line and sat down, my head in my hands. A voice on a megaphone blasted in my ears:

Dr Wren. This is the Spanish Civil Guard. Put your hands up and drop to your knees! We are boarding your vessel!

CHAPTER 17
NO EXIT

What happened to me in the next 48 hours is still a blur. I recall, as they led me away, seeing the letters "Ga" on the back panel of the ship. No doubt, that was a result of my rushed and shoddy paint job the morning we departed for Morocco. I also remember sitting in a cell in Marbella, the same cell that had housed, in 2006, Carlos Lopez Gutierrez, the former mayor of that town, who was held there briefly on corruption charges while he awaited trial. (Gutierrez is still serving time in Spanish prison, along with 26 other conspirators in twenty-first century Spain's biggest corruption trial.) The police had also asked me to supply the combination to the safe in my cabin, which contained almost 10,000 British pounds, 2500 American dollars and 1500 Euros. I did so. I thought at this point I would cooperate with the Spaniards as much as I could; don't ask me why. Perhaps I thought I might pay them off. Perhaps I was tired of running, tired of the stress and tired of looking over my shoulder. I don't recall. I was hoping they didn't find Michael's body. They made no mention of Colin.

While in Marbella, I was visited by two FBI agents: Thoreau and Locatelli. They told me that I had been handed over by the Spanish Police, for which I was grateful. I did not want to be at the whim of foreign authorities and oddly, it was nice to talk to some Americans for a change. Besides, Thoreau was quite easy on the eyes, and LocatelliI found him amusing.

It was Charles, in our many discussions of our respective professions, who had always told me that people accused of crimes should always remain silent. "Say nothing until your lawyer arrives, then speak only to him or her." For the most part, other than the safe's combination and verifying who I was and the name of my ship, I stuck to his advice. I was surprised when the agents did not ask me any questions. They also didn't read me my Miranda rights. (I learned later that if no interrogation was going to place, the Miranda rights are not read.)

Thoreau and Locatelli, it turns out, were just baby-sitters. I had been given a clean pair of my own clothes, removed from the jail in Marbella in handcuffs and spent the night under guard in a hotel. The next afternoon, on a plane whose make and model I didn't recognize, I flew the ten hours from southern Spain to Andrews Air Force Base in Prince George's County, Maryland, brooding over my mistake in north Africa. By the time we arrived on a hot afternoon in early August, the depth of the trouble I found myself started to sink in. I was no longer concerned about how shapely Thoreau's legs were or how Locatelli reminded me of "Lenny" from the TV show "Law and Order." No, I was beginning to realize that in mere days I had gone from a wealthy adventurer to a miserable SOB who could very well expect to spend the best years of my life in prison.

The FBI Agents turned me over to a man in an expensive

suit who called himself "Mr. L." Mr. L, a tall, thin blond-haired gentleman of light complexion and soft speech whom I estimated was about 35 years old. He was dressed too well to be a policeman, and his artful wielding of the English language, gracious manner and clear intelligence placed him on the upper extreme of the bell-shaped curve in brains and class for a Fed. In a private room in Andrew's, Mr. L asked me if I had had a good flight and whether I'd like something to eat.

"Yes I want something to eat! And what I really want to know is why you haven't read me my rights?"

He looked at me coolly and took a cigarette from the pack in his breast pocket, tapped it on the table to concentrate the tobacco and lit it, blowing a large blue plume above my head. . Clearing his throat, he began, "Dr. Wren, there will be no need for 'reading of rights'. That's TV crime drama stuff. I've come to talk to you about a matter of national importance."

I looked at him and said nothing.

"This is not going to be the kind of encounter you'll see on one of those high-drama detective shows. This is going to involve something you are not expecting and is coming from the highest echelons of our government. "

"Don't I at least get a phone call?"

"You do and you will. But before that, you don't have to talk; just listen."

Mr. L then took a piece of paper from a folder on the desk next to him and, clearing his throat, read from it:

"*The President of the United States, for his own personal and political reasons, favors of the death penalty. He sees value in this method of punishment in certain cases, not all, and while he is an extrajudicial figure in our government, he still feels there is a place for its employment. In the past few years, there have been multiple botched executions by the lethal injection method, most notably in 2015 when the Arkansas debacle occurred.*

The press and mainstream media have stoked the controversy regarding this form of execution, and execution in general, often and in many ways. As a result, the public's distaste for both the death penalty and the lethal injection method has continued unabated.

That is why the apprehension, on criminal charges of great magnitude, of a board-certified anesthesiologist, a professional who is best versed in the administration of this method of execution, has attracted the President's attention.

The President, therefore, is ready to offer a deal, the essentials of which involve clemency, privacy, remuneration and protection."

He went on to describe in detail the government's secret offer, the entire plan dubbed "Project Penrose." To think that the incredible events of the last nine and one half months had come to this: an offer from the President of the United States to serve him, or his party, or my country (I wasn't sure which at that point) in a way that anathema to the oath I had taken upon graduation from medical school decades ago. It was too much for me to digest. What I really wanted, suddenly, was to eat something and sleep in a comfortable bed. I told him

"Mr. L or whoever you are, I'm tired. Really tired. And I'm hungry. And I can't think straight. I hope you don't want an answer to this, this fantastic proposition, immediately? I think I need time. I also need advice. Legal advice. Speaking of that, what about my phone call? I need to talk to my brother Charlie. Is that possible?"

Mr. L tamped out his cigarette in the government issue ashtray and blew a final snort of smoke out of his nostrils. Looking me in the eye, he snapped his fingers to an assistant and added,

"I can do that one better."

The assistant went to a door at the far end of the large room, opened it and in walked my brother Charles; tan, thinner than I had seen him in years, and with a stern look.

Charlie walked to the desk where we sat. My mouth was agape. He turned to Mr. L and said, "Excuse us."

With a wave of his hand, Mr. L got up from his seat, pushed in Charles' chair and turned on his heels, escorting his assistant out of the room. Charlie sat across from me, erect, hands folded and silent.

"Charlie, what is this all about?" I felt as if there were a real possibility that I was either dreaming or hallucinating.

"What this is about, Adrian, is saving your foolish ass. You should be counting your lucky stars about now."

Same old Charlie, I thought. Always has to be the superior one. Just like all the lawyers I've known over the years, I thought. They always thought they were smarter than you.

"How did you get involved in this? How did they know to contact you and…?"

"Never mind that. Just close your mouth and listen. Right now, your best option is to consider what I say very seriously. It's like this: I know some important people who you never knew I knew. Known them for quite a while. Because of whom I know and how I know them, there is a chance here for me to save your sorry self. Save you from prison. A long stint in prison, you understand?"

"But how do you know…?"

"Look, I know you are tired. And hungry. And perhaps now is not the best time to talk. But understand this: I am the only thing between you and a prison cell, get it? Mr. L has told you the terms. They want you, Adrian, and they want you because you have a skill. A skill they need. And you are in a jam—a big jam. And the only way out is to do what they say. Listen, they could've driven a much harder bargain, but because of me and my association with them, a relationship that goes back many years, I have convinced them to make some minor concessions. Suffice it to say they owe me."

I rubbed my eyes and looked at Charles. The tan threw me off. He must have just come from the beach with the wife and kids. Suddenly all I wanted to do was sleep. Forget the food, I needed to lie down and close my eyes.

"Listen Charlie, I'm very tired. I need to sleep. Can I at least sleep? Can we discuss this, say, tomorrow?"

"Yes Adrian, we can. Tomorrow. They have a bed for you waiting. I'll be here tomorrow but only for a few hours. You can give Mr. L your answer. But take this to heart; if you don't take their offer, don't do what they say, you're toast. I can't help you. Nobody can help you. And don't think about divulging anything you've seen or heard. Nobody would believe you. Just the ravings of a dishonest, discredited, and law-breaking lunatic, see?"

I put my head on the desk and buried my face in the back of my palms. Through a muffled voice I muttered, "Yes, I'll have an answer. I understand. Just let me sleep. Please."

Charles got to his feet and motioned through a small window for the two men to return. Before they entered, he said, standing over me. "Adrian, it will all be spelled out in detail tomorrow. Do the right thing, brother. Don't fuck this up. Sign the paper and be done with it."

Charles put his hand on my shoulder and walked out, just as Mr. L resumed his seat at the table. Mr. L assisted me to my feet and took me to a room that had a hot cooked meal, some water, and a bed. There was also a box with some of my clothes from the ship on a stand at the foot of the bed, as well as my toiletry kit. I took a few bites of the food and went directly to the adjacent bathroom, where a fresh towel, shampoo and soap were laid out, just like in a hotel.

I took a five-minute shower in comforting hot water, dried off and clothed myself in underwear and a t-shirt. I brushed my teeth and got into the bed. The clock on the wall read 7:25. I didn't care. I turned out the bed stand light, fluffed the pillow, pulled the clean, fresh bed linens up to my chin and disappeared into the blessing of sleep.

The dream came quickly and vividly. It was so well-seated to the reality of the actual event that it seemed as authentic as the meeting I had had with Charles. I'm in OR 10 at Hamilton, and it's 2 am. The nurse anesthetist and I, along with vascular surgeon Brian McCloud, are frantically working to save a retired admiral who has suffered a ruptured abdominal aortic aneurysm. McCloud, short, balding and pugnacious, is a professor of surgery at Georgetown who also had privileges at Hamilton. Before the surgery, in the dream as in real life, he comes to me and says, "You don't induce (anesthesia) until I say, got it?," poking a stubby index finger in my chest. In the dream, I nod and the next thing I see, he's on the other side of the ether screen giving me the signal. We push the midazolam, the fentanyl, the etomidate and the succinylcholine, the nurse anesthetist and I, and it's off to the races.

With a flourish, McCloud splits the abdomen down the middle, the fish-belly white flesh contrasting with the dark red-purple blood like the admiral is some stockyard side of beef. The blood pressure plummets. Next it's all blood on the floor, on the walls, on the scrubs, visors, masks I'm yelling to the circulating nurse we need more units of blood, more fresh frozen plasma, more platelets! The admiral is like a human sieve; the more we pump into him, the more that comes out. In spades. We're losing him, losing him, and McCloud yells for me to start CPR.

I rip the drapes away, get on a stepstool and start pumping the chest, hearing the sickening crack of a few ribs. I look over at the capnograph (the CO_2 monitor), and the exhaled CO_2 waveform is disappearing, an ominous sign. Then, I ask the nurse to take over the CPR, and I turn up the big guns full spigot: neosynephrine, epinephrine, ephedrine, dopamine. One step forward, then two steps back. The IVs are running in blood products full bore. Then, I pull out my ace-up-the sleeve, calcium chloride. I squirt in syringe after syringe, and we start to gain ground. The CO_2 starts stabilizing, the surgeon has a clearer field and the blood pressure is rising. McCloud is now able to get the synthetic graft around the mince-meat aorta. I fall back into my swivel chair, like some James T. Kirk whose been told by Scottie that the engines weathered the storm. The nurse whispers in my ear, "This guy's gonna walk outta here!"

I woke up in a cold sweat and peered into the dark. The clock next to the bed read 12:48. I put my head back down on the wet pillow, flipped it over, and fell back to sleep.

Gail and I used to interpret each other's dreams. Whether playing mad-libs or squiggly-lines, we'd while the hours away up in her room while Charlie was out doing one sport or another. Mom used to have to drag us down to dinner personally to get us to stop.

Gail would have had no trouble with this dream: "We are seldom offered second chances in life," she'd say. Especially when the stakes are high. And they were as high now, for me, as they'd ever been. Gail would have told me in two secs what the dream meant. "Take the deal; don't dicker and don't screw around. Take the deal and don't look back."

Mr. L, greeted me after my breakfast of scrambled eggs, rye toast and coffee. We sat across from each other at the same table we met the day before. The clock on the wall read 8:45. He presented me with a document outlining the terms of Penrose. I read it with keen interest.

214

"Dr. Wren, have you made a decision on our offer?"

I wiped some toast crumbs from the corner of my mouth. "Before we discuss that, I have a question."

Mr. L fixed his eyes on me. "Shoot."

"Something doesn't make sense here. If you want this to be a long-term set-up, and one that is outside the ken of, what shall I call it, 'mainstream government', how would our arrangement be carried out over multiple administrations?"

"You mean different presidents, different parties, if that came to pass?"

"Exactly."

"That's an astute question, Adrian, but I have an answer that may put your mind at rest. You see, there are many such "arrangements", things that go on behind the scenes of normal, everyday politics and governmental functionalities, that John and Jane Public cannot even imagine. The average American does not even know what he or she does not know; the idea that we live in an open society where government and governing is, and I hate this particular buzzword, "transparent," is an illusion. That was revealed, at a heavy price, by Ed Snowden back in, '13. Goodness, Adrian, if you only knew what I know: the names and acronyms would make your head spin! TURBINE, STELLARWIND, PRISM, CHICKWIT, RAGTIME, FASCIA, Bullrun, The Hemisphere Project, XKS, the list goes on. And those are just the more recent. God, in my training days we learned about Rampart-A, COINTELPRO, Ghetto Informant, XKS...Anyway, Adrian, rest assured that we have mechanisms in place to address your concerns. We plan for these things."

I coughed, preparing for the response to my next question. "Is it possible for me to see a friend?"

Mr. L smiled and tightened his silk Hermes tie.

"I was wondering when you were going to get to Ms. Porter. I actually thought it was going to be your first question."

"How could you know…?"

"Adrian, we know everything. Cleesh, Styles, Gimble, Devlin; everything. We've had plenty of time to put the pieces together. And it was really your fatal mistakes that helped us: you should have never donated *The Catcher in the Rye* to the BCC book sale. That and the name you chose for your boat and company. Anyway, getting back to your question, we've already considered that you might ask this of us. The consensus was: absolutely not. Too risky. But after reconsideration, the decision was made to allow it. It and only it. Our sole concession.``

I silently cursed the BCC book sale.

"Really?"

"Yes, incredibly."

Mr. L took out a cigarette, tamped it, lit it with his silver engraved Zippo and blew a plume high in the air.

I said, motioning to his cigarette, "You know those things will kill you."

"Let me worry about that. Anyway, back to Ms. Porter. We know that she was and is important to you. And if you're not happy, we're not happy. We can't have a mopey executioner, you see. Besides, there are mechanisms in play should Ms. Porter decide to not play ball."

"How do you mean?"

"Well let's just say that should Ms. Porter attempt to go public about the fact that you're in custody, we have swift and effective ways to deal with that. Trust me on this."

I squirmed in my seat. "I want to see her, but I don't want to put her at risk."

"We appreciate that, but you can't have it both ways. If you feel you're willing to take that chance, we'll allow it. "

Grinding the cigarette butt in the Andrews AFB ashtray, Mr. L concluded, "You've read our offer. Charlie's explained it to you, and we've settled on the Porter issue. Do we have a deal?"

"When can I call her?"

Mr. L took out a cell phone, not his normal one, from his jacket pocket.

"As soon as you sign on the dotted line."

I was faced with a big decision. I had spent my entire professional life in healing the sick, even saving people's lives. I had helped bring babies into the world, save trauma victims from a probable death, given anesthesia to install pacemakers, access grafts for dialysis patients, harvest fresh veins retooled as bypass highways for coronary circulation, remove brain tumors, fix pediatric heart valve abnormalities, place intraocular lenses so people could see their grandchildren's faces.... Now, the government was asking me to kill. And it was all because of my own greed, carelessness, and grandiose ideas.

The government had me, squeezed my balls and my brain. There was no way around it. It was either do as they say or go to prison. It was merely a matter of days, incredibly enough, that I had gone from free-wheeling multi-millionaire, with the world at my feet, to prisoner. I was in shock over how precipitous my fall was.

And there seemed to be no room for negotiation, for, what could I negotiate? The money? The government didn't care that I had stolen millions from my ex-wife and two-bit companies. Why should they, after all? Twelve-plus million dollars meant nothing to them. But it meant lots to my creditors.

What didn't make a lot of sense to me, at the time, was: why is this death penalty issue so goddamned important to these people? Why now? The death penalty had been around for years in the United States. What happened, whose interest did it serve, to suddenly have another conduit through which the government could carry out what was already being done? Yes, it occurred to me that I could do it better than the people doing it now, but so what? Was it that important?

Clearly, for whatever reason, it was. I looked at Mr. L with what could only have been an expression of sheer desperation.

Gail would have told me "take the deal."

I thought to myself: "Can't change the wind; read—just the sails."

"Where do I sign?"

Mr. L smiled.

"A smart decision. It's settled, then. And by the way; from now on, Adrian Wren and Juan de Nebra—they no longer exist, understand?

CHAPTER 16
SELLING SOULS

Francis Devlin's attorney had just finished extricating his client from the grips of an FBI investigation, but not until the K Street lawyer's life had been significantly disrupted. There was the collateral damage the investigation had wrought: The DC Bar was up his ass, the billable hours he lost cleaning up this mess were gone forever and his own legal fees had exacted a price. Devlin searched his mind for ways of getting back at Wren for what he did but came up empty. He had heard the initial rumors he had been nabbed in the south of Spain but like everyone else, hadn't seen anything in the news since. Indeed, there was talk that the man apprehended was not Wren at all, but a true Spanish national on holiday in the Mediterranean nabbed in error.

Gimble was sitting pretty in rural Virginia, his dog, and his Wild Turkey to keep him company. Ever the master of deception, he had been able to keep his most recent identity intact, evading the prying eyes of former associates and the authorities. Styles too had managed to keep clean, denying any knowledge of Wren's motives and activities. Clete Shea had quit his job at the SEC and was now working in the private sector, for more money and more respect. Mobray, ex-agent Thoreau and Locatelli were all kept in the dark. The word "Penrose" would have meant nothing to them. Locatelli's inquiries into the progress of the case and prosecution of the man they apprehended went mysteriously and suspiciously unanswered. He too even began to doubt the veracity of the arrest. It all was very strange.

Natalie's office phone rang the third Monday in August. Caller ID displayed a number she did not recognize.

"Tricia Porter. How can I help you?"

There was a pause on the other end.

She continued

"Ms. Porter. Hello?"

"It's me."

A pause.

"I can't believe it. Wait; let me shut the door."

Natalie's heart banged in her throat as she looked both directions into the hallway and closed the office door.

"Where are you?!"

"Nat, I can't say now but listen to me. I'm safe and free, for now. I need to see you."

"Adrian! Why should I want to see…?"

"Listen. Nothing is as it appears. You've got to trust me. You're the best thing that has happened to me in the past ten months."

"Is that why you left. Is that why you used me?"

"I did leave but I did not use you. You were just a bystander. I can explain. I will explain if you'll let me."

Natalie wanted to torture me a little longer but thought better of it. She saw no point in it.

"How and where can you 'explain'?"

"Can you meet me at Pike and Rose, tomorrow night at Café Rustica. 7 pm? I promise it will be worth your while. No games, just truth. Truth and dinner."

She assented.

"And listen, Nat. I look different. I'll come to you."

The next evening in Rockville (or North Bethesda, as the locals insist), Mr. L parked himself at the table behind me with one of his flunkies, toying with a Southern Comfort Manhattan. The stiff had iced tea. Mr. L was in casual wear tonight: Khakis and a blue pinstripe Thomas Pink buttoned down shirt. He had his best Johnston and Murphy shoes on. He was clearly chafing for a cigarette.

At 7 sharp she walked in, wearing a pink sheath. She looked like an angel descended freshly from on high. I got up and took her hand, leading her to the booth.

"Adrian! You look like Jesus Christ Himself. The hair, the beard!"

"Shoosh! Just sit and let me look at you."

I took her in like a glass of cold lemonade.

I took off my sunglasses but not my cap. I could tell she loved me.

For the next hour, over dinner and wine and with Mr. L listening in, I recounted the past ten months. The whole thing. Silverstone, Styles, Gimble, Devlin, the Manx Crown Bank, The Gail Force Winds, the Irish boys, everything. Well, most everything. Her mouth stayed open, for food, drink and merely in awe of the story, the entire time. I kept grabbing her hands, but she insisted on pulling away.

"And that's what happened. And here I am. And here you are."

"And why am I here?"

"Why? Because I've missed you. I can't get you out of my mind. You're a stabilizing force for me."

"Is that the only reason? To be your 'stabilizing force'?"

"That and because I need you. And want you."

"Want me for what?"

"Natalie, stop playing. I don't have time. I want you with me. From now on. "

She looked at me and took a sip of wine.

"What are you saying, Adrian? That I drop everything and run off with you, into the…the…whatever?"

"That's exactly what I'm saying."

"I have a life, Adrian, a…"

"Do you? Do you have someone special? Do you love your job, slinging securities and proprietary mutual funds for Muriel and Stanley Retiree?"

"Adrian!"

"Sorry, that did not come out right."

Pause.

"Well, do you have someone? Special?"

She looked down at her plate and chased an olive around with her fork.

"No, but…"

"Then come with me! You know the great times we had, as brief as they were."

I removed my hat and brushed back my long hair.

"I'll even shave and get a haircut!"

She smiled and turned red. I took her hand and she laced her fingers into mine, our palms facing.

"Whaddya say, Nat? I won't disappoint. I promise. You've got to give me a chance."

She looked up from her plate and tossed her hair back. Clearing her throat, she began, "I'll need time."

"How much?"

"Adrian, I don't know! A week? Days at best..."

"We...I... don't have that much time."

She dipped her head and took my chin in her hand. She kissed me.

"Give me a few days. Today is Tuesday. Give me until Friday, okay?"

"I can do that. Friday. I will call you on your cell Friday. What time?"

"Give me until 4 pm, when the markets close."

"Done."

I took both her hands in mine. She said, "You didn't even tell me what the plan is. Or if you have a plan."

"I have a plan... I just can't tell you now. You've got to trust me."

"Wren, if you fuck me over I swear I'll..."

"No one is fucking anyone. Not that way, anyway."

She stifled a laugh. She got up and I hugged her.

"I'll call you Friday. Don't disappoint me."

She smiled at me and left, just like that. A pink breeze and the door was shut.

Mr. L sidled up to where Natalie was sitting and stabbed the olive from her plate with a toothpick.

"Well done, Dr, Wren. I'd come back for her too. You have excellent taste."

I looked at him above the rim of my wine glass.

"Let's just hope she says yes."

On Wednesday they moved me to a hotel in Northwest DC. Mr. L told me that Thursday was going to be a day of meetings, to go over my transition from prisoner to secret government contractor. I could meet with Charlie on Wednesday to work out how to deal with my parents. Over lunch in the hotel in my room on that day, Charlie and I decided that we'd tell my parents I was still in Europe and at large, contrary to the news reports. He'd tell them that the government's case against me was flimsy and unfounded, and that with time I would be exonerated. The whole thing was a big mistake, a misunderstanding. Although not a perfect solution, kicking this can down the road afforded me time to work out a better resolution; a way to re-establish my relationship with my parents without screwing up the arrangement. I knew that was going to take time. Besides, truth of it is, I was never that close to my mother. And my father, well, as I've said, he just was not the same man.

At 9 am Mr. L met with me at the hotel. He brought fake documents, credentials, forms to fill out, a barber and a photographer. There, a new me, for the second time since my days at Hamilton, was created. My name was Alexander M. Crisfield, a native of Los Angeles. I was born 1/1/86, attended the University of Chicago and earned a degree in Chemistry in 2011. After that, I went to work for Parthenon Partners, a defense contractor in Greenbelt, Maryland. I left Parthenon in 2018 and moved to Scottsdale, Arizona, where I now resided. I was running my own small business and lived not far from Pinnacle Peak. I was single.

Mr. L put up a white background and told me to go into the bathroom and shave my beard into a goatee. Once done, he sat me down and had the barber shave off most of my hair. It fell in blond/grey clumps onto the hotel room carpet, where an assistant vacuumed it up. I peered into a hand mirror and saw myself. I felt cold and violated. He gave me a new pair of glasses, wire-rimmed and spare, and asked me if the fit was alright. I told him it was.

Without the glasses on, I sat in front of the white backdrop and allowed the photographer to take a series of pictures for my new passport and Arizona driver's license. I was fingerprinted, rendered a cheek swab for DNA and was measured by the photographer for clothing. I guess he doubled as a tailor. I felt like a lab rat.

After the shearing and the measurements, I sat down with Mr. L to go over the details of Project Penrose. I listened like an attentive schoolboy. If Natalie would agree to go with me, the powers behind the plan would go along. She would not have to take on a new identity. But any deviation on her or my parts from the arrangement would result in her immediate return to Bethesda, or wherever she might want to go, and my incarceration. The government would disavow any and all of the activities that had taken place to set me up in a new and covert existence. I would be compensated in the way the government had outlined and agreed to. I would be furnished with a home, a car of my choosing under the retail value of $30,000 and I would be responsible for the rest of my expenses: utilities, food, and personal travel, which I was free to undertake within the United States. I was not allowed to hold my passport; that document would be held by Mr. L or his designee. I would pay my taxes, filed like any other citizen, on time and in order. I would not be allowed to contact my parents, old friends and associates or anyone else except for my brother Charles. I would especially make no attempts to contact Clete Shea, Francis Devlin, Horace Styles or Max Gimble, under any circumstances. Any moves to do so would void the agreement and lead to my prosecution.

Of utmost importance was that I would never divulge the arrangement to anyone under any circumstances. That included Natalie. If and when she, or anyone else, would broach the subject, the gist of the answer would be, "My employment and employers do not allow for me divulging this information. However, the activities are legal and sanctioned by the United States government."

I protested that this answer was bound to raise more red flags and questioning. "You're a resourceful and skilled liar, Mr. Crisfield.

I'm sure you will come up with some way, within the bounds of the agreement, to satisfy anyone. You have no choice, really. You have to."

It sounded so strange to be called Mr. Crisfield.

All of that took most of the morning. After lunch in the room, Mr. L, with an assistant at a laptop computer, went over what I would need to carry out my job. I felt like a patron of a Chinese restaurant ordering off of a tasting menu. I told Mr. L that. He laughed and "took my order."

"Tell me what you will need, Alexander, and the government will do its best to provide it. "

And that's where I thought things would get tricky. It wasn't merely like ordering off a Chinese restaurant menu, I told him, since many of the dishes and even ingredients were restricted due to the type of "meal" I was ordering. I warned Mr. L about this. "You do realize that drug companies that supply some of the agents I'll require, particularly the propofol and the muscle relaxants, will be resistant to supply you."

Mr. L took out a cigarette and tamped it on the table. I warned him that this was a non-smoking room.

"I'll pay the no-smoking fine, Alexander. As to your concerns about the supply of 'ingredients' in your Chinese meal, that's already been handled. The companies will believe they are supplying the VA various hospitals in the DC, Baltimore, Philadelphia, Boston, and Miami areas. We will get you all the material you require."

"And what about the IV fluid? You must be aware that ever since Hurricane Reuben whipped Puerto Rico back in '19 there's been a shortage of saline and dextrose in water."

"We're well aware of that and have made the proper arrangements. If our country can make enough gin, marijuana, and bubble gum to supply the wide world we certainly have a handle on salt- and sugar- water. Reuben was a private-sector fuck-up. We have mechanisms at our disposal."

We went on about my list. I wasn't greedy; I knew I had the talents to deal with any of the basics he could muster. Propofol, sodium pentothal or etomidate to induce sleep. Midazolam or, in a pinch, injectable diazepam, to sedate and reduce anxiety. Fentanyl, morphine, hydromorphone, sufentanil, remifentanil or even meperidine to induce euphoria and depress respirations. Potassium chloride to induce arrhythmias. And the muscle relaxants (read "paralytics") to make triple sure they're dead: vecuronium hydrobromide, pancuronium bromide, atracurium, rocuronium, even d tubo-curare in a pinch. But not succinylcholine; too much muscle twitching and movement. Besides, it was too short acting. And in essence, paralytics were over-kill anyway. Window dressing, for the public, so the prisoner would not move.

It was simple, really, to kill someone who was in the right hands. And I owned those hands. So did thousands like me; but they weren't over a barrel.

Mr. L seemed pleased that I was both flexible to work with and had the supply requirements on the tip of my tongue. He said, "Anything else?"

I answered that I would need a portable ultrasound machine and access to central line kits. The ultrasound machine he had anticipated; it was to be used to find veins in the neck or groin in people who, though IV drug abuse, obesity, or unfortunate genetics, did not display healthy veins so readily. The central line kits threw him. Mr. L was taken aback, surprised that there was a detail he had missed.

"What is a 'central line kit', Alexander?"

I explained to him that these pre-packaged IV access kits, containing a combination of needles, catheters, syringes, local anesthesia and tubing, were designed to allow the practitioner to gain intravenous access to the internal jugular vein in the neck or the subclavian vein just under the collarbone. They were used mostly in critical care settings, like the ICU, CCU, burn units and ER. I rattled off the name of the major manufacturers as the assistant took special note of the spellings on his laptop. I told him I'd probably not use them more than 1 percent of the time, but that we'd have to be prepared.

I pushed myself away from the conference table and looked at the clock. It was 3:30 already!

"Are we done yet, Mr. L? I'm tired."

Mr. L extinguished his third cigarette of the afternoon and loosened his tie.

"Not quite yet, Alexander. There's one more hurdle, and it is not minor."

I looked over at the assistant, whose hands stayed poised above the laptop's keyboard, his eyes down.

"What's that?"

"Therapy."

"Therapy?"

"Yes, as in psychotherapy. Think for a moment. You've spent all of your professional career helping people, even saving lives. Now you are going to take life. And you will need help along the way."

I sat for a minute and let his words settle in. Normally, my first instinct would have been to dispute the need for what I thought was an unnecessarily intrusive measure. But rolling his statement over in my mind, I saw that he was right. In my life as a doctor, I had never killed anyone. Not even close. I'd had patients die on the table, but that was different. Their illnesses did that, not me. But to have as my new life's work the deliberate and cold termination of other peoples' existence was a prospect, in the rush and whirr of the decisions that had faced me, that I had not fully pondered. Of course, I would need help; any normal person would.

"What plans are there for that?"

Mr. L smiled, seeing that I did not put up a fight on this point.

"You are making a wise and measured decision, Alexander. This bodes well for you. It won't go unrewarded. We have a person in place, a Dr. William Rosengrave, of Phoenix, who will be handling that. We have used Dr. Rosengrave's services for many years. We have full confidence in him. In the beginning, you will meet with him, once you have relocated, once a week. During assignments, at least the first few, you will meet with him the day after the performance of your duties. There are no exceptions to this. If, at any time during your employment, he feels that medication is warranted, you agree to comply. Is that clear?"

I took in Mr. L's erect posture, his impeccable grooming, his clear, blue eyes. "Completely.."

Mr. L stood and offered his hand. I did the same. On his way out the door, he looked over his shoulder and, in a stage whisper, added, "Let's just hope she says 'yes'. Oh, and Alexander…"

"Yes?"

"I forgot to mention. We'll need complete access to your Manx Crown Bank account. Remember? All your money there goes to us, to help defray the cost of our little project.

"What about all my creditors; my former wife, the mortgage company, the physician-signature loan corporations–?"

Mr. L smirked. "Alexander! Let's just chalk that up as patriotism…donations to a worthy cause, shall we say?"

And with that he was out the door and gone.

CHAPTER 17
NEW HORIZONS

Friday afternoon came and she said, "Yes." My heart soared. We had it all figured out. We would move to the government-furnished home, a small rambler up near Scottsdale, in early September. She was able to wrangle a lateral move to the Titus/Dixon office in Phoenix, telling her friends and family that she had wanted a change in surroundings and wanted to make a go of it. I was to begin therapy with Dr. Rosengrave the first Wednesday of that month, in anticipation of my start date of September 23, which was the date of my first assignment at The Louisiana State Penitentiary. Mr. L had sent me an encrypted email that had me scheduled out as far as the end of the year: there'd be two in October (Missouri and Alabama), three in November (two in Florida and one in New York) and three in December (Florida again and two in Texas). They apparently wanted me to hit the ground running.

On Wednesday, September 5th, I drove my new Jeep Cherokee

down to Old Phoenix where I sat waiting in Rosengrave's reception room. I had not seen a psychiatrist since the days surrounding my divorce and had never been on medication for a psychiatric issue. The closest I had come to needing psychopharmacology was a short-term use of Ambien and clonazepam to help me sleep.

Rosengrave's office was modern, spare, and clean. The furniture was IKEA-bare, populated by the usual suspects: *Sports Illustrated*, *Golf Digest*, *The New Yorker*, *Woman's Day* and *Town and Country*. I pretended to be engrossed in the article "Cure Your Ugly Slice NOW!" when he stepped out, all grey beard, long grey hair and khakis, tucked in Oxford pinstripe shirt, leather belt with a south-western turquoise belt buckle and Mephisto shoes. He extended a slender, spidery hand. I shook it and followed him into the room, where a couch and two overly comfortable chairs sat facing each other in front of a bookshelf groaning with books by authors such as Freud, Jung and Skinner. I took a seat facing him, moving the obligatory box of Kleenex out of my way on the table between us.

Rosengrave crossed a long khaki leg over his knee at the ankle and opened a substantial manila file in his lap. He scratched his beard, looked at me over his glasses and said, "You know, Adrian— excuse me—Alexander, you know this will be different from my usual patient encounters. I already have a great deal of information on you, so we can save a lot of time and effort on the essentials."

"Essentials?"

"Yes: ethnic background, family structure and upbringing, education, health, hobbies, habits, career, sexual orientation, travel history. It's all here. And there's a lot of it."

Well isn't that just lovely, I thought. "What would you like to discuss, then?"

Rosengrave paused and snapped the file shut. "Well, for starters, I'd like to know how you feel about the arrangement. About Penrose."

I opened my palms toward him. "How can I feel? I essentially have no choice. It was either comply or go to prison."

"True, but you must have feelings regarding your new life. Your new role?"

"I do. Look, first, I'm thrilled that Natalie said yes to me. We've had a great time the past few weeks. She seems to be adjusting to her new job and to having me in her life. I know she was bored in her old life in DC. She told me she felt stuck. I think for the first time in my life, I'm in love. She is, too."

"Fine. And what about you? You do realize that in a few weeks, you will be executing people for the United States Government. How do you feel about that?"

Rosengrave tilted his head slightly and waited for my reply. The air seemed suddenly thick, even stuffy.

"I'm not crazy about it, but I have no choice. I am pleased about a few things, though."

"And what are they?"

"Well, first off I'm glad to get a file on the 'condemned'. Each one."

The word seemed so foreign as it exited my mouth.

"Go on."

"Well, it's like I said. I get to review the crime, the proof, the background of the person, and so on. That's all good.

"And did you, before this arrangement was reached, have an opinion one way or the other about the death penalty?"

I thought for a minute.

"To tell you the truth, yes and no. Yes, in the sense that, like anyone I saw it discussed in the news and gave it some peripheral thought. But I must say I was never really a student of the issue. I never really paid attention."

"Peripheral thought?"

"Yeah. I mean, it's like this. Part of me feels that violent, proven crime should be punished. Why should the taxpayer, for example, have to pay for some shitbag languishing in prison and appealing, tying up the courts and criminal justice system? I feel that in the face of overwhelming evidence, heinous crimes should be met with severe punishment."

Rosengrave took off his glasses and cleaned them with a tissue. He looked up with a squint at the newly cleaned lenses and replaced the glasses onto his face. Squinting he said, "Actually, statistics prove that the government spends far more on the process of appealing the death penalty than keeping a death row inmate alive for his or her natural life. But go on."

"Well, that's one aspect of it. The other, which you might be guessing, is deterrence. There, I part ways with the pro-death penalty folks."

"Yes?"

"Yes. I never bought into the idea that it was a deterrence. And the studies prove me out. I believe them."

"The studies?"

"Yes. Deterrence is a fallacy. The death penalty, for me, is all about economics. That, and vengeance."

"I see."

"I don't mean to sound harsh but, it's like this: I think the death penalty folks have a point: no one pays attention to the victims and their rights and the rights of their families. I'm a pretty liberal guy on most issues but I can see the irony in this. Also, like I said, it must cost millions every year to keep those people alive and on death row, with their lawyers and appeals and so on."

"And vengeance?"

"Well, I know. The good book says 'vengeance is mine, saith the Lord.' I get it. But, you know, humans are flawed. We have emotions.

And sometimes, the public need to satisfy those emotions is great. Great, and serves a purpose. Like NFL football."

I winced as I said that.

"I see you have given this issue more thought than you give yourself credit for."

"I guess I have. So, if your question is whether I can handle my new job, the answer is twofold: yes, because I have no choice, and yes, because I'm solid with the concept of the penalty itself. It's 'moral footprint,' if you will."

"Well. That seems to settle that. And what about the chance of executing an innocent man?"

I was waiting for this question.

"I knew that would come up. I'm well familiar with the 'tis better to let a hundred guilty men go free than put one innocent man to death' spiel. But, with today's technology, DNA testing and so forth, I think we've reached a point where we are as accurate in proving guilt as we can get."

"Are you trying to convince yourself, Alexander? Or do you believe that?"

Once I was out of the office, Dr. Rosengrave phoned Mr. L in Maryland. He answered, "This is L. Go ahead, Bill."

"Well, I just finished our first session with our boy."

"And?"

"Well, it's a mixed picture. On the assignment front I feel things will be fine. There's not enough opposition to fight there. However, it seems our friend has some unresolved anger issues."

"I knew he had problems with authority figures. Is that what you are referring to?"

"Not exactly. It seems, through probing his relationship with his late sister, that I've mined some emotions about his view of people in general. He's not quite a misanthrope, mind you, but he harbors some strong feelings about personal responsibility."

"'Personal responsibility'? How so?"

"Well, let's just say he expects the world to be a certain way, and when it isn't, he gets worked up. I'm not explaining it very well, but I will cover it all in my email. You'll have it by 9 am tomorrow."

"Well Bill, as long as Penrose is not in jeopardy I…"

"No, no. It's nothing like that. We'll be fine there. I'll work out the kinks in our next few sessions. I don't think there will be cause for concern. I've seen his type before."

"Whatever you say, Bill. You have our full confidence. Looking forward to your report. Bye, now."

"Goodbye."

By Election Day in November 2024 I had completed two more executions for my employers with the same ease in which I had dispatched my first subject, Billy Ray Devereaux, at the Louisiana State Penitentiary in September. Mr. L had called me in Scottsdale to tell me how pleased he and "the administrators" were with my work. He also wanted to know how my personal life with Natalie was getting on, as well as my relationship with Dr. Rosengrave. I told him Nat and I were settling in nicely to our lives together, that Natalie was enjoying her new office in Phoenix and that Rosengrave was doing his job. That meant he was keeping me on a steady course. I also told him we had rescued two dogs.

Stanton had won election handily. Ever since he had ascended to the presidency upon the death of the sitting president, this was his first victory in his own right at the national level and he exuded the confidence and vigor of a man, a politician, who had come into his own.

A little over 5200 miles to my northeast, however, actions were transpiring that I could not have imagined. The death of Michael McPhail, a British subject whose battered body was discovered washed up on a rocky shoal near Gibraltar earlier that summer, had caused a stir in Scotland Yard. McPhail's bloated corpse, complete with apparent blunt trauma to the right side of his skull, was found by two British teens who lived near the massive and iconic rock. They called their parents, who then alerted the authorities in Gibraltar. Identification of the body was easy; McPhail was still wearing his Royal Navy dog tags, tangled in the remnants of his shirt, at the time of his death. Dental records from his time in the service confirmed his identity.

Inspector Thomas Jakes, a veteran detective of The Yard, was ultimately placed in charge of the investigation of McPhail's demise. It did not take long for Jakes, a 60-ish man of tall stature and slim frame, who sported a pencil thin moustache and slicked-back salt and pepper hair, to piece together McPhail's last day. He had Colin Tynes to thank for that.

It was Tynes who had gone to Manx police shortly after his dismissal from his work on The Gail Force Winds to report what he had seen and experienced in the service of Captain Juan de Nebra. Tynes had seen in the early news reports that summer that the man who he had worked for was most likely the now-captured American doctor Adrian Wren. Tynes was eager to see if the reward money of $300,000 was still to be had. Manx police connected him to Scotland Yard, and thus to Jakes, who was so eager to talk to the Irishman that he took the earliest fight he could to Douglas to meet with him.

It had been only a few days since Tynes had been back in Douglas when Jakes knocked on his apartment door. He let the inspector in. It was 10:30 in the morning.

Jakes sat across from the former Royal Navy sailor, looking

around the sparsely outfitted and drab apartment and sipped his tea. Brushing flat his thin moustache, Jakes said, "Well then. Tell me what you know about Juan de Nebra."

Tynes went on about how he got to know the Spanish Captain, how he and the deceased McPhail had been hired on as crew for the seemingly wealthy bon-vivant, and how they were paid and treated while under his service. Tynes then said, "I knew something was strange the minute I saw the news reports."

"You mean the one about the American doctor?"

"Yes, that's right. I lived with the man for months, me and Michael did. There was no mistake; de Nebra was Wren, only with a beard, long hair and glasses."

"Tell me again what you told the Manx police when you returned to The Isle."

"Well, it was like I says: The morning we was to leave for North Africa we were all on deck and Michael, I'll never forget it, he pulls a gun on the Captain! A cannon it was! A .44 magnum. Like Dirty Harry!"

"Had you ever seen Michael carrying a gun before?"

"No sir. I didn't even know he owned one. I was shocked. Shocked and confused as to why he had a gun on the captain and insisting that I get in the lifeboat. We were friends, after all…"

"And then?"

"And then, Michael gets *really* angry. He says if I didn't get in the boat something bad was going to happen. I thought he had gone daft. So I get in the boat and they shove off. I'm sitting in the stupid boat, wondering whether I'm going to stay alive in the open water with what little he left me or get eaten by a shark. And then, before I can even get my bearings, about half an hour or so, the boat returns! Only this time the Captain is the only one on board. He says to me that Michael had been acting strangely and that he had shot himself, fallen overboard and drowned."

"Go on."

"Then, the Captain, calm as can be, decides we're going to make a run for Morocco. He tells me because of what had happened with Michael and all, that the plans have changed and the summer cruise was off. He told me he didn't need my services anymore. He said he would file a police report about Michael and that I didn't have to worry about it. To make up for it, he said, he would pay me the rest of what had been promised me plus passage back to Douglas. That's when I saw in the papers that they caught this American doctor, Wren. There was no mistake de Nebra was him. I'm not stupid."

"So you went to the Manx police who then came to me."

"That's right. They said that The Yard was the best place to handle this sort of thing. Now, if you don't mind me asking, what about that reward money?"

"Yes, the reward money. Well, Colin, that's where we have a problem. You see, the Americans, who are in charge of that, say that Wren was never caught. That it was all some kind of mistake. They are making it sound as if de Nebra, a true Spanish national with no relationship to Wren, was erroneously taken into custody. That's where I come in. I don't believe it. I think Wren has been captured. And I'm trying to find out why the Americans are hiding it. But if you want to maintain any chance at getting the reward, you'll have to leave it to me. You making noise about this will only hurt your cause. Am I clear on that?"

"Yes but…"

"No 'buts', Colin. That's the way it is. You see, things have changed. We are now in the midst of a murder investigation."

"Murder? Who?"

"Well, Michael McPhail, of course. His body's been discovered off Gibraltar by two kids. There's evidence of trauma to the head. We have every reason to believe Michael did not merely drown; we believe he was hit by a blunt object first. And this was no 'self-in-flicted gunshot wound'. We found blood on The Gail Force Winds, starboard side, that matches Michael's DNA and the blood type from his royal Navy records. We're going over that ship closely; nothing that has significance will escape detection, I assure you. That changes things for us, the Americans, even for you."

"How for me?"

"If we can establish, and that is a big 'if', that Wren indeed had been taken into custody, that moves your reward claim along nicely. You see, the reward calls for the apprehension of Wren, and if the Americans are stonewalling for Lord knows whatever reasons, we are all fighting an uphill battle. So, my advice to you is keep quiet, let us do our work and don't talk to anyone about what we've discussed. Colin, I don't want you to get charged with impeding a police investigation."

Jakes's abrupt departure left a disappointed Tynes staring out the window.

Jakes continued working every angle of the case before him. He had called American counterparts, people at Interpol, even a contact who was the friend of the American ambassador to the Court of St. James, in the hopes of mining information as to why Wren would be protected. His suspicions were stoked in that whoever was calling himself Juan de Nebra had apparently disappeared off the earth. No one had come to claim the Gail Force Winds, which had been impounded by the British government and anchored in the south of England. De Nebra's apartment in Douglas had gone unvisited, the mail piling up at the doorstep. The landlady said the rent had not been paid in months and she had been looking for a new tenant.

To worsen matters, the Manx Crown Bank held firm. They refused to reveal, like the other Isle of Man banks, whether Juan de Nebra, Adrian Wren, Gail Force Holdings (the registered owner of The Gail Force Winds) or any related entity held or had held accounts in their institutions. But to Jakes's satisfaction, it was an American court order presented to the State of Wyoming (whose officials Jakes had attempted to contacted through his research into the name "Gail Force Holdings") that established the crucial link between Adrian Wren, Max Gimble, Francis Devlin and the corporation that had tied them all together.

Francis Devlin remained bedeviled. He saw the early news reports that summer that Wren had been snared. And then, nothing. It was like many of the cover-ups the DC lawyer had been witness to over the years: a break in a major story rapidly changes course, with amendments, obfuscations, and then downright denials. What initially was so clearly obvious had apparently not occurred. Like Jakes, Devlin toiled mightily to get at the truth. He called Charlie, hired a private investigator, probed his contacts at the Justice Department and State Department; all to no avail. The trail and scent of Dr. Adrian Wren, like the quick passing of summer, was gone.

CHAPTER 18
PEOPLE AT WORK

By the new year, Natalie had agreed to marry me. In a civil ceremony in Phoenix one sunny morning in January 2025, she became Natalie Patricia Porter-Crisfield. Had quite the British ring to it, we thought. She had decided to go part -time at Titus/Dixon and devote more of her free time to photography. That, and a return to fencing. Our dogs, our travels in the desert and my work all kept us busy enough. To my delight she had been diligent and good about not asking me what I did when I went away on "business trips" each month. On my visits to Rosengrave downtown twice a month she accepted the fact that it was "work related."

I asked Mr. L if there was any chance I could contact my parents. He said he'd "run it by" the people in charge and get back to me. Weeks went by without an answer, and when pressed again, he responded within 24 hours that I could send a letter and that was all, but only after he had read it. It said

Mom and Dad,

I know it has been a long while since you've heard from me or about me. But circumstances beyond my control dictate that I had to wait to contact you. There are things I can and cannot say, so here goes.

First you should know that I am safe and happy. I live a good life, have a good wife, and am gainfully employed and financially secure. I am healthy, as well. All that you may have heard in the news does not come close to the truth. There is not a lot I can tell you, but I will try to ease your fears and concerns.

The news media said a man caught in north Africa last summer was me. I'm sure you saw those early reports, like the rest of the civilized world. Whether it was or not, I am unable and unwilling to tell you. But it matters little anyway. I am safe. Trust me fully when I say I have good reasons for this.

Do not press Charlie as to my whereabouts; he does not know them.

Our relationship, yours and mine and Charlie's, changed a lot when we lost Gail. There is not a day that goes by that I don't think about her and miss her. It is said the worst thing a person can do is lose a child. I cannot imagine, after having lost such a sister, the pain you must continue to have.

There may come a time when I can see you, but I'm not sure how soon that is. I don't want to get your hopes up. Perhaps when that time comes, you'll be rewarded with grandchildren.

I wish I could be more forthright, but I cannot, due to an arrangement I have with my employers. I know this all seems very mysterious but, trust me, it's for the best.

Just know I've never stopped being your loving son,
Adrian

PS: Please do not speak of me to anyone. If asked, just tell them I am fine and working abroad.

I mailed the letter after making a copy. The copy I placed in an envelope near the nightstand drawer near my bed. I planned to show Dr. Rosengrave the letter during my next visit. After Mr. L had read and approved the letter, he called me on his cell phone. Natalie was at work. The call was all business talk. Mr. L said that as of January 15, 2025, there were 2888 people on death row in 31 states, and that the majority of those states employed the lethal injection method of execution or offered it as an option to electrocution the condemned. He told me that my employers had made firm arrangements with ten states and were working on the others. The states that I could expect to stay busy in (and he intimated I was to only get busier) were California, Florida, Texas, Alabama, Georgia and Kentucky. He said his operatives were in communications from officials in Pennsylvania, North Carolina and Oklahoma, and that other contacts in other states were soon to follow.

He told me that these negotiations must, by their very nature, be handled slowly and carefully. Any breach of the confidentiality of the arrangement could be catastrophic, leading not only to the end of the President's pet project but the commencement of investigations, accusations and the necessary denials and cover up that would naturally ensue. I asked him what all this meant for me. He inhaled a breath of tobacco, over the phone, and remarked, "Fair question. Because you have performed so well in your duties and because 'botched executions' appear, for now, to be a thing of the past, your services are in even higher demand. You see, whether one follows this issue or not, as we do, there hasn't been much in the press about inmates dying long and tortuous deaths. In other words, the Christopher Newtons of the world have for all purposes slipped off the radar.

"Christopher who?"

"Newton. He was an inmate in May of 2007 who had the nerve to take two full two hours to die by lethal injection. "

"Two hours! I take…"

"Yes, Alexander. We've kept the stats. The average time it takes from the time you start the I.V. until the demise of your client is an astounding eleven minutes. Eleven!"

A gust of shameful pride I felt swept over me like a wind full of sand and grit. He went on. "So, what this means is twofold: one, as I've said, is you can expect to get busier. Two, we will make every effort to arrange your schedule so as to consolidate your duties into convenient groupings. For example, if you have five jobs for a particular month, say, we will try to get them all done in eight to ten days, so that they are not spread out all over the calendar. We will think geographically. If you have two gigs in California and then one in Nevada we will try to get them lumped into the same week."

I wondered what suit he was wearing today, and how many cigarettes he'd chalked up so early in the day.

"I appreciate that. So will Natalie."

"We know. Natalie's a big part of the reason we are considering this, because a…"

"I know. A happy executioner is a good executioner. I get it."

I heard a small chortle.

"We'll be in touch, Alexander. Enjoy the next few weeks and get some rest. You're going to need it. And give Rosengrave my regards. You're supposed to see him Wednesday, is that right?"

"Correct."

The line went dead. I roused the dogs, loaded them into the Jeep, and set out for the desert.

It turned out Mr. L was premature in his assessment of the press. In late January, an investigative reporter for the *Washington*

Morning Star, Ann Avison, published an above-the-fold story in the main section of the paper, a three-part series entitled "What's Behind the Uptick in Executions?" In the first part of the trilogy, she reviewed the history of the death penalty in the United States, paying particular attention to the 1972 court decision Furman Vs. Georgia that had temporarily banned capital punishment in The United States, and the 1976 ruling in Gregg vs. Georgia, the so called "July 2nd cases" that reinstated it. She also profiled many of the anti-death penalty advocacy groups, in particular the Citizens United Against Cruel and Unusual Punishment. In the second part of the series, she covered many of the state's individual stories about the penalty: who used what method, how many people were on each state's death row, what is the protocol for lethal injection in each state and so on. Apparent was the fact that thirty-one states allowed for the death penalty, most of them employed the lethal injection method and, until recently, that method was carried out with the use of a single drug, a massive dose of sodium pentothal.

The final, and longest, installment of the trilogy dealt with detailed eyewitness reports that had come out of many state prison execution room galleries. These reports were unusual in their description of the new efficiency and rapidity of the practice under discussion and of the person who so effectively carried out the executions. Descriptions of the same "tall slender man" who dispatched his victims "rapidly and without a struggle or whimper" emerged. Details also came forth about a multiple injection protocol: witnesses, when questioned, spoke of three and four separate injections used by the man, who, unlike some prior executioners, stayed in the same room with the condemned, not separated by a curtain or a partition. The viewers were all consistent in their descriptions, especially of the man "in the cap, tightly fitting mask and protective eyewear." The story offered no hints as to the identity of the man.

But the mere presence and length of such a newspaper series bothered many. The trilogy raised more questions than it had answered.

The story was well received, particular by those who opposed the death penalty, and caused many to write about the article in other papers. Many people wrote letters to the editor on the story, taking both sides on an issue who contentiousness had never waned. The story made a temporary celebrity out of Avison, who made the talk show circuit in Los Angeles, New York, and Washington.

Many others with a special interest in the story were captivated as well. This included President Stanton, Izzy Rappaport, Charles Wren, Mr. L, and Agents Mobray and Locatelli of the FBI. Missing from this list was former FBI agent Thoreau, who had resigned her position with the Bureau the prior November and was living in Spain with a certain Civil Guard captain. Francis Devlin was intrigued too.

Stanton poured out his growing discomfort on Rappaport. He went on about the dangers of the story leading to unfavorable conclusions and demanded to know if there was a spy in his White House. Rappaport assured him that the cadre involved in the scheme was loyal, while at the same time searching his mind for the potential mole. Through third parties untraceable to The White House he called upon, on the President's orders, the services of a public relations and damage control agency on M Street, Howston and Associates, to feel them out on the best ways to handle the story. It was important to get this out of the news as quickly as possible. They were only too glad to accept the assignment.

Then in April, after twelve additional without-a-hitch executions had gone by, big changes were afoot. Avison won a Pulitzer Prize for Investigative Reporting for her three-part article. Suddenly, she was on the world stage, and along with her came her story. The anti-death penalty folks celebrated. Stanton grew more nervous and horrified. And on the other side of the Atlantic sat Inspector Jakes, who while sipping his morning Assam, read about the prize-winning journalist in *The London Times*. This caused him to find Avison's original article series, which he read in one sitting on the *Washington Morning Star's* website. His first move after doing so was to pull out his notes on the interview he had conducted with Michael McPhail's sister the year before. He paid close attention to this passage:

Jakes: Tell me, please, about what your brother was doing after he told you of his new job.

Mrs. McPhail: Well, as I said, Michael had called me in the spring to tell me this Spaniard had hired him and another boy from the Navy, Colin, to crew a boat that summer. Said that this fellow seemed to have a lot of money. Said the pay was good.

Jakes: Yes, continue.

Mrs. McPhail: Thing of it was, he went on about this captain. Michael said he sounded more like an American than a Spaniard. He paid attention to such things, Michael did. It was his background in intelligence that kept him that way. Or the other way 'round.

Jakes: Had he ever contacted you after he left Douglas?

Ms. McPhail: Oh yes, once or twice. I remember the last time I had spoken to him, he told me something big was going to happen and that I need not worry any more about money. He was concerned, you see, that I was going to lose the house.

Jakes rifled through the material in the file: the newspaper clippings from *The Washington Post* when Wren had gone missing, the police reports he had requested from Montgomery County, Maryland and District of Columbia Police departments covering the slip of paper found in the B-CC High School book drive, the interview transcript of nurse Stepanczyk and the sparse notes the FBI had supplied of the report filed by Thoreau and Locatelli. He also read the notes that The Spanish Civil Guard had made when the man on The Gail Force Winds, whoever he was, was apprehended.

But none of this would have interested him had it not been for the recollection of a conversation he had had with his brother-in-law, Nigel Downes, five years prior at a dinner party at his own home. It was at that party that he and Downes, an anesthetist and member of The Royal College of Anaesthetists of Great Britain and Northern Ireland, somehow got into a discussion of the way countries around the world punish violent criminals. He being in law enforcement and Downes being in medicine, Jakes went along as the conversation veered toward the topic of the death penalty and recalled Downes' subsequent statement, "There's nobody better than me and my colleagues in taking care of that."

Ever since McPhail's body had washed up in Gibraltar, there was something bothering Jakes. Reading through the Wren file only furthered his suspicions. It was just too coincidental. A man fitting Wren's general description is captured in the summer. Then, the trail disappears. There's no mention of Wren's transfer to the States, no prosecution, no case, no punishment, no nothing. Only a first-hand interview with a man who had spent every day with the man arrested and the late McPhail, who insisted that de Nebra was indeed Wren. The first question is: what happened to the man arrested?

The second question required a larger leap of faith. Not long after all this, in a mere matter of months, a major report comes out of the United States about how condemned inmates are dying at an increasing rate, and with more ease, finesse, and facility than a firing squad or hanging ever did.

Jakes was not nor had ever been a conspiracy theorist. And yet, his pet theory about what might really be transpiring caused him to lose sleep. He knew the chances were slim. After all, the Americans just said that the man caught was this de Nebra fellow. That it was all just a mistake. Wren for all the world knew, was still god-knows-where. But still…

Jakes decided to do two things. The first was to find out if Juan de Nebra really existed. The second was to try and reach Agent Thoreau. Both would not be easy but also not impossible for an Inspector with decades in Scotland Yard behind him. Now a widower with two grown children, Jakes had the time, energy and innate curiosity to chase leads to their exhaustion.

Jakes used all the resources at his command to answer the first question. Turned out De Nebra had been a real person and he did spend time in California. But the only Juan de Nebra whose records he could trace was born in Spain in 1966 and moved to California in 1980. That would have made de Nebra almost sixty years old at the time of his arrest on The Gail Force Winds. The man taken into custody was said to be in his early to mid-forties. That made no sense to him.

His research, using information only available to an inspector of his rank and security clearance, also revealed that Agent Dana Thoreau was no longer an FBI agent; had not been one since December of last year. No, Thoreau had had enough of life as an agent. She happily left her cats and ex-Marine boyfriend in the United States and was now living in southern Spain with Enrique Lorca. Jakes had an address. He soon had a plane ticket.

Within two days Jakes was on Lorca's doorstep on the Costa Brava. He knocked on the door and a young woman answered, dressed in a silk dressing gown and wearing leather sandals below her shapely ankles.

"Ms. Thoreau?"

Dana looked at him cautiously.

"Yes? Who wants to know?"

"I'm Inspector Jakes of Scotland Yard. Do you mind if I had a word or two?"

Reluctant at first, Thoreau insisted on seeing Jakes' credentials and then let the distinguished looking man through the door. She soon grew curious.

She offered Jakes a drink, which he declined, as she poured herself a half glass of Tempranillo.

"What can I do for you, Inspector?"

Jakes looked her over. Young and attractive. He thought "those Spaniards have a reputation, don't they?"

"Well, Ms. Thoreau, I'm here in an unofficial capacity. Even paid for my own plane ticket. Everything I'd like to ask you is off the record."

"Do tell."

Jakes changed his mind. He actually would like a small glass of the red, it being the afternoon and all. Thoreau handed him a glass and set out some almonds and olives.

Jakes took a long sip of the wine.

"Good stuff, this. Underrated as clarets go, I think. Anyway, I'm here to talk about Adrian Wren."

"That's a name I hadn't heard anyone speak in a while."

"Yes, and that's just the problem. No one seems to know where he is."

"And you think I do?"

"Well, I thought you might enlighten me on a few things. Again, strictly off the record of course."

Thoreau paused and placed an olive pit into a small dish.

"I'm listening."

Jakes went on: "The man apprehended last summer in north Africa near Ceuta, he was…"

"Without question he was Adrian Wren, M.D."

Jakes smiled and put his wineglass carefully on the table. He sniffed, sat back in his chair, and raised his eyebrows at the young woman before him.

"You seem to be so sure."

"And why not? I was there. I saw him."

"There's no chance that…"

"Look, Inspector. I had been in The Bureau long enough to know a suspect when I saw him. I had studied the man's face for much too long. No long hair and beard could hide the truth. It was Wren, without a doubt. I even did a computer analysis of his face."

Jakes rubbed his hands together.

"An analysis! What type of…"

"The usual facial recognition software that we and no doubt, you, employ. We use MorphoTrust."

"As do we."

"Then you'd have found what we found. There's 98.7 percent confidence that de Nebra is Wren. Plain and simple. Actually, 98.7 percent MorphoTrust and 100 percent my own eyes."

Jakes then leaned forward and picked up his wine glass.

"That concurs with what Tynes told me. He was the sailor employed by Wren who made it out alive."

Jakes briefed Thoreau on the interview he had conducted with Tynes, as well as the ongoing developments in the case of McPhail's mysterious death. Jakes posed another question.

"Did you leave the Bureau because of what happened?"

"You mean because of what 'didn't happen'? That Wren "didn't" get extradited; that he disappeared?"

"Precisely."

"Well, that was part of the reason. The rest was personal. I was tired of the Bureau. I looked at my partner, Locatelli, and said to myself 'I don't want to be that guy in thirty years.' Nothing personal. I like Peter. But I like my life with Enrique better."

"Understood."

"Well, Inspector Jakes, what are you going to do now?"

Jakes drained the last of his wine and smacked his lips.

"Ms. Thoreau, I really don't know. I don't know what I'm up against. You see, I have a pretty wild theory."

Jakes proceeded to outline his thoughts to an open-mouthed Thoreau. She said, "Wow! That certainly is one wild theory, Inspector."

Jakes rose to his feet and shook Thoreau's hand.

"You've been awfully kind and helpful, Ms. Thoreau. I won't forget it and I won't mention any of this to anyone. If I do discover something, I will let you know. Professional courtesy and all that, even though you've seemingly left the game. Good luck."

"Good luck, Inspector. Have a safe trip."

Thoreau watched as Jakes' tall figure receded down the street and disappeared into the alleyway.

CHAPTER 19
BUSY TIMES

It was a busy spring, aside from Pulitzer Prizes. California, Texas, Florida, Alabama, Pennsylvania, Arizona—they all needed my services. My easiest weeks were when California and Arizona wanted me; we could consolidate those assignments in a matter of days. Heading east was tougher for me, for obvious reasons. Florida was my least favorite assignment. It was remote geographically, inconvenient and, unless I had jobs in the Carolinas, which I often did not, was just a pain in the ass.

I was sure to wear the same clothing in airports, on planes and on assignment. A hat was mandatory, and I mixed that up between baseball caps, tennis visors, straw fedoras and Indiana Jones-type covers. I had to strike a balance between not drawing attention to myself and not being recognized so, the less flamboyant and colorful, the better. I consistently wore sunglasses, even indoors, and kept a well-trimmed goatee, which was my best compromise between being clean-shaven and sporting a full beard. My height I could not help. But my bulk I could. I had put on a good fifteen pounds since my days as de Nebra, lifting weights and filling up with protein powder.

I marveled that Mr. L and his cohorts were able to coordinate my assignments: how they got the various states to hold their executions on a schedule that gelled with Mr. L's, how the secrecy surrounding my identity held so well and about the professionalism of those who transported me to jobs and back to the hotels and airports. It soon became apparent that the only variables not under our control were stays of execution and drug supplies. The former no one could do anything about. That was a judicial issue and beyond the reach of Mr. L and his team. The latter I dealt with easily, much to my handler's satisfaction. If there was a shortage of propofol in one location, I just went with pentothal, etomidate or even high dose midazolam or ketamine. For paralytics, vecuronium or pancuroniumit made no difference to me. And potassium, always easy to get, was a non-issue. And I.V. access, always a big problem in the older botched executions were a thing of the past. I hadn't even used my ultrasound machine or central line kits, which the driver carried with him, since my second month on assignment.

In March we got great news. Natalie was pregnant. I was bursting at the seams, wanting to tell the world—to tell Cleesh, Charlie, my parents. But I knew that, at least then, I could not.

On a mid-week trip to see Dr. Rosengrave I was handed an article written in *The Atlantic* by writer Matt Ford in 2014. Dr. Rosengrave had clearly handpicked this article among many others that dealt with the myriad issues related to my employment. The article, whose tone I took to be anti-death penalty, afforded people who were willing to use my lethal skills some back-handed compliments. I read it with great interest. Ford spoke of two men, Joseph Wood and Clayton Lockett, who suffered particularly brutal deaths

at the hands of less than able executioners. Ford quoted historian
Joel Harrington,

*"Medieval executioners had basically two goals: first to shock and
then reaffirm divine and temporal authority... A steady and reliable
executioner played a pivotal role in achieving this delicate balance ritu-
alized and regulated application of violence. Poorly performed executions
could lead to the community losing trust in or retaliating against the man
who swung the axe..."*

Ford went on to write about states that had enacted laws
shielding the identities of the drug companies that supplied
lethal-injection drugs. He concluded,

*"...what remains is a system in which prisoners are killed with drugs
of uncertain provenance...administered by executioners of unknown
credentials with unpredictable results..."*

I took a few minutes to read the article, which was relatively
brief, while Rosengrave sat silently across from me.

I looked up and he said, "You see, Alexander, the progress we've
made since that article was written a mere seven years ago?"

"I do."

"One has to wonder: if you and I have no control, as individuals at least, over the existence of the death penalty, isn't is good and
fair that people like you are bringing a much-needed service to the
table?"

I felt for the first time that Dr. Rosengrave was trying to
convince himself of the moral righteousness of our activities. "Are
you trying to convince yourself or me?"

"I'm not attempting either. I've reconciled that the death

penalty is a reality in this country, and that years of contentious debate have led us to a still hotly-argued status quo."

"Does that make it right?"

"Right or wrong, it just *is*."

"And? Are we just like good soldiers, following orders?"

"Now we're getting somewhere. Are you just a good soldier, Alexander?"

I looked out the window and saw the trees swaying in the early spring breeze. I was suddenly feeling uncomfortable. Was it Natalie's pregnancy, the possibility of bringing new life into a world where it was my job to take it, that was making me so uncomfortable? I blurted, "Natalie's pregnant."

Rosengrave removed his glasses and rubbed his eyes.

"Congratulations."

"Thank you."

"By the way, there are no accidental exhortations."

"What do you mean?"

"Why did you choose to tell me that when we were discussing your good-soldiering?"

"I guess because…because…I'm conflicted."

"Yes?"

"Yes, I'm conflicted. Someday, god forbid, someone might kill my wife or kid. Or, as likely perhaps, my kid may murder someone."

"Those are fantastic thoughts!"

"Yes, but…"

"But you are right to think so. It's a sign of good health, critical thinking. Keep it up."

I looked down at the article in my lap and offered it back to him, folded.

"No Alexander, you keep that. I want to read it again. We'll talk about it next week."

I folded the article into quarters and stuffed it into my pocket.

There were other things going on that spring of which I had no inkling. In a bid to look more presidential, President Stanton had met with his advisors and The Secretary of State to discuss ways to enhance his stature. One idea floated was to attempt to convince the Brits to get Queen Elizabeth the Second to make a State Visit to the United States for the first time since May of 2007. Her Majesty, who was remarkably sharp and spry even at this advanced age, had expressed her desire to see "the colonies" for perhaps one last time. There were proposals to have her celebrate her 99th birthday with a bang, which was to occur on April 21, 2025, at The White House at a State Dinner, and after much behind-the-scenes maneuvering and deals, the English agreed. Stanton was overjoyed.

So was Inspector Jakes of Scotland Yard. Having been part of the Royalty and Specialist Protection Unit tasked in 2015 to guard politicians, diplomats and royals, Jakes had served in this capacity on that 2007 American, and other, royal trips abroad. This squad, a retooling of the Royal Protection Squad that was formed in 1983, was an improvement that The Queen Herself had sought to shore up security. It cost the British taxpayer £27 million per year and was part of the 34-person entourage (including the 8 police officers) that traditionally accompanied Her Majesty on trips overseas.

Jakes saw an opportunity. He had been reading and following confidential reports available to him through his high position concerning the March, April and May execution schedule in seven states. April's schedule revealed that there were two executions scheduled for April 29 and 30 at The State Correctional Institution/ Greene, in Waynesburg, Pennsylvania. When he learned that the visit fell around those dates and had been approved and scheduled, he immediately put in for the assignment. The go-ahead nod came quickly.

Jakes then put his plan into motion. Recalling the unusually strong relationship he had forged with Philadelphia Chief of Police Alton Briggs during their mutual casework back in 2017 regarding a Nigerian British national who was involved in criminal activity in both London and The City of Brotherly Love, Jakes called his old friend and asked some favors. He wondered if, on his upcoming trip to America in April, he could make a visit to the Waynesburg facility to get a tour from the warden and view the executions themselves. This was done under the guise of "learning more about the American system of criminal punishment" and to see "first-hand how America deals with its most violent and dangerous criminals."

Briggs was glad to assist in the request. Jakes was to break away from his duties with The Queen at the end of her visit on April 27 and extend his visit until the first of May "to see colleagues in Pennsylvania to tie up loose ends on a former case." He would take a tour with Warden George Bianchi on April 2, seeing the execution room, the ingress and egress of the staff involved in the execution, the facility itself and the security measures employed. Briggs called Bianchi to set everything up. It was just that simple.

Jakes added that he'd likely have an assistant with him, a former Royal Navy seaman named Colin Tynes, who was accompanying him on his visit. Jakes lied that the Royal Navy too had an interest in how the Americans dealt with incarcerated criminals. Briggs and Bianchi voiced no objections.

Neither did Tynes. When he learned that someone else was footing the bill for his first trip The United States, he was intrigued. When Jakes dropped the bomb on him that the primary purpose for his presence was to confirm the identity of Dr. Adrian Wren, he was elated. Perhaps, he thought, this would be the crucial step in getting him the reward money he deserved.

Jakes wanted to leave nothing to chance. He asked Briggs if he could call Bianchi to go over the visit's itinerary. Briggs complied and in an April 2 phone conversation, Jakes had his hand-written list in front of him. It was 4 pm London time when Bianchi picked up the phone in his office.

"Warden Bianchi here."

"Warden, this is Inspector Jakes of Scotland Yard. I believe Chief Briggs told you I'd be calling?"

"Why yes, Inspector. Nice to talk to you. How can I help?"

"I understand you've kindly agreed to give a tour of the facility to me and my Royal Navy assistant, seaman Colin Tynes."

"Yes, that's right. Let's see; the 28th of April, and then two days following to witness executions."

"Correct."

"Fine. Are there any questions you have?"

Jakes licked his lips. "Well, can you give me the basics of your layout?"

"To begin with, SCI/Greene is what we call a SuperMax, meaning the highest level of security among the state prisons in Pennsylvania. We house presently 159 death row inmates, which accounts for about 75 percent of our state's death row inmates. Two inmates, as you know, are scheduled to be executed, barring stays, on April 29 and 30 of this month. They are Emilio Sanchez and Tyrone Scutter."

"Yes, those are the names Chief Briggs gave me."

"Yes. So, if you want to come on the 28th, you and your assistant can visit Blocks G and L, which are the death row blocks, as well as get a feel for how our security works."

"That's just fine, Warden. Will there also be an opportunity to see how your visitors, the press, your officials, and execution team enter and leave the facility? We are particularly keen on learning about the logistics of your security protocols. We have a particular challenge with that here in Britain and are always looking for ways to improve."

"Certainly, Inspector. Be happy to. Anything else?"

"No, Warden. Thank you. We look forward to seeing you later in the month."

Nat's ultrasound visit was just about finished, and Natalie and I had made a split-second decision. We decided to let the sonographer tell us, after we had told ourselves otherwise, the sex of the child. It was a boy. A boy! My mind fast-forwarded to catching baseballs, rough-housing, fishing, launching him overhead in the pool and camping trips. I was over the moon happy.

The week before I was to head east for my assignments in Pennsylvania, I had my visit with Rosengrave. He was unusually circumspect.

"How does approaching fatherhood sit with you, Alexander?"

"I'm thrilled."

"Tell me."

"I never really thought I'd have a child. After my divorce, I didn't see it happening. And now it is."

"Why did you not see it happening before, but now it is?"

"Well, after what happened to Gail, I did not want to bring a child into the world. In case you hadn't noticed, I'm a cynical kind of guy. I don't think there's much hope for people. They are too stupid, in general."

"Really?"

"Sure. The average person, I feel, isn't that bright. Look at popular culture. How dumb and pointless it is. What people seem to think is so importantsports teams, fashion, popular music, you name itit all seems so, so *common*. There's very little that's *refined* anymore. And the wars. What's the point? Do you know we've been

262

in Afghanistan for more than twenty five years. And for what? What have we accomplished? And climate change. Just look at what we've done to the planet since the Industrial Revolution! Billions of years of evolution and human progress is now threatened by carbon-emissions. It's terrible."

"So what changed. Why a baby now?"

"Well, for one thing, the woman I married. She's special. And another, I'm not getting younger, obviously. Having a child, the experience of it, is the one thing I wanted to do now before I die. What's different now, besides the woman, is that, with my new arrangement, I'll actually have time to see my kid. I only work a few days a month. We're secure, financially. There's no more on-call, no one is going to sue me for malpractice. I'm in a different place, you see?"

Rosengrave did his glasses-off-and eye-rubbing-act.

"I do see. And you work, how do you see it affecting your relationship to your child? To have a new life in the world?"

"Why should it?"

"Well, after all, you do take life for a living. And now you are creating it. How does that affect you?"

"We've discussed some of this before. You know how I feel. I've read that all lives possess infinite value. I can accept that. But is everyone deserving of life? Have some among us relinquished their rights by their acts?"

"Is it for you to decide, Alexander?"

"I'm not deciding. The government is, in the case of my work, deciding."

"And is that 'right'?"

"Right or wrong, it's what I do. It's what I have to do, if I want to survive."

"So, in your case, the ends justify the means?"

"They have to. For me, Natalie, and our child, they have to.

CHAPTER 20
JUDGMENT DAY

Late April came and Queen's enormous party had landed. Members of the Royalty and Protection Unit met with White House staff and The Secret Service to coordinate security for the State Dinner. The guest list had been vetted and the Chief of Protocol had gone over the menu, schedule of events and arrangements for The Queen's stay at Blair House. Inspector Jakes had arrived with Her Majesty's entourage and Tynes had made the flight over as a private citizen. Jakes stayed with the rest of his party but kept in contact with Tynes many times a day. Tynes was staying at the Washington Hilton, where John Hinckley had shot President Reagan on March 30, 1981.

The night of the State Dinner 118 guests dined at the White House. The President was effusive in his praise for Her Majesty, speaking of her "unprecedented stewardship under her magnificent reign" and the strength of the "unshakeable bond between The United Kingdom and her former colony."

Among the guests sitting at a table was Francis Devlin, Esquire, and his third wife, Susan. What he didn't realize was that, standing a mere fifteen feet behind him and sharing a mutual interest in Dr. Adrian Wren, stood Inspector Jakes of Scotland Yard.

The State Visit had been a success for the President. His approval rating after the visit was up considerably, and he and Izzy Rappaport seemed, at least for now, to have forgotten Ann Avison's lengthy article.

On the morning of Tuesday, April 27, on a warm and sunny spring day, the cherry blossoms just past their peak, Thomas Jakes took an Uber to The Washington Hilton to collect Colin Tynes. From there, both of them rode to Union Station and boarded the 9:30 Acela train to Philadelphia's 30th Street Station. Just after 11 am they hailed a cab to the Chief of Police Brigg's office at The Round House at 750 Race Street in downtown Philadelphia.

After a lunch with the Chief, where Jakes and Tynes had insisted on cheesesteaks from Sonny's Famous Steaks at 228 Market Street, the Irishman and the British inspector checked into the Marriott in Downtown Philadelphia, across from Reading Market. The next morning at 6 am, the two took a rented car on the almost six-hour drive to western Pennsylvania and met Warden Bianchi. There they had lunch, toured the prison, acted particularly interested in the security features and inspected Blocks G and L and the execution room. Just before the tour concluded, they walked the route the execution party would take the next day to enter and leave the facility. Jakes was careful to take notes on how long it took to walk the route, reconfirm the times of the scheduled executions and where the guard towers and security cameras were stationed along the way.

I had awoken two days prior to a brilliant desert day on Sunday, April 25, kissed Natalie goodbye and headed for Phoenix's Sky

Harbor Airport. I caught the 10 am TransAir flight 117 to Chicago and then on to Rochester, New York, with a scheduled arrival for late Sunday afternoon. The plan was to have Luis pick me up, take me to my hotel, and transport me to the Attica Correctional Facility on Monday to execute two inmates there. I was then to drive on Monday afternoon with Luis to Waynesburg, Pennsylvania, where I would check into my hotel and then perform two additional executions, one on Tuesday and one on Wednesday, at SCI/Greene. My flight back to Phoenix was booked for Wednesday afternoon.

On the plane to Chicago in the seat next to me sat an elderly man, probably pushing eighty. I had the window seat and he had the middle. The aisle seat was occupied by an off-duty airline captain. Midway into the flight the captain had announced that there would be some significant turbulence ahead and that we should stay in our seats, seatbelts securely fastened. After some initial mild choppiness, the weather got bad quickly. Some early spring thunderstorms were kicking up and the plane was taking a beating. The worst of it lasted about fifteen minutes, with tray-tables coming undone, overhead compartments opening and some crying children a few rows back. The man next to me gripped my arm at one point with his bony, white hands.

After the turbulence subsided and the announcement was made that we could unfasten our seatbelts and use the lavatory, the man next to me said, "I'm so sorry. I am a nervous flyer. I didn't mean to intrude."

"Think nothing of it."

"For a while there, I thought we weren't going to make it. "

"Turbulence happens all the time. These planes are built to withstand those conditions."

The man shrugged his shoulders and smiled. "Not that it would matter much anyway. I've lived a full life."

I wasn't sure whether he was joking or not.

"Stan Gellman's my name. I'm heading east to see the grandkids."

He extended a cold had. The skin on it was pale and tissue-like. I shook it gently.

"Alexander. Alexander Crisfield. Nice to meet you."

"What brings you east, Alexander?"

I had to think fast. "Oh, a convention."

"What type?"

"I'm an undertaker. We have conventions; like plumbers, dentists, lawyers."

"Well, that's tough work. Not everyone could do that."

I tried to steer the conversation away from that. After an awkward silence, I said, "And you. You said you've lived a 'full life'. Did you mean that?"

"Oh, that. Well, just talk, you know. But, after 82 years, with the kids and the grandkids, I'm content now. I could die happy."

"How many grandkids do you have?"

"Oh, five. I'm going to see three of 'em in Buffalo. Getting big now. Too bad my wife isn't with me. She died last year."

"Sorry to hear."

"No need. Life goes on."

"Any advice for a man about to have his first kid?"

"Oh, wonderful. Congratulations!"

"Thank you."

The man scratched his wispy-haired chin.

"Advice? Well, let's see. That's a tough one. There are so many lessons to be learned."

We sat quietly for a moment.

Then the man turned to me, grabbed my arm, and with a smile said, "Everyone talks about being 'proud parents'—how when they have kids they are proud of this and that. School grades, sports, what school they get into and such. That's all well and good. But how about this? Be the kind of person that will make your child proud of you someday. The admiration of your child is priceless!"

I thought about what he said and thanked him for the advice. He nodded and I got up to use the restroom. "Undertaker," I thought. What a dumb-ass thing to say.

We landed on time and I helped the old man with his suitcase from the overhead bin. He thanked me ambled to the aisle, ahead of me. As we reached the terminal gate, he turned to me: "Enjoy your convention. If you can 'enjoy' that sort of thing. And think about what I said. I can tell you have it in you."

I said goodbye to him and headed out to the waiting area, where a silent and unsmiling Luis grabbed my bag and led me to the car.

On the car ride from Philadelphia to Waynesburg, Jakes and Tynes were discussing the upcoming prison visit. Tynes turned to Jakes and began, "I have a question, Inspector. What if this executioner is actually Wren? What do we do about it?"

Jakes peered out the window and, without looking at the young sailor, said

"Seems to me we have three choices: we can do nothing and let the Americans continue on with their charade. Or we can out him to the press, and let the court of international opinion weigh in. The third is we can try to get the Americans to cooperate in our investigation into the death of McPhail, which bloody-well has little chance of happening. None of these is optimal. The best outcome is for Wren, if it is he, to wake up to all that he's done and do the right thing. He needs to own up to his actions, pay back whatever is left of the money to the people he owes and stand trial. But that'll never happen."

"Then what is this all for? I deserve my reward money, you know."

Jakes looked back at Tynes.

"Then you've answered the question, Colin. The only way that will happen is to get Wren prosecuted. And the only practical way I see that transpiring is to expose the Americans and their plan. We go to the press, give them the story and proof we have and let whatever happens happen. It's the only way, as I see it, to get some justice out of this."

I arrived at SCI/Greene early Tuesday morning and presented myself to Warden Bianchi. Inmate Sanchez's execution was scheduled for 9 am and I went to the execution room to check my equipment and medication. It was my lucky day: all the meds I needed were well stocked. I had 10 vials of propofol, 5 vials of pancuronium bromide, plenty of fentanyl, midazolam and 50cc bags of normal saline in which to mix my potassium chloride. I had my portable ultrasound machine with me but clearly had no need for it. When Sanchez arrived strapped to a gurney at 8:50, I saw he was muscled and trim.

I had read his dossier on the plane. Sanchez, 31, a Mexican by birth with U.S. citizenship, had murdered a Pennsylvania State trooper during a routine traffic stop on Pennsylvania State Highway 10 almost three years ago. The officer felt he had probable cause to search Sanchez's car, and when he requested the driver to open the trunk (which contained 5 pounds of methamphetamine Sanchez was delivering to a buyer/dealer), Sanchez shot him and sped off.

Sanchez was clearly agitated. I had not yet dealt with an inmate so volatile since I started my work. I knew there must be a full gallery behind the one-way mirror this morning—no man who kills a police officer is going to die with a paucity of onlookers. My first instinct was to quiet him down as soon as possible. I did so by hitting him with 15 mg of intramuscular midazolam, right through his shirtsleeve. Within three minutes he was docile.

I hooked up my monitors and started his I.V., which was easy since he had a huge antecubital vein that I could have hit from across the room. The lactated ringer's solution was flowing nicely, and I was ready to launch. I pushed 400 mg of propofol, 10 cc of fentanyl and 10 mg of pancuronium, in that order, through the I.V. line. Sanchez quickly turned a sickening blue, and I began running the potassium chloride in saline through a piggy-back line hooked to the lactated ringer's. The pulse oximeter on his right index finger, which had sunk to the low 70's, suddenly failed to detect a pulse and the BP cuff showed an error code. The EKG went wild with fibrillation and, by the time the 50cc bag of potassium had run its course, so had Sanchez. He was gone. It had taken all of eight minutes.

For the first time since I had accepted the plea deal, I thought I heard muffled clapping through the thick wall separating me from the gallery. By 10 am I was escorted to the secure waiting room greeted by the Warden who shook my hand and said

"Nicely done, Dr. Crisfield. We will see you tomorrow then, same time?"

"Yes, Warden. See you tomorrow."

I walked out into the fresh spring air, a warm breeze kicking up, and traversed the 100 yards or so to the semi-circular parking/drop-off area. Luis took me back to my hotel room, where I called Natalie. She said the baby had been kicking her a lot. I told her I couldn't wait to see her tomorrow afternoon. I spent the rest of the day walking around a nearby park, grabbing a quick lunch at a diner and taking in an evening movie.

The next morning I had taken care of Tyrone Sutter in much the same way I had Sanchez. He was a small man and took less drugs and less time (seven minutes, door to door) to send across the River Styx. My work was done by 10:30, and I said goodbye to the Warden. I was eager to get home. As I walked out the prison door and strode toward the parking area in the distance, I saw two men approaching me, coming the other direction. As they drew closer, I noticed the slightly shorter one suddenly stop and stand, legs firmly planted on the ground, placing his outstretched palm on the other man's chest. As I neared the two men, I slowed to look at them. A wave of nausea spread over me and my knees weakened. My God, I thought. It was Colin! How could this be?

I heard Colin say to the other man

"Yes, it's him. It's even his walk. You can't disguise a walk. That's Juan de Nebra. Rather, that's Adrian Wren."

The other man looked closely at me and asked me to take off my glasses. For some inexplicable reason, I stood there frozen like a statue and did what he said. He remarked, "Dr. Wren. We've come a long way to find you. And now, at long last, we have."

All I could think about was Natalie and my unborn son. "Be the kind of person that will make your child proud of you…"

We stood staring, the three of us, in the glaring light of a brilliant spring day, the trees rustling in the distance and the fragrance of the daffodils wafting through the air.

"I need a moment. Just give me a moment to collect my thoughts." Without waiting for a response, I turned and walked back into the prison, with the blood rushing into my leg muscles in a true fight-or-flight response. I strode down the hallway ten yards to the rest room, went in and whipped out my cell phone.

"Mr. L?"

CONTENT
NOTES

The reader may find the following information helpful:

The Role of the Federal Reserve Bank of The United States

The Federal Reserve's most important mission, of course, is monetary policy. I wish I could say that there is a bound volume of immutable instructions on my desk on how effectively to implement policy to achieve our goals of maximum employment, sustainable economic growth, and price stability. Instead, we have to deal with a dynamic, continuously evolving economy whose structure appears to change from business cycle to business cycle....

Because the Fed is perceived as being capable of significantly affecting the lives of all Americans, that we should be subject to constant scrutiny should not come as any surprise. Indeed, speaking as a citizen, and not Fed Chairman, I would be concerned were it otherwise. Our monetary policy

independence is conditional on pursuing policies that are broadly accept-
able to the American people and their representatives in the Congress.
Augmenting concerns about the Federal Reserve is the perception that we
are a secretive organization, operating behind closed doors, not always in
the interests of the nation as a whole. This is regrettable, and we contin-
uously strive to alter this misperception.

– Alan Greenspan December 5, 1996

ACKNOWLEDGEMENTS

I would like to thank my agent, Maryann Karinch, for her faith in me and her hard work in bringing this book to life. My thanks also go out to Judith Bailey of Armin Lear Press, who was instrumental in acquiring the manuscript. My special thanks also goes to my son, Liam Sherer, who was so helpful in technical matters related to formatting this work.

AUTHOR BIO

David Sherer was born in Washington, DC and spent his childhood and adolescence in Bethesda, Maryland. After earning a BA in Music with a concentration in piano from Emory University in 1979, he moved to Boston where he completed his medical school studies. After an internship in internal medicine in Baltimore, he completed his anesthesia residency at The University of Miami/Jackson Memorial Hospital in 1986 and practiced clinical anesthesia in a variety of settings until his retirement in 2019.

Since 2018 he has written the blog "What Your Doctor Isn't Telling You" for Bottom Line Publications and has written numerous articles and appeared in many videos on healthcare, medicine and related topics.

During his clinical career he was Physician Director of Risk Management for a major American health maintenance organization, helping to design and implement policies that made patients less likely to suffer the consequences of medical malpractice and medical error.

His work and writing has appeared in The New York Times, The Washington Post, The Wall Street Journal, Esquire, Bethesda Magazine, U.S. News and World Report, USA Today and other publications.

He lives in Chevy Chase, Maryland, where his hobbies include classical piano study, running, biking, reading, functional fitness training and travel.

Into the Ether is his first work of fiction.

His personal website is www.drdavidsherer.com

ALSO BY DAVID SHERER

Dr. David Sherer's Hospital Survival Guide: 100 + Ways to Make Your Hospital Stay Safe and Comfortable (with Maryann Karinch), 2003

The House of Black and White: My Life with and Search for Louise Johnson Morris, 2014

Hospital Survival Guide: The Patient Handbook to Getting Better and Getting Out, 2020

What Your Doctor Won't Tell You: The Real Reasons You Don't Feel Good and What YOU Can Do About It, Spring 2021

CPSIA information can be obtained
at www.ICGtesting.com
Printed in the USA
FSHW011702020221
78093FS